FATAL ERRORS

C. L. PAUWELS

His reverse-attack coding could erase all the evidence I'd gathered to clear my name. The flash drive in the USB port had been wiped through his external access. I couldn't let that happen again. I pulled up my laptop and rerouted my network access through three proxy ghosts and a server hi-jack, adding a few lines of code to protect my external port. I launched another flash drive on the laptop and resumed copying files. He was fast, but I was faster, so far. I kept an eye on the blinking light from the flash drive at my wrist. It fluttered in pace with my heart rate. The download box onscreen showed 3.9 gig of 4.5 copied and safe.

Only a few more seconds.

I inhaled sharply as he executed a reboot command trying to force me off the system.

Not yet, you bastard.

I overrode his code, relieved I'd had time to configure that special admin account earlier. 4.2 gig...4.4... The download box flashed full, the USB light shown steady. I hit my escape key sequence to disconnect and the screen went blank. I pulled the flash drive with one hand and dropped it in my pocket while yanking cables free with the other before shoving the laptop into my backpack.

On my way out the door, I dropped a second flash drive onto the front counter. I was counting on Raymond's efficiency and the lab's lack of high-end security. When Raymond found the flash drive Monday morning, he'd plug it in to see who it belonged to. The auto-run BackTrack program I'd installed on the drive would wipe the private network and leave nothing to trace the shambles to me, linking instead back to the computer lab itself and scrambling some of the system files. I'd carried it as insurance, hoping I wouldn't need it.

Sorry, Raymond.

Dedication

To Lori, who always believed in Fatál even more than I did

Pen Testing, aka Hacking

"Penetration testing, also known as pen testing, security pen testing, and security testing, is a form of **ethical hacking** [that] attempts to pierce the armor of an organization's cyber defenses, checking for exploitable vulnerabilities in networks, web apps, and user security."

~ Contrast Security

~ http://www.pentest-standard.org/index.php/Main_Page

Prologue

My name is Fatál, emphasis on the second syllable, please. And skip the jokes, I've heard them all. Grandma Zigana, bless her heart, thought she was doing me a favor, warding off whatever evil spirits that killed my mother when I was born. Try telling that to a seven-year-old, taunted every day with "Fay-*tahl*, Fay-*tahl*, touch her and you're *dead*."

I found out years later that Zigana had cornered the ringleader of my tormenters one evening after I came home in tears, knees skinned and jacket torn from being worked over on the playground. She'd spun a yarn about wizards like in the *Harry Potter* books everyone was reading, threw in a dash of her garbled Catholicism and karma, and left him quaking in his high-priced Nikes. Zigana's always been very good at leaving things unsaid, letting the imagination take over. She knows a person's own fears are much worse than anything she could suggest. That's the basis for a good curse—fear.

See we're Romani, what most people would call Gypsy. At least I'm one-quarter Romani. Zigana had the bad luck to fall in love with a *gajo*, a non-Rom. So did Harmony, my mother, but I didn't learn that until I was older. Zigana raised me. It was just the two of us. She's proud of being Roma, but there's a little shame, too, after growing up on the receiving end of the all-too-human tendency to mistreat what we don't understand. It's not so bad now, but from little things Zigana says, it wasn't always good to be labeled "Gypsy" here in southwest Ohio, or anywhere, really. Europe is much worse, even today. But Zigana doesn't believe in dwelling on the past, says it encourages the spirits of those times to intrude on us with *prikaza*, bad luck.

I took her word for it, mostly, until I found a photo taken in one of those arcade booths. The guy was thin, maybe early twenties. Ray-Ban sunglasses peeked out of blond tinted spikes on top of his head. His eyes were fixed on the young woman on his lap and the camera caught him mid-laugh. Harmony's image was like looking in the mirror, except she was smiling. I don't do that much. Scrawled on the back, in what I guessed was Harmony's loopy cursive, was "Mr. & Mrs. Matthew O'Connell," with the ampersand replaced by a heart. I stared at the picture for a long time, hoping for an emotional response.

Maybe someday.

A Google search didn't find anyone named Matthew O'Connell in the area who was even close to the right age, so I'd tried a few other less legal sources. Eventually that led to a formal name change linked to a bookstore in Dayton's bohemian Oregon District, now owned by an M. Taylor Schmidt. I paid them a visit on the off-chance someone would recognize the picture. Turned out not to be a problem. An older guy carrying a stack of books met me at the door. He took one look at my face and dropped every single volume.

Now I know where I get my green eyes.

After we picked up the books and found a spot to stack them on an overflowing table near the door, we faced each other for a long minute, not speaking. It's a good thing business was slow. Once we got past the initial shock we talked for hours, overcoming any lingering resentment at abandonment with a shared realization of the implacability that is Zigana. He kept apologizing for letting her chase him away.

"Harmony was seventeen when she came in looking for a job," he said. "God, she was beautiful, and smart. Our first date was dinner for her eighteenth birthday." His eyes misted over. "When we found out she was pregnant, I wanted to get married, but Zigana...I ignored the curse she threatened me with, but then she said she'd have me arrested if I came around. I scraped together some cash, sent a check to help with the hospital and stuff. She sent it back, shredded."

I searched for something to defuse the emotion. A framed certificate near the cash register showed he owned the place. "Why the name change?" I asked.

"After Harmony—" Matthew cleared his throat. "After she died, I kind of went off the deep end for a while. Sold everything, shaved my head, lived in my grandpop's cabin in Hocking Hills for almost six months. I knew I was a different person without her, so when I came back, I took Mom's name. Dad was gone by then, died in a motorcycle crash a few years before, so it didn't seem to matter what I called myself."

"M. Taylor?"

"Hey, first initials like that were all the rage. Made me sound more important, right?" His grin lightened the sadness etched on his face and revealed a glimpse of his younger charm.

I could see why Harmony had been smitten. I grinned back.

Even though Zigana still keeps Matthew at arm's length and then some, finding him filled a hole in my life I didn't know I had. Life was pretty good, all things considered. My federal probation was on its last few months (long story). One more semester of college, and with a small scholarship and my job in the school computer lab, I'd graduate debt free—not an easy thing these days. While I have only a nodding acquaintance with being "happy," I was content.

Until my boss's boss got antsy over the "special skills" I'd been hired for and had me fired. In 15 minutes, my life turned upside down in ways I could never have imagined.

Pre-engagement Interactions

"Present and explain the tools and techniques available, define scope"

So, I'm a hacker—get over it. My boss Patrice sure did, as long as she could use me. But I didn't realize *that* until I got fired. That Gypsy sixth-sense Grandma Zigana insists I have failed me miserably.

Patrice had appeared at my cubicle in the Gem City Business College computer center the week after Thanksgiving and offered to buy coffee. Of course I accepted, figuring she wanted another hack. Officially, I'd been hired because I knew my way around a computer network. Unofficially, my "special skills" helped her keep an eye on her boyfriend—and boss. Only after we were seated at Beaner's did she blindside me.

"You're firing me?" I echoed.

I clutched my mug of *chai*, hoping to ward off the chill her announcement caused. My strident question silenced the chatty barista at the counter behind me, and I wanted him and the trio at the next table to stop staring. They did when I glared at them.

Patrice looked everywhere but at me as she fidgeted, adding more sugar to her already syrupy coffee, checking her watch.

"You're firing me," I repeated, only a tad calmer.

"It's been brought to my attention that you've been bypassing security protocols to gain access to confidential files." Patrice could have been reading from the employee handbook.

Silence stretched while a scathing response eluded me. My mood dropped to match the gloomy weather. Twice in my twenty-four years, my hacking had backfired, leaving me betrayed by someone I trusted.

Bypassing security protocols my ass. "At your request," was all I could squeeze through a clenched jaw.

She flushed. "Anyone violating security policies can be summarily dismissed without the standard—"

"I wrote that policy, and now you're using it against me? What about Tatum?" I asked, referencing the school president and her boss.

"I would prefer to keep *Dr.* Tatum out of internal office problems. Your fascination with him is common knowledge."

"*Revulsion* is more like it." I shoved my mug of *chai* away, sloshing a bit on the table. Hands-on Tatum liked his women young. He'd hit on me a week after he was hired almost two years earlier. I shut him down, and he'd moved on to the next co-ed. Until Patrice snared him. I leaned into her range of vision, forcing her to look at me. "You're the one who's obsessed, after your little fling."

Patrice pulled back. "There was no...it wasn't a fling. Dr. Tatum and I have an understanding."

"And would he understand your tapping a student to spy on him?"

"It wasn't spying." She swallowed hard and coughed her way back to a professional tone. "Dr. Tatum's activity on the date in question was of concern to the status of a...special project. My request was designed to protect that project. It in no way authorized you to view those restricted files. He learned of your intrusion and directed me to...handle the situation."

I stared at Patrice while she squirmed, understanding now why she'd gone out of her way to be friendly. "I have your emails."

She checked her watch again. "Your Admin account and all network access were deleted as of nine-thirty this morning."

Ten minutes ago. That explained the invitation for coffee off-site.

"You came to me after you read that Stieg Larsson book," I said, as if she needed reminding, "wanting to know if I could pull off the same kind of stunt. And now I take the hit?"

Patrice ignored my question. "I trust you won't make a fuss that might harm the reputation of the school while we're in the middle of accreditation. We'll note your termination as workforce reduction and you can claim unemployment if you want. Your *probation officer* doesn't have to know about the breach. If you go quietly."

"Big of you." I counted to ten using the passing cars as markers, brooding over the veiled threat.

Patrice knew how to play the system, and the media, with her calculated social activism skillfully wrapped in administrative brown-nosing. I should be grateful, my PO reminded me every month. Patrice had hired me, gave me access to computers again when the court loosened its grip. She liked playing the good-hearted rehabilitator.

Even though she's a manipulative bitch.

Guess she figures that's how to get ahead in the IT world if you aren't male. Me, I prefer to depend on my skills, which are considerable. Patrice has yet to understand the difference between a router and a switch, although the higher-ups don't know that. Probably don't know the difference themselves.

Even though I only had a few months left in my supervised release, if she went to my PO, I could end up serving the rest of my suspended sentence for federal computer fraud—legalese for hacking. The Feds don't take kindly to college students browsing unsecure databases, especially with links to Wright-Patterson Air Force Base. I'd been expelled, convicted, banned from any online activity for two years, and put on five years' supervised release. Three months, one week, and four days before my PO and I could part ways, and not a minute too soon. Only good thing he'd done was connect me with Patrice and the private college after my Internet restrictions were lifted.

Now this.

"I have personal stuff in my desk," I told Patrice, looking for a back door. "And the new database isn't finished."

"Carmen's packing your things. You can pick them up at the front counter." Patrice's shoulders dropped a notch, her tension releasing at my apparent capitulation. "I'll need your badge and keys."

"So everyone else knew about this before me."

She stiffened again but said nothing.

I unwound two heavy Master Lock keys from my penguin key ring and laid them on the table with a sharp click. The ID badge and computer room keycard were in my backpack. When I tossed them next to the keys, the cards smeared through the splatters of *chai*. Patrice grimaced and looked to me to clean them off. I didn't. She eventually picked them up with two fingers, wrapped them in a napkin, and slipped them into her purse with the keys.

"I'll need a receipt for those," I said.

She opened her mouth to argue, then closed it again. I waited.

"I don't have any paper," Patrice said to the Ficus in the corner.

"Email it to me. Now."

Her lips formed a hard line but she pulled her iPhone out of a voluminous Coach handbag. After the message appeared on my Android cellphone, I stood up. "Anything else?"

"You'll let this go, right?" she asked, a slight tremor in her voice the only obvious crack in her composure. "It's over. I only wish—" She stopped.

You wish what? That I hadn't trusted you? That I didn't let you talk me into snooping on that leech? I'd bit back the angry words and fingered the flash drive in my pocket. "Sure, it's over."

Now, after Patrice's ambush, I felt more like a victim than ever. Not a position I care to be in. Tuition doesn't pay itself, and I have to graduate—from college and from the Feds—or no prospective employer will look past my criminal record. Patrice left me sitting in Beaner's, and after an hour of moping and scheming, I retreated to the school library. I tried to set aside my anger and focus on logic.

First, I checked to see how much of the computer network I could still access. I'd left a few strategically placed hidden access points in the bits and pieces of code I'd contributed to projects in my years in the lab. RATs we call them—Remote Access Trojans, and they worked as intended. I was in. I kept my access light so as not to set off alarms. Someone was sure to be monitoring the system closely for a few days until they decided I was no longer a threat. That's fine. I can be patient when I have to be. I found enough open portals to ease my fears at being locked out. Now to decide what to do with them.

I still had a few hours to kill before I could safely pick up my things from the lab without running into Patrice, so I headed for my part-time job at my dad's bookstore.

Matthew and I had come a long way in our relationship in the short time since we'd found each other, but today he took one look at my scowl and left me to tend the front counter alone. He's still not too good at interpersonal relations, something I inherited from him along with the green eyes. Unfortunately, that lack—combined with Patrice's betrayal—triggered a nasty impulse I would come to regret.

See, Matthew has a buddy, Sammy, who hangs out with him most days. He's a fire plug of a guy, shaved head, impressive ink. Looks like he'd be more at home on a Harley than in a bookstore. Like so many others in Dayton, Sammy's a vet, on disability with PTSD and a slight limp from an unfortunate encounter with an IED over there. He usually avoids me.

Every morning, Sammy stops at the coffee shop down the street and brings Matthew and himself a tall Americano, delivering it with all the dignity of a tuxedoed *maître d'*. It shocked me the first time I saw Matthew let Sammy take money from the register for the coffee. When I asked him about it, Matthew looked hurt.

"Me and Sammy go way back," he said. "He's like my big brother, only I take care of him now instead of the other way around. He doesn't have anybody else."

Something about it didn't feel right. Zigana had taught me the value of hard work and personal responsibility. Her example kept my hacking in check, more gray-hat than black, but I also have more than my share of curiosity. She says I've got a sixth-sense, some special Romani insight. I don't go for that stuff. Tarot, divination. Let's just say I trust myself more than her spirits, as much as I appreciate their occasional nudge. I doubt any of them really want to share answers to the silly questions people ask over a deck of fancy cards. I watch. I listen. Eavesdrop here and there if someone's foolish enough to talk loudly in a public place. Snoop a little, maybe. You'd be surprised the information people give away with very little prodding. Social engineering, my professor calls it. I call it being observant. It's a hobby. But I don't use it to rip people off.

Two weeks before my scene with Patrice, I'd convinced Matthew to let me open the register for him and made it a point to be at the counter when Sammy was due to arrive. He stumbled a bit when he saw me there, but he handed over a receipt, and I reimbursed him for the coffee. I was loitering near the register again during my next shift, waiting for him, when I caught a glimpse of his reflection in the glass door as the mail carrier left. Sammy was standing just around the corner out of sight, watching me. By then I knew how much was in the register, knew how much the coffee run cost. I wandered into the bay window and picked up a stack of books from the display.

"Matthew, I'm going to switch these out for that new batch of Elmore Leonards you took in yesterday. They're in the storeroom, right?" I made sure my voice was loud enough to carry through the open transom window before slipping down an aisle away from the door.

Not more than a five-count later, the bell jingled as Sammy entered the store. I poked a hole between the books on the shelf so I could see. He went through his usual routine of greeting Matthew, delivering the coffee to the worktable where we sorted incoming books before returning to the cash register up front to get his money. When I stepped behind him and tapped Sammy on the shoulder, he jerked away.

"Didn't see you there, Missy," he said. His laughter sounded forced. It irked, that "Missy," but he refused to call me by my name. Said "Fatál" gave him the creeps.

He had no idea.

After Matthew and Sammy disappeared into the office, I counted the cash in the register. Seems that two-buck coffee had gone up quite a bit. The drawer was down ten.

I'd puzzled over Sammy's petty thievery all week. Tell Matthew and ruin his old friendship? Say nothing and let him keep getting ripped off? Ten dollars a day—okay, five and change after the coffee—adds up. I'd always believed if a victim was dumb enough to get taken, he deserved what he lost. But this was different. There was a face on the victim now: my father.

Today when Sammy strolled in with the coffee, my anger at Patrice spilled over onto an injustice I could do something about.

"Pretty good scam on the coffee, huh, Sammy?" I sidled up next to him like I had a secret. "My Gypsy grandma would say if someone hurts a friend of mine, they hurt me. And I don't like being hurt, do you?"

Sammy's face blanched. He slopped coffee on the counter trying to set the carrier down and escape.

"No, don't go," I said, blocking the door with my foot. "Matthew likes you. You're his friend." I leaned in close and whispered, "Act like one."

He disappeared into the back office with Matthew. I didn't see him again all afternoon. I tried to focus on hacking into the school network again, but that closed door irked, too. Matthew had yet to invite me into his inner sanctum. I'd guessed he dealt some of the pot he smoked after hours, or maybe did a little bookmaking to cover his minimal gambling debts. Instead, Matthew runs an exclusive little pawn shop, making loans on all sorts of oddities and selling them to select buyers when they go unclaimed. Mostly jewelry and small collectibles, and he has a thing for sports memorabilia, vintage baseball cards and the like. He gives clients a better deal than any loan shark with minimal interest and he treats them with respect. Plus he isn't into breaking kneecaps.

When the church tower down the street chimed five, I left the bookstore, still not having told Matthew I'd been fired, and went to the lab to pick up my things. No sense showing up while Patrice might still be around. Carmen met me at the front desk. She started around the counter to give me a hug, but I warned her off with a look when the security guard walked in. He must have followed me from the parking lot.

"I packed the personal items from your desk, nothing business-related, per Ms. Gerrard's orders," Carmen said as she slid the copier paper box onto the counter. Even though the guard was practically hanging on my shoulder, she raised her voice to make sure he heard.

"Your class notes are there, too." She tapped the edge of an orange folder to get my attention before shoving it out of sight under a dog-eared paperback of *Nicomachean Ethics*. "You'll need to sign this inventory."

I scanned the paper she laid in front of me. Mug, tea strainer, agave sweetener, Kleenex, a spare sweatshirt I'd used to fight the squirrely air conditioning in the lab, my autographed copy of *Cuckoo's Egg*, and the philosophy text. A stuffed Y2K Bug desk mascot wasn't mine. It was one of a pair that guarded Carmen's cubicle like ancient griffins. I smiled my thanks. "Looks like everything." I scrawled my name at the bottom of the page and handed it back to her. "Take care of yourself." I ignored the guard and left. He followed me all the way to my car.

I resisted the urge to open Carmen's folder until I made the half-hour drive home from Dayton to Yellow Springs. When I was ten, Zigana had sold the crumbling north Dayton farmhouse where I'd been born and moved us to this quirky town just east of the air force base. She bought a shop on the main drag and set up her jewelry-making studio in one corner of the sales floor. In the back room, she offers the occasional Tarot reading to friends, never strangers. We live upstairs.

I curled up in the window seat under the peaked roof of my attic room and leafed through Carmen's notes. The dozen or so pages contained a print-out of the network's activity log for the past week.

Bless you, girl!

I scanned the lines, highlighting a few instances for closer scrutiny. Carmen isn't a hacker so much as a wanna-be, but she knows her way around a network. I had shown her a few tricks. She was thrilled when I explained a basic MD5 hash and had immediately changed all her screen names to C@rm3n. Kind of defeated the point of the coding, but it made her happy. She knew what Patrice was up to with Tatum, at least as much as I did, and we groused about their "special project" together.

It was after hours now, but Zigana was in the shop getting ready for the merchants' holiday open house weekend and I'd promised to help. I gave myself an hour to scan the file, then stashed the folder in my desk and went downstairs. Zigana finished stringing handmade beads onto thin silver wire for earrings and bracelets while I tacked twinkle lights around the front windows. *Asfalt Tango* by the Romani band Fanfare Ciocarlia filled the air. Usually the energetic brass tune moved me to dance. Tonight it jarred my nerves.

The staple gun ran out while I was balanced on the edge of the front display ledge, stretching for the top corner of the window. Of course.

"I think there's more in back," Zigana said when I tossed the empty staple box onto the counter next to her work lamp. She squinted at me over her reading glasses. "You okay?"

I grunted a non-response and pushed through the bead curtain separating the rooms. After searching for a good five minutes, I found another box of staples in a basket of silk flowers stuffed under the card table holding wine making supplies. I tripped on the table leg and caught one of the decorated bottles just before it hit the floor, spilling a carton of corks in the process.

"Don't break anything," Zigana called from out front.

An impolite response died in my throat while I shoveled the corks back into the box. She'd be angry enough when I told her I got fired, but hopefully not at me. No sense front-loading her.

After I got all the lights up and found replacement bulbs for a half-dozen that were burned out, I dusted the shelves and refilled the trinket jars Zigana kept on hand for kids. The music ran out, but she waved me off when I tried to change CDs.

"Enough for tonight, I need food. My treat." She slid the last pair of earrings into the display case and stored her toolbox under the counter. "The Tavern okay?"

We bundled up and headed out into the night. A dusting of snow slicked the sidewalk and added sparkle to the barren tree branches. Zigana looped her arm through mine as we crossed Xenia Avenue.

"You're awfully quiet," she said. "Problem at school?"

I pointed out a passing neighbor to distract her and stood by while they chatted about slow business, the latest class of freshmen at Antioch College, and who knows what. I stopped listening, fretting instead about my final tuition bill.

We made it to Ye Olde Trail Tavern just before the kitchen closed. Zigana ordered her usual portabella sandwich. I skipped my favorite bacon cheddar burger and settled for the house special, a multi-layered pesto grilled cheese on marbled bread. I didn't need her lecture about eating red meat tonight. She raised one eyebrow when I downed half of my beer as soon as the server set it on the table.

I focused on the smokers huddled around the flickering fire pit on the patio and avoided Zigana's questioning look. She's not much more patient than I am, so it didn't take long.

"So, what's up?" she asked.

I took another gulp of Guinness. "I got fired."

Her eyes grew hard, and her color rose as I detailed Patrice's manipulation. Zigana didn't like computers, but she bragged to her friends about my expertise. She had stood by me when the Feds showed up with their warrant five years ago and only later, after she made sure I hadn't hurt anyone, berated me for getting caught. But like she handled my bullies in grade school, she wasn't about to let anyone mistreat family.

"Look at me." She lifted my chin, nearly impaling me with her red talons. "You're not going to let her get away with it, are you?"

I half-smiled and drained my beer. "You taught me better than that."

She leaned back in the booth and laughed, nearly drowning out the jukebox. "That's my girl."

We're not vigilantes or anything, Zigana and me. I would never physically harm another human being, except maybe in self-defense. What Zigana taught me is justice. As Romani, we share a long history of justice denied, so we've learned to exact our own understated vengeance. Subtle, maybe delayed a bit, but karma needs a hand now and then, and I'm happy to oblige. Tatum and Patrice deserved to be as unsettled as they'd made me.

After dinner, I returned to Carmen's file and made notes. First, I isolated all the emails between Tatum and Patrice, and highlighted the timestamp in yellow. Then I marked all entries for access to their project database in red. While I'd had a hand in designing the backend,

Tatum and Patrice managed all the input. I never paid much attention to the specifics since it appeared to be a standard records management file, lots of documents, contacts, financials, stuff like that. Now I was interested. If he was worried enough about my access to get rid of me, there must be something in the files I'd missed.

Several months earlier when Patrice had asked me to hack Tatum's email, she was a jealous girlfriend looking for signs he was cheating. She didn't realize the search left me in possession of his security codes, and I didn't tell her. He diligently changed the password every sixty days, but I'd left a keystroke logger in place out of habit, so updates were easy to find. I added that search to my to-do list.

My flash drive contained a complete copy of Tatum's database. It was against department policy, of course, but when Patrice tagged me to hack, I looked at it as insurance. I'd run a backup of the file only yesterday, even though I hadn't worked on the database in several weeks. I called up a single ghost proxy and tried logging in with Tatum's most recent password. Somewhere in the interim, he'd encrypted the file. Not that I couldn't get in, but now it was going to take real work. *Damn.*

It was after midnight before I worked my way through all the log entries. I'd promised to be at the bookstore for Matthew at eight in the morning to handle a delivery, so the database would have to wait.

Matthew met me at the door of the bookstore with a huge grin on his face, waving a fistful of papers. "Know what today is?"

His unusual enthusiasm clashed with the lingering foul mood from my sleepless night. I tried to play along, delaying the moment I'd have to tell him I'd been fired.

"Oktoberfest?" It was worth a guess. A bit late in the season, but he was always talking about "our" German ancestors, even when I reminded him his last name, O'Connell, was Irish.

"Mom was German, Dad was Irish. Either way, family get-togethers meant lots of beer," he'd told me.

Matthew laughed loudly at my lame joke, more excited than I'd ever seen him. "It's mortgage burning day!" He led me toward the back. A shiny new metal wastebasket sat in the middle of the scarred worktable reflecting a weird Dali-esque image of the stacks of books he'd shoved out of the way. Matthew pulled a pack of matches from his jacket pocket and handed them to me. He shook the papers again, still grinning like a maniac, before ripping them in half. He tore them in half a second time, and a third, and tossed the shreds into the wastebasket. "Light 'er up!"

"You sure about this?" I checked the ceiling for a sprinkler head. Nothing too close, so maybe we wouldn't get drenched.

"Go on, do it," he said. "I've waited twenty years for this."

I shrugged and lit a match. When the first try didn't catch, I ignited the whole pack and dropped them onto the pile. The flame flickered briefly before flaring up above the metal edges. He laughed again as we watched the papers disintegrate. It didn't take long. An acrid metallic odor from the scorched can mixed with the smell of burning paper. Made my eyes water as much as Matthew's display of emotion did. At least that's the excuse I gave him.

He set the can in the alley outside the back door to continue smoldering and reached into the drawer for his bottle of Jameson.

"This deserves a toast." He poured us each a shot in the mugs he kept by the coffee maker. "Cheers!"

I winced when the whiskey hit the back of my throat. Jameson neat at eight in the morning is a bit much. "Congratulations," I said through a cough. "Twenty years, huh?"

A funny look came over his face.

"What?" I asked.

Matthew had another surprise. He slipped a folded sheaf of papers out of his jacket pocket. "Congratulations to us." He downed another shot while I read through them.

"What the hell—the deed to the store? Why is my name on it?"

He wiped a hand across his mouth. "I sent Harmony money for…you. When Zigana sent it back, I didn't know what else to do with it, so I put it in the bank. A few years after you were born, when old man Peters decided to sell this place, I bought it. With your money." Matthew took my hand. It was the first time he'd ever touched me. "It's our store now, yours and mine. If that's okay with you."

Glimmers of hope for some kind of income to get me through school now that Patrice had fired me clashed with what I knew of the store's precarious finances. Plus, I'd never told him about my mishap with the Feds. I couldn't ruin his celebration with my troubles. That would keep. Since I wouldn't be driving for another four hours, I poured myself another shot.

The celebratory mood lasted until my phone rang while I was driving back from the bookstore to my one o'clock ethics class.

"When did you plan to tell me you lost your job?" my PO asked, sounding even more annoyed than usual.

George Pendleton had been a probation officer longer than I'd been alive. He counted down the days until retirement on a large wall calendar behind his desk. Last March on our four-year anniversary together, he told me the end of my supervision would be his going-away present. I was touched by his unusual sentiment, but it didn't last long.

Now he was just pissed, and so was I. Patrice had double-crossed me again, and faster than I'd anticipated.

"I want you in my office this afternoon," Pendleton said.

We settled on three-thirty, after my classes were done, and he hung up before I could offer an explanation. Not that I knew what I was going to say. My afternoon lecture was a waste of time. I missed most of the discussion on Kant's categorical imperative brooding over how to maneuver through this fiasco. I needed to know what Patrice had told Pendleton.

A quick call to Carmen took care of that. She filched a copy of Patrice's fax to the probation office and read it to me from a stall in the bathroom. I could tell by the echo.

"'Dear Mr. Pendleton…blah, blah, blah…regret to inform you that due to budgetary and other internal considerations, we can no longer employ your client, Fatál Wood…,' 'internal considerations,' what a bitch." Carmen tacked on her commentary and asked, "You okay?"

"I'll live. Dinner later?" I pulled into the Sunrise Center on Fifth Street where the Montgomery County probation offices are housed. The Feds handed me off to the county for supervision which at least saved me the drive to Cincinnati every month.

"I'm really sorry," Carmen said, her voice changing from bathroom echo to cafeteria clatter. "Bruce won tickets for the StarBase Indy convention. I'm picking him up in an hour." She shuffled the phone. "Large café mocha," I heard her tell the cashier before she shifted back to our conversation. "We won't be back till late Sunday. Call you then?"

"Sure, have a great time." I pocketed my phone and made it to Pendleton's office with two minutes to spare, only to be kept waiting for ten. I spent the time rehearsing my story in light of Patrice's ambiguous notice.

"Since I'm graduating in June, when they had to cut staff it made sense to let me go rather than an underclassman they could use for another year or two," I told Pendleton when he finally called me in. "It's not a big deal."

His eyes never left my face, looking for signs of deception, I'd imagine. It's what people in his line of work do, and he's good at it. But I'm good, too.

"The court requires you to hold down a job," he said, tapping the open file folder on his desk.

"No problem." I'd deliberately not told him about working for Matthew so he wouldn't call the store to check up on me. Now I had no choice. I filled him in on my job at the bookstore, leaving out the father and part-owner details. I'd make sure Matthew knew about that before Pendleton had a chance to confirm my story.

He let me go after another five-minute lecture, reminding me I only had three months left on supervision. "Don't screw it up."

As if.

I headed back to the bookstore to make sure Matthew could handle a call from Pendleton and called Zigana on the way to tell her I'd be late.

"Bring food," she said. "I haven't had a break all afternoon." Satisfaction mingled with the *ka-chunk-ding* of the ancient cash register as I heard her ring up another sale. She counted on the holiday season to improve what had been a slow business year. With everything else that's spiraling out of control in my life, her request was a comfort. Food I can handle.

Matthew wasn't so easily appeased.

"What do you mean you have a federal record?"

The disappointment on his face stung. At least Sammy wasn't around to watch.

"It was a long time ago," I said, "Over five years since they hauled me in."

"Five years is nothing." He counted a stack of resale books twice before continuing. "How could you not tell me?"

So that's it, the whole communication thing again. I closed my eyes and took a few deep breaths, searching for an answer that would satisfy him.

"We've been getting to know each other, and I'm supposed to dump a rap sheet in your lap?" I tried to laugh, but it sounded hollow, even to me. I trailed around the store at his elbow as he shelved the books. "This is exactly what I didn't want to have happen, you mad at me for being stupid."

"You're not stupid."

I waited for more. Nothing came. "But you're mad at me."

"I'm not mad."

"Disappointed?"

"Not because you were arrested. I mean, that's not something a father wants to hear, but I can deal with it." Matthew leaned against the edge of the worktable, his eyes sad. "You don't trust me."

"Trusting a man got me into this mess." In my eagerness to erase his hurt, the whole story poured out in a rush. How I'd met Rake just before graduating high school and fell stupidly into my first love. We had so much in common. Loners raised by grandparents, bullied for years. Classic rock. And computers. It was like finding a missing part of me, the *duad* Plato talks about. I had no experience with men. I'd learned from Zigana to keep them at arm's length like she did, but Rake's charm stamped out my misgivings. I dumped my scholarship to Ohio University and followed him to the local community college. We studied computer science together in class and honed our hacking skills in his crummy studio apartment at night, along with my first forays into sex. I was a late bloomer.

Zigana had tried to warn me, said she saw disaster in my future when she read the Tarot. I didn't listen. Instead, I let Rake convince me to help him crash the school network with a denial-of-service attack right before finals week. A practical joke, he insisted. Thing is, I was already a better hacker than he'll ever be. I tweaked the code he'd cobbled together, I planted it in the system when he said it was time. When the Feds showed up because of all the Homeland Security paranoia, Rake dumped it on me and cut a deal. So much for true love.

Matthew listened without interrupting. His clenched jaw when I talked about Rake's abandonment gave me hope.

"I was young and stupid, with no priors," I said. "I'll be off paper in March."

He crossed his arms, head down, and stared at the floor for a long minute. "So how'd you get a job in a computer lab?"

"Patrice needed a splashy social activist gig to get her into the 'Twenty Under Forty' media parade. Someone convinced her it'd look good to give a non-violent ex-con female a second chance. My PO wanted me employed and back in school, and Patrice's offer did the trick." Mentioning the PO reminded me. "He'll be calling you soon, guy named Pendleton."

"What for?"

"Verify employment is all, make sure you're legit." I shifted. "I didn't tell him you're my father."

Matthew straightened. "I embarrass you?"

My eyes widened. "Of course not. I just don't want him harassing you like he does Zigana if I miss a check-in."

That calmed him down a little. "Any other secrets?"

"He doesn't need to know you put me on the deed. It would only complicate things." I hadn't even told Zigana I owned half the bookstore. She wouldn't understand.

Intelligence Gathering

"Perform reconnaissance against a target to gather as much information as possible to be utilized when penetrating the target during the vulnerability assessment and exploitation phases"

When I got home, Zigana was in the shop chatting up customers. Since I rarely cook and she'd tasked me with food, I called Lucky Dragon for take-out and walked over to the storefront to save delivery time. We ate at the store's back counter during a lull, slurping up egg drop soup before splitting the fried rice and an egg roll. Patrice's clumsy attempt to cause trouble with Pendleton dominated the conversation as we considered how best to return the favor. Zigana still doesn't like computers, so possibilities from that angle left her confused.

"Trust me, there are ways," I said. I gathered up the empty cartons and left her to business. "Need a bathroom break?"

A trio of Red Hat ladies entered the store, so Zigana shook her head. "I'll be late. Christina's coming after closing."

Christina's an annual visitor who comes for a Tarot reading on her birthday. She claims to be a devout Catholic, but she also believes the cards tell her what God has in mind for the coming year. Just don't tell her husband. She always takes home a piece of Zigana's custom jewelry "for Mom" as an excuse for the visit. Whatever works.

I prowled around the apartment, too restless to concentrate on the database. I tossed in a load of laundry and called TK, my sometimes bed partner, but he had a real date for a change. I found *Fair Game* playing at the Little Art Theater down the street. Watching the reenactment of the politically-motivated smear campaign against

Valerie Plame inspired me. I spent the rest of the night looking for a way into Tatum's database and planning my next course of action.

Even with Tatum's passwords from my earlier email hacks, I couldn't break the encryption. I tapped into his Facebook account to look for clues. No luck. By two-thirty, my frustration was making me stupid. I logged into my old hacker group on the dark web to check my credits and found I still had enough for a good-sized distributed network access to run encrypted key cracking. I set up a script under my *Att3rc0p* user name and went to bed. The crack could take a few hours, or forever. Such is hacking.

I spent the weekend helping Zigana in the shop. Her regular assistant was off in Wyoming somewhere waiting for her first grandchild to be born. For a change, Zigana didn't argue when I brought my laptop with me. She knew I needed it to work on Patrice. I kept it on a ledge behind the counter so it wouldn't interfere with business. It split my brain power, probably took longer to find the answers since I couldn't focus, but I owe Zigana the time. She's been mother, father, and grandmother to me all these years since my mother—her daughter Harmony—died giving birth to me. No way I'd let her down.

Fortunately, Matthew didn't argue when I told him he'd have to manage on his own for a couple of days. He holds out hope Zigana might forgive him eventually, so he's nice to her whenever possible. I have my doubts. She won't even talk to him. Guess she still blames him for taking her daughter away. For somehow causing Harmony's death. When I was a kid, vicious bullies convinced me *I* was at fault, so I figured she blamed me, too.

She put the kibosh on that in a hurry.

"Things happen," Zigana said. "And we don't always need to know why." She had never mentioned it again.

The shop was so busy I barely had time to glance at the database. When I finally checked, the script had been running for thirty-two hours without a crack. Not a good sign. I found a few minutes before falling into bed Saturday night to run another scan of Tatum's email, and Patrice's, just in case, looking for patterns. A couple of interesting entries showed up, but I was so brain dead I couldn't do much more than sort them into groups for later study. Sunday night Zigana's book club meets at our place. Only way I can get out of reading the sappy books they pick is to serve as host, keep the hors d'œuvres hot and the wine glasses filled.

My first final for the semester was scheduled for Monday morning. School takes precedence over righteousness for now, so after the group broke up, I spent the rest of the night reviewing network protocols for the exam practicum.

What with finals, extra work at the bookstore so I could pay my tuition, and helping Zigana restock her seriously depleted inventory, I had to put Patrice and Tatum on hold, frustrating as it was. No matter how I try, there are only so many hours in a day. I never did find that hacker groove of being online for days on end. I enjoy sleep too much.

———

Lunch with Carmen on Wednesday was depressing. Whatever part of her brain isn't wrapped up in finals can't see past Bruce, the twit. He's using her, lets her pay all the bills while he spends his time on the computer playing the latest version of *Call of Duty* and surfing porn. Hasn't held a real job in almost a year. But I can't say anything. She's in love. I gave her a list of things to watch for in the computer lab since it would be easier for her, not having to get through the firewall. I can only infiltrate in short bursts or they'll track down my access, and there's stuff she can learn just by keeping an eye on Patrice. If she remembers.

———

Matthew's been awfully quiet since I told him about my arrest. If I didn't know better, considering his little backroom pawn shop and all, I'd think he was worried about my breaking the law. As it is, I'm not sure what's bugging him.

Thursday morning Matthew met me at the front door again. That time he wasn't smiling.

"Sammy's been evicted," he said.

It was too early for the coffee run, but I looked around for him anyway. The store was empty. "I'm sorry to hear that." I didn't know what else to say to his simmering anger. He just glared at me. "What am I missing?"

"When did you chase him out of the till, before or after I signed over the deed?"

That set me back. I dropped my bag under the counter and shrugged off my jacket, buying time. "You knew he was skimming?"

"Course I knew," Matthew said. "You're not the only smart one in the family."

Family. Funny, I'd almost gotten used to the idea, here it was slipping away.

"You think I did that because of the mortgage?" Now I was angry. We faced each other, nose-to-nose, in a stare-down we were both too proud to break.

The antique wall clock was the only sound in the room for several minutes. Finally, without looking away, I asked, "So how long are we going to stand here like idiots?"

Matthew exhaled loudly and slumped onto the high-back stool by the register. "How is it you're so much like me when we hardly know each other? No, I don't think it's 'cause of the mortgage."

"I thought Sammy was ripping you off."

"He thought so, too. No, he'd say he just borrowed the money." Matthew wrinkled his forehead in thought. "What's that line from *White Christmas*, when Bing Crosby's talking to Rosemary Clooney in the night club, first time they meet? 'Everybody's got a little larceny operating in them.' That's Sammy."

Leave it to Matthew to dredge up an old movie quote to make me laugh.

"So why'd you let him get away with it?"

"Sammy and I go way back, went to high school together over at Belmont. His old man talked him into joining the Army after we graduated. Taunted him more like it, said it'd make a man out of him." Matthew's eyes clouded over. "Bastard."

"His old man," I said, to be sure I followed.

He nodded and cleared his throat. "After two tours in the Mideast in whatever the hell the government called the latest war that wasn't, Sammy wasn't the same. Post-traumatic Stress Disorder they call it now. His head's so screwed up he can't hold down a job. Took him three years to get sober and another two before the VA broke down and gave him disability. It's almost enough to live on, if you can call what he does living."

Any words that came to mind were lame. I hung my head and waited for him to finish.

"Even as messed up as he is, Sammy won't take charity. I tried to give him a job here. That didn't work out. He gets rattled too easy. He's good at the coffee run, though, gives him a routine so he'll get out of bed in the morning. I made it plain I trusted him with the cash because knowing Sammy like I do, I knew he'd help himself. And he does, just enough to get by."

Stupid. Stupid. Stupid. The clock punctuated my internal chastisement.

Matthew roused himself and looked at me, the hint of a smile giving me hope.

"I don't know what you said to scare the shi…sorry, daughter, the living daylights out of him. If he hadn't been drunk last night, I doubt he'd ever have told me about it. First time he fell off the wagon in a dozen years."

I returned his smile, relieved at the "daughter" but still hesitant to believe he didn't hate me for screwing things up. "I thought I was protecting you. That's what we do for family."

He snorted. "Families also communicate, least that's what Dr. Phil says. Guess we got a lot to learn."

"What about Sammy?"

"I worked it out with the building manager. He'll tell Sammy the government's picking up the rent as part of his disability and send me the bills."

"Send *us* the bills," I said. "We take care of our friends, too."

Matthew's smile had broadened, erasing the last of my anxiety. "So who's going for coffee?"

I survived finals week, somehow. With Patrice and Tatum weighing on my mind, I have no idea what I wrote for my philosophy exam. My GPA is high enough I can wiggle by with a low score, but I'd rather not. I pride myself on my ethics, even if not everyone would agree on my standards. Kant's not my philosophical benchmark. I lean more toward utilitarianism, but with limits.

Saturday morning, I was at Matthew's front counter when Sammy showed up with coffee. For the first time since I'd started at the bookstore, he handed me a cup on his way to the back table. Matthew must have convinced him I was okay. I finished opening the register and followed him to say thanks. Matthew disappeared into the office when he saw me. I slumped against the table in disappointment.

Sammy patted my shoulder. "He'll get over it, you know."

"Having a daughter who's a felon?"

"Hell, that's not what's bothering him. He's afraid his loan stuff could get you in trouble. Trying to figure out how to work around it, still be there for folks who need him." Sammy shuffled his feet, staring at the floor. "You and him are a lot alike."

Gratitude for the apparent truce between us humbled me. I needed all the friends I could get these days. "So why does he run away?"

"Keeping his distance. Probation says you can't be around any criminal activity."

"Pendleton called."

He sipped his coffee, almost slopping it as he nodded at the same time. "Matthew said he seemed like a decent guy."

Matthew called Sammy into the back office, so I grabbed a stack of books and started shelving. His words unnerved me. I don't like people worrying about me. Spent my school years hiding all sorts of things from Zigana so she wouldn't. Now Matthew. And I was the one worrying.

Business was slow, so I brought up my laptop. I used an unsecured downtown wi-fi to tap the school network through one of the more obscure back doors I left on the server and ran a new log file from Tatum's email. I sorted the addresses, deleting the mundane administrative stuff. Patrice's I dumped into one folder. Somebody called Khan37, with nearly a dozen exchanges in the past month, went into another.

After lunch, I went back to the database script hack. Persistent cracking finally turned up a password—I was in. I scrolled through a list of dates, email addresses, and cryptic document names. Each doc file was linked to an external folder. I needed to find access to each one on the server if I wanted to see the contents. I copied the URL for each document into Notepad. A late afternoon rush pulled me away from the laptop and kept me busy until close. I called Carmen on the way home to check the server maintenance schedule. Her answer deflated my recovered enthusiasm.

"After grades were printed late last night, they shut down the entire network for a system upgrade while they move the server," she said, her voice muffled. "Won't be back online until the end of next week maybe, and I'm off till the semester starts in January."

"Where are you?"

She giggled. "That tickles, Brucie!...What'd you say?"

"Never mind. Call me when you come up for air."

———

The apartment was empty when I got home. Zigana's note said she was at a gallery opening down the street, if I wanted to come. I didn't. I preferred to mope. All I had were logs, no real data, and now I was locked out of the servers for a week or more. Tatum could take advantage of the downtime and move his files. Or whatever maintenance they were doing might wipe out all my access points. I don't like to lose. I needed a back-up plan, but until I knew what changes were being made, I was stuck.

An hour later, Zigana shrieked when I greeted her from my cocoon on the loveseat as she flipped on the lights.

"Damn, girl, why are you sitting in the dark?" She patted her chest a few times, feigning palpitations.

I growled something non-committal.

Zigana squinted at me for a minute while she shrugged out of her faux leather trench coat. "Be right back." She disappeared into the kitchen and returned with an open bottle of her homemade chocolate raspberry port. She poured a generous amount into two stemless wine glasses from the corner cupboard and handed me one. "Drink. Then talk."

I took a cautious sip, knowing the forty-proof alcohol would sneak up on me. "It's computer crap, you don't want to know."

Zigana waved off my objection. "It's about Tatum and what's-her-name? Talk." She nestled sideways into her Art Deco club chair and slung her legs over the arm, kicking off her stiletto heels in the process. "Should never have worn those out in this weather. My feet are frozen." She let me finish half the glass before prodding again. "What's up?"

Even though all the people she'd terrified over the years wouldn't believe it, Zigana is kind, fiercely protective, and a great listener. She's just choosy about who she lets into her life. The look on her face when she mentioned Tatum made me glad I was one of the favored few.

I talked. The port seeped in, warming my chilled body and heightening the passion in my words. I replayed Patrice's backstabbing, her callous dismissal. I railed against Tatum's high-handed treatment of us lowly students. I bitched about Carmen's single-mindedness for Bruce when I needed her. The wall I'd locked my emotions behind crumbled. Somewhere in the midst of it all, Zigana leaned over and refilled my glass. I kept going. I talked about Matthew, how I'd disappointed him, and avoided Zigana's eyes as I did, sure she couldn't care less about his feelings. I confessed my misjudgment of Sammy, complained about Pendleton's intrusion, and whined a bit about the unfairness of life. That's when she stopped me.

"How many times have I told you, life isn't fair?" She swung around to face me. "As for the rest, we can deal with them, one thing at a time. I can't help with the computer stuff, but…." she stopped, staring into her port for a long minute before emptying the glass in one gulp. "I should probably explain about Matthew."

Zigana bolted from the chair and disappeared into her bedroom. She came back with a shoe-box size wooden chest. The lid was covered with a bright floral mosaic, her mother's handiwork I'd bet, from what little I'd picked up over the years. A fine-spun silver chain looped through an intricate key rested on top.

She handed me the box. "Harmony left this for you. I never opened it. I was saving it for…." she trailed off to concentrate on the port.

While she split the last of the bottle between us, it was her turn to talk. I sat motionless, cradling the treasure box, afraid of breaking the spell of this rare moment. I learned more about my family in an hour than I had in my entire twenty-four years. About how her father left when Zigana was barely six and her baby sister just toddling. About how her mother, Pashka, supported them by making jewelry and mosaics to sell at local flea markets and festivals, always just getting by. About the notorious Irish Travelers, one of the few remaining nomadic Gypsy tribes in the country, who come through the Dayton area every year or two. About the widower who took a liking to Pashka and convinced her to join them on the road. Zigana was sixteen. She refused to leave with them, preferring to stay with the dashing young *gajo* who was courting her. Pashka disapproved of Tobias and left without Zigana. She never came back.

"I couldn't believe she wanted to live that way, always wandering, blamed for whatever crime happened nearby. But she went. That was the last time I saw my *daj*, my mother."

I had to strain to hear those last words. She pushed herself out of the chair again and went to the kitchen. I heard water running, the stove click on, the rattle of tea cups. When Zigana reappeared, her expression was calm, although her eyes were bright with tears.

She perched on the arm of the loveseat. "About ten years later, I heard Pashka died in Mississippi somewhere."

For several minutes, the only sound was the hiss of the tea kettle. When she didn't offer more, I spoke for the first time since she began her story. "And your sister?"

She shrugged. "She could find me if she wanted to. I haven't gone that far."

"But you haven't looked."

Zigana's glare stopped me.

"Family takes care of family," she said. "They left. I didn't."

The kettle whistled. I pressed Zigana back into her seat and made the tea. I was afraid she was done talking, but over a steaming mug of chamomile, she continued.

"Toby took care of me. When the Army drafted him, he insisted we get married before he shipped out. Harmony was our honeymoon baby. He was ecstatic when she was born. Tore him up when he couldn't get leave to be with us." She sat quietly, lost in her memories while the tea cooled untouched. "He died when Harmony was four, so it was just the two of us all those years." Her smile was sad. "Kind of like you and me."

I heard the guilt in Zigana's voice when she told me how Harmony contracted rheumatic fever the year after Toby died. "I was still mourning, never even noticed how sick she was until it was too late. It damaged her heart, and the doctors said she should never have children. I didn't care. At least she was alive. Then she met Matthew." Zigana stopped again. She sipped the tea, making a face at the now-tepid liquid, and set it aside. "When she got pregnant, I was so mad at her, at them both. She knew it was a bad idea, but she was in love, and stubborn. She wouldn't tell Matthew how dangerous it was, wouldn't let me tell him, threatened to run off with him if I did. When she died, all I could do was scare him off so I wouldn't lose you, too."

I knelt on the floor next to her chair and laid my head in her lap, like I'd done so many times growing up. She stroked my hair.

"Matthew is a part of my life now, but you and me…." I hugged her knees. "You're stuck with me."

Alone in my room after Zigana went to bed, I opened the box. A musky floral scent slipped into the room. I'm not convinced it wasn't Harmony's spirit.

Inside the box, nestled among a few dried sunflowers, a long bright patterned scarf, and a stack of faded pink envelopes secured with a blue ribbon, I found Harmony's diary. I flipped through the gilt-edged pages, hesitant to read much at first. I felt like an intruder. I set it aside, pulled the ribbon off the envelopes, and sorted through them. There were seven, one for each month of her pregnancy. The first three were addressed to "My Little One." By the fourth, she must have figured out I was a girl. The rest of the envelopes were decorated with hand-drawn hearts and labeled "Princess Angel Wood." Yikes. For as much trouble as my name has been, I'm glad Zigana didn't stick me with that.

I stayed close to home after that evening, wanting to reassure Zigana of her importance in my life, needing reassurance myself that we'd get through this mess with Tatum together, like we'd always conquered life in the past.

I couldn't figure out Tatum's scheme until the servers were back on line, maybe not even then. And after paying my last tuition bill and buying token holiday gifts for a chosen few, my bank account was tapped. What I earn at the bookstore puts gas in the car and pays my half of our living expenses, not much else. But I keep that to myself. No sense worrying Zigana or Matthew more than I already do. If I can finish my degree and get off probation, a new tech firm south of Dayton has offered me a job in their development office. The IT community around here is in-bred, and if Patrice's version of events gets out, their offer would vanish along with any other prospects within a hundred miles. I can't let that happen.

The holidays descended, and while we don't celebrate Christmas as a religious event, the winter solstice is a good milepost. We decorate with pine boughs and candles. New Year's Eve is a big event in Yellow Springs, too, with special art gallery exhibits, late night screenings at the Little Art, and a multi-colored disco ball drop at the intersection of Xenia and Short streets filling in for the glitzy Times Square celebration. Carmen and Bruce joined us for the festivities, and with Zigana humoring the latest gentleman who wanted to get close to her, I felt like a fifth-wheel. I have no love interest on tap right now. TK is more of a convenience, so I invited Matthew. Probably not a good idea, but I was feeling contrary.

Zigana's face tightened when Matthew showed up at the ball drop. I'd had enough sense not to invite him to dinner in the apartment beforehand, but I also didn't warn her he was coming. Better to ask forgiveness than permission. I made sure to keep them at opposite ends of our little group and hoped for the best. Between an assortment of buskers and the rigged-up loudspeaker at the official viewing stand, the gathering on the street was deafening, so it wasn't difficult to run interference. Open container laws are fairly loose for pedestrians in Yellow Springs on New Year's Eve, and the crush at the intersection was well-lubed.

Carmen and Matthew get along pretty well. He treats her like another daughter and shares my opinion of Bruce. Carmen and I found seats on a bench outside the shop with one of the men standing at each end. Somehow I got stuck with Bruce. I tried to ignore him, but when Zigana and her companion wandered off to join a group in front of the theatre, he struck up a conversation.

"Don't look old enough to be your grandma," he said, gesturing toward Zigana with his plastic cup of beer.

I almost wore its contents. I shifted as far away from him as I could on the narrow bench without crushing Carmen. I craned my neck to find Zigana's lithe figure in the crowd and had to admit, in her red wool cape, bright patterned skirt, and black leggings, with those ridiculous stilettos, she didn't fit the grandmotherly norm. Only one reason I love her so.

"She'll never be old, grandmother or not," I said to Bruce. "She'll be sixty in a few months and couldn't care less."

He lost track of the conversation when a gaggle of co-eds not dressed for the weather skirted past. His eyes followed them until they disappeared into the throng. I hoped Carmen didn't notice. She's sensitive about that sort of thing, fretting over how she looks, always battling her weight. Another strike against Bruce for not realizing how she feels.

I planted a heel on his foot and stood up, ignoring his yelp of pain.

"Matthew, keep my seat warm, will you? I'll refill our drinks."

Carmen scooted across to let him sit down. I collected the empties and went upstairs. When I kicked open the door to return to street-level, juggling four full cups, Carmen was standing, her gaze fixed on a spot in front of the bank across the street. She handed Bruce and Matthew their drinks before nudging me away from the bench.

"Look, over there by the ATM." She crooked her elbow and pointed with a finger held close to her side. Like anyone could see what she was doing, or cared.

I scanned the crowd overflowing from the sidewalk onto Xenia Avenue. Shadows and winter caps distorted recognizable features, so it took me a minute to find what had her so worked up. A tall man in a black leather fedora raised his head to watch the crew fiddle with a couple of broken bulbs on the suspended ball, and the streetlight hit him.

Tatum, with Patrice clinging to his arm.

It was like a gut-punch. *How dare they invade my turf?* Stupid, irrational, but real.

"What's wrong?" Matthew joined us near the door. Bruce plopped onto the bench, dislodging a pair of 12-year-olds who darted for the empty seat.

I took a deep breath while the mental arguments collided. "Nothing."

"It's Tatum and Patrice," Carmen said, my sharp look of warning missing her entirely.

"Where?"

She did the odd little pointing thing again. I turned my back and concentrated on the wine.

"You want I should break his kneecaps, boss?" Matthew asked.

I snorted the pinot noir. Damn him and his silly movie quotes. I dismissed Tatum and Patrice and concentrated on the celebration, determined not to let them ruin the evening.

My pledge lasted as long as most New Year's resolutions. Less than half an hour after the ball descended, the streets were mostly empty. My fretting returned with the stillness. Zigana and her beau were back with the four of us at the door to the shop, debating where to continue the party, when Tatum and Patrice passed in front of us with a quick two-step to avoid a staggering Bruce.

"What a coincidence." Tatum pushed Bruce upright and away before facing me. "I didn't know you frequented Yellow Springs."

"I live here." I gripped Matthew's arm and warned Zigana off with a look.

Patrice's pale face was washed out further by the glare of the streetlight. She studied our footwear and said nothing.

"Why don't you introduce us?" Tatum asked.

"No."

I relished the confusion on Tatum's face as he tried to puzzle out our connections. My resemblance to Zigana is undeniable, to Matthew not so much.

When Tatum recognized Carmen trying to steady Bruce, his eyes narrowed. "Well, Happy New Year to you." Patrice mumbled what might have been a greeting before he propelled her toward the town parking lot.

Zigana took charge. "Upstairs." She pulled her date aside, whispered in his ear, and sent him away. When Matthew hesitated at the door, she said, "You, too," and led the way.

I helped Carmen steer Bruce to the loveseat while Matthew hovered in the entryway like a stray puppy unsure of its welcome. Zigana started a pot of coffee. She locked eyes with Matthew across the room, and I saw a flash of anger cross her face, followed by uncertainty and fear. I moved in to fill the tray with mugs, squeezing her shoulder as I passed. The pressure broke her concentration on him and earned me a resolute smile.

"So that was Tatum?" she asked. "He looks familiar. Her, too."

"Can't imagine why, he's a big-city type." I cocked my head at Matthew, motioning him to sit down. He slid onto the edge of the nearest chair.

Zigana added a plate of deli pastries to the tray, along with cream and sugar. I followed her into the living room with the coffee pot. Bruce's snores punctuated polite chatter as everyone settled down. I felt sorry for Carmen, wondering again why she put up with such an oaf. Zigana pulled out a stool, positioning herself as far from Matthew as possible. I parked on her club chair in between. The pointless chit-chat faded away, and awkward silence pushed me to answer Zigana's question for everyone.

"Yes, that was Tatum and Patrice. They usually socialize in Cincinnati, or the casinos. Never expected to see them here."

"Have you figured out what to do yet?" Zigana asked.

"Do about what?" Matthew cleared his throat, flushing under Zigana's sharp look. "The job's gone, move on."

"That's your answer, 'move on'?" Her eyes darkened. "Explains a lot."

His mug clattered onto the side table as he leaned into the debate which took a sudden shift away from Tatum. "What's that supposed to mean? Fighting a losing battle is a waste of time and energy."

"It's only a losing battle if you give up," Zigana said.

Matthew stiffened. "I didn't give up. I gave in to the inevitable. Harmony was more important than my ego. I wasn't going to jeopardize her health, or the baby, fighting with you."

Zigana snorted. "Uh-huh."

Carmen stared wide-eyed, bouncing from Zigana to Matthew like she was at a tennis match. "What are they talking about?" she whispered to me.

I shook my head, not breathing. She leaned against Bruce's shoulder and watched in silence.

Matthew gripped his knees, white-knuckled. "She stopped coming to work, wouldn't answer the phone. You threatened me with the cops if I came to the house again. What was I supposed to do?"

"Fight for her, if you really cared." Zigana eyed him over the rim of her mug, daring him to continue.

I'd seen that look before when she pushed me to defend myself, prodded me to find the words to justify my argument, taught me to stand my ground. I sat back and let the scene unfold without interference. It was twenty-five years overdue.

For several mesmerizing minutes, they traded barbs and snipes, disagreed over memories of Harmony, and lobbed not-so-veiled accusations of who was to blame.

"I sent money for the doctor," Matthew said, desperation in his voice. Up against the force that is Zigana, he was outmatched.

"You sent money for an abortion."

I gasped, Zigana's words echoing in the sudden stillness.

Matthew's shoulders slumped. "If it would've saved her life, yes." He jerked upright and met Zigana's accusing stare. "I wanted our baby as much as she did. But I wanted Harmony more."

"She preferred the risk of dying rather than give up her baby," Zigana shot back.

I'd had enough. "Stop it, both of you! 'Her baby' is right here, remember?" I vaulted out of my chair and up the stairs to my room, returning with Harmony's treasure box. I tossed the diary to Matthew and dropped the letters in Zigana's lap. "Do you have any idea what you did to her? All your bickering, trying to control her life? All she wanted was the man she loved and their baby. Me." I faced Zigana. "Just like you wanted Toby's baby, even after he died."

Zigana caught her breath. I held mine, too, knowing I'd breached an invisible barrier. Trembling, she clutched Harmony's letters and left the room. The quiet closing of her bedroom door deflated my anger.

Before I could figure out what to say, Matthew stuffed the diary in his coat pocket and left. After a seemingly endless stretch of silence, I exhaled softly and gave up myself. I dug a blanket out of the closet to drape over Bruce before Carmen and I gathered the dirty dishes, emptied the coffee pot, and turned out the lights. When I hesitated outside Zigana's door, Carmen pulled me up the stairs to my room.

"Not now," she said.

While she did bathroom things, I curled up on the window seat. Xenia Avenue was empty, bits of confetti mingling with light snow flurries as the wind picked up. I toyed with the stuffed Y2K bug for a minute before slamming it onto my desk, its audio chip producing a wholly unsatisfying artificial sound of breaking glass. My world was shattering, ten years later than the new millennium predicted.

I didn't expect to sleep, but the smell of brewing coffee and yeasty baking woke me to a pale sunlight. Carmen was already up, fixing her make-up at the bathroom mirror. I rarely bothered with anything more than eyeliner—a remnant of my high school Goth days, but it fascinated me to watch her routine. It also delayed the inevitable confrontation with Zigana.

I shouldn't have worried. We found her bustling around the kitchen, a fresh quiche cooling on the counter. She handed us each a mug of coffee, her smile aimed at a spot over my left shoulder.

"Look, about last night," I said.

"I remember where I saw Tatum and Patrice," she said, deflecting my comment. The oven timer conspired with her, buzzing loud enough to wake Bruce, and the conversation ended before it began. Zigana set a loaf of sourdough on the cutting board and shooed us all to the table. The elephant in the living room was going to stay hidden behind the oversized philodendron.

For now.

"I remember where I saw them before," Zigana said again while we ate. "They were at last month's village council meeting."

"Why would they be there?" I savored the nutty Gruyère in the quiche and allowed her to avoid personal matters until we were alone.

She handed me a sheaf of papers. "I found a copy of the minutes in my folder. She spoke against the gas drilling company that's soliciting around town."

The *Yellow Springs News* had covered the project in detail. A drilling company out of Michigan was trying to lease farm and residential land for natural gas exploration. Local environmentalists were in full protest mode over the controversial method of hydraulic fracturing, or fracking, used to extract natural gas from rock reservoirs. Opponents say it contaminates groundwater and destabilizes bedrock. Give Yellow Springs an issue and the activists come out in force, with Zigana usually at the front of the pack. We're not called the Berkley of the Midwest for nothing.

I leafed through the notes. "Patrice is always looking for a cause to keep her face in the news, but she never struck me as a tree-hugger. What does she care about what happens in Yellow Springs?"

"Apparently she's from Arkansas."

"So?"

Zigana sighed and pushed a clipping across the table to me. "Don't you ever pay attention to the world outside town? Fracking's a real problem there, and northeast of here in Youngstown."

The news article detailed protests in Arkansas over almost five hundred earthquakes in the area in four months' time compared to thirty-eight in all of the previous year, linking the tremblers to increased fracking activity in the state.

"Still doesn't explain why she was at council." I scooped up the last bite of quiche with a chunk of sourdough and washed it down with the rest of my coffee, coughing frantically when I inhaled the liquid.

"I know I taught you to chew your food," Zigana said as she cleared the plates.

Carmen stifled a giggle and got up to help. Bruce staggered to the loveseat, his plate untouched, and collapsed in a heap.

I scooted behind them to load the dishwasher, my chore since childhood. "So now there's another question mark around those two. Just what I need."

Two hours later when the Rose Bowl Parade rounded the last corner in Pasadena, I helped Carmen load Bruce into her car, and they went home.

"I'll be at work Tuesday. Call me if you need anything," Carmen said before pulling away. Bruce flipped a half-hearted wave in my direction and slumped in the seat.

Back in the apartment, Zigana was engrossed in hand-drawing labels for her first batch of wine for the new year. I waited until she finished the last calligraphic stroke of her signature to interrupt.

"We need to talk about last night."

She cleaned her pens with a deliberateness bordering on obsession before laying her work aside and joining me in the kitchen. I refilled the coffee cups, started another pot, wiped the counter. Procrastination's a family trait.

"I read the letters." Zigana's voice quavered just a bit. She gulped her coffee, then fanned her mouth over the hot liquid.

I scrambled for a glass of water.

Cooling off her tongue tempered her emotions, too. When she collected herself, she laughed softly. "Harmony was smarter than I thought. Kind of like you, huh?"

"Maybe." I grinned, glad she wasn't mad at me. "We come from good stock."

Zigana tugged the ribbon out of her hair. She tousled the dark tresses, hiding behind her hair for a moment before sweeping it back. "I was too hard on Matthew," she said. Her eyes glistened. "He loved her, but I wouldn't let him in."

"You did the best you could at the time." I took her hand from the napkin she worried on the table and sandwiched it in my own. "You all did. I was hard on both of you last night, and I'm sorry."

"If he hadn't pushed for an abortion, we might have worked things out."

"He said it was to save her life. I believe him."

"Maybe, but it's still wrong." She was adamant, refusing to absolve him completely. "How would you feel if he'd convinced her?"

"I wouldn't be here to feel anything, would I? And Harmony might be."

Zigana jerked her hand free, but the idea stilled further protest. The coffee maker gasped one final gurgle and fell quiet. We sat lost in thoughts of what might have been, what is…and what will never be.

"I suppose you're right. It was so long ago." Zigana topped off the mugs and moved to the living room. We settled into our usual seats and she repeated, "It was so long ago. Matthew seems like a good guy, I guess, but how can you be sure?"

"He is." I thought about his unquestioning acceptance of me, of the bookstore deed, but settled on a marginally safer example. "One of the first things he asked me, when we connected, was where Har…she was buried. So I took him to Woodland Cemetery."

Dayton's historical Woodland Cemetery is the final resting place of numerous celebrities of various infamy, including the Wright Brothers, humor writer Erma Bombeck, and Levi and Matilda Stanley, the legendary King and Queen of Dayton Gypsies. A *New York Times* article from 1878 reported twenty thousand people came to Queen Matilda's funeral in Woodland. Their descendants and assorted other Romani, including Harmony, are buried in plots surrounding the obelisk erected in her honor.

Matthew had never heard about them and he's kind of a history buff, so it was an interesting visit. Until I showed him Harmony's grave. Then he got real quiet. We stood in front of the small headstone for a long time. Even the breeze stopped blowing, like nature held its breath so as not to disturb his grief. I didn't know what to say, his tears were more than I'd ever shed. It took a fire crew roaring down Wayne Avenue, sirens blaring, to bring him back.

"I never knew where she was," Matthew said, brushing the tears away with his sleeve. "Seeing her name in stone like that…." He'd cleared his throat. "Thanks."

Zigana listened thoughtfully while I talked, then gave an exaggerated shudder. "I don't do cemeteries. But I'm glad he mourns her like I do."

"Give him a chance. You have more in common than you think."

"Maybe."

Daylight melted to dusk as peace returned to our little corner of the world. Matthew I could deal with tomorrow.

Monday morning, after helping Zigana clear the party debris from in front of the shop and salting down the thin layer of ice on the sidewalk, I drove into Dayton to find Matthew. The bookstore was closed for the long holiday weekend, but I found him there anyway, sorting boxes we'd snagged at an estate sale on Thursday. Harmony's diary was on the shelf under the register where I always stored my backpack. I zipped it into the outside pocket before joining Matthew at the back table. His eyes were bloodshot, and his head looked like a black and silver Brillo pad.

"You look like hell," I said.

"Morning to you, too." He shoved a box in my direction. We worked through the dusty books, stacking the usable volumes by category and tossing the tattered, water-stained, or those with missing covers into the recycle bin. It wasn't until all the boxes were emptied that he spoke again.

"I went to the cemetery this morning to talk to Harmony."

I caught my breath. Not what I expected, by a long shot.

He spent a long minute scrubbing the grime off his hands while he leaned against the table next to me. I waited, afraid any movement would shut him down.

A heavy sigh, and Matthew looked at me with a piercing sadness. "I apologized for not fighting harder for her. And for you."

"You did the best you could at the time." Echoing my words to Zigana might be a cop-out, but it's all I had. I toed his foot. "I don't blame any of you for what happened, you know? It's just life. I was out of line last night."

He shook his head. "No, you were right. Zigana and I got so caught up in what we wanted, or thought was best, we forgot about Harmony." The bell jangled over the front door and Sammy came in with coffee. Matthew squeezed my hand. "Not holding out hope on Zigana forgiving me, but I hope you do."

Sammy joined us before I could answer. I was glad to see Mama Elephant slip out from behind the stacks and vanish, leaving a pair of her calves hovering under the window seat.

I wish I could say the tension between Zigana and Matthew vanished as easily, but no such luck. The next few weeks were like walking a tightrope. I had to be careful not to mention him to her, or vice versa, unless I wanted another round of ancient guilt, blaming, and excusing. Business dropped off in both shops after the first of the year, and when classes started again, it gave me an excuse to cut my hours working for either of them. I don't have enough "family" experience to tackle anything more from the murky past right now.

Covert Gathering

"Wireless scanning, Dumpster diving, Types of Equipment in Use"

Carmen called Wednesday while I was driving to class. "Tatum showed up at my desk this morning." Her whisper sounded hollow. Must be in the bathroom again.

"What'd he want?" Tatum rarely came to the computer lab. Seeing Carmen with me must have triggered an alarm.

"It was weird. He acted like we were old friends, made some stupid comments about the crowd New Year's Eve, stuff like that."

"Did he mention me?" I heard a distant voice greet Carmen.

"No, he...hold on." A short sound of muffled scurrying, the thud of a door, and she was back. "Patrice came in. She never uses the hall bathroom."

"Where'd you go?"

Quick breathing rasped through the phone. "I'm in the storage room at the back of the lab. Are they following me?"

I replayed the New Year's Eve encounter, Tatum's expression when he saw Carmen. "Could be. But Tatum didn't mention me?"

"Nope. Said something goofy about being glad I was on the team. Then he left."

A traffic back-up at Patterson and Third gave me a minute to think. "Don't do anything more about their emails or the database. And if you have any notes, shred them or take them home."

"You're scaring me."

"Not my intent, just playing it safe." I wheeled into a parking spot next to the library. "There's one thing I need before you back off though. The final protocol documents for the new server. When I worked with the team, the sysadmin kept a copy in a blue notebook on his desk."

Her voice went up a notch. "How do I do that and not get caught?"

"Just borrow the notebook after Patrice's gone for the day. Scan a copy and email it to me. From home." After I was fired, I'd told her not to email me from the lab, but she keeps forgetting.

———

Late Friday, Carmen sent me the configuration documents for the new server. I got in easily enough from the public wi-fi, which doesn't say much for school security. Tatum's files were another matter. He'd locked them behind a triple layer of firewall protection. Fancy stuff.

What's he hiding? I mulled the possibilities over the weekend, considering how best to breach his network without getting caught. After discarding more elaborate methods, I called Carmen Sunday night. A few minutes of chit-chat before I put her on the spot for the last time. "When's your next evening shift in the lab?"

"Tomorrow."

"I'll call you. If Tatum and Patrice aren't around, I'll stop in."

Anxiety exploded in a single word. "Why?"

"You don't need to know. It's better that way. Remember what I told you about plausible deniability?" I ended the call before her fears stirred up more guilt in my chest.

The next morning, Carmen texted me. *Admin meeting in Columbus today and tomorrow. Patrice and Tatum just left.* With the two of them out of town, I'd be able to poke around during evening hours without fear of getting caught.

I showed up forty-five minutes before the lab closed for the night. Philosophy class and Ockham's razor told me the simplest answer was best. Why bother with an elaborate hack into the new server when I could walk in through the front door? I'd deliberately kept my clothes generic with a hooded sweatshirt to hide my face from the security cameras, and I waited until night security was on rounds before I slipped down the hall to Patrice's office. Figured I'd start there, since she's more likely to be lax.

Carmen's master key got me through the door. I flicked the blinds closed over the interior window so security wouldn't spot the light before I started on the computer. Her log-in was stored, so I didn't have to hack through sign-on. *Lazy bitch.* I popped a flash drive into the USB port. In the two minutes it took my installed auto-run script to process, I studied the rogues gallery dotting the wall next to the desk. Patrice and the mayor. Patrice and the county commissioner. Patrice and the head of the Chamber of Commerce. A gilt-edged Twenty Under Forty certificate hung next to an MBA from Stanford. Below the polished oak frames, a matching triangle case displayed a folded American flag under glass. I leaned in to read the gold plaque: Lt. Col. Patrick Gerrard, USAF Ret. He'd died young, only sixty-three, just four years earlier. A framed photo on the desk showed a stern man in uniform next to Patrice in her commencement regalia. No picture of Mom.

The light on my flash drive blinked out. It was now filled with all her passwords and access codes, as well as recent file list and emails. Thumb-sucking, it's called by those of us in the hacker world. Patrice would never know.

Tatum's office wasn't so easy. The master key didn't work. I had to resort to jimmying the lock with the picks I'd borrowed from Matthew's pawn shop inventory. I'd practiced for hours following the YouTube video I found, but actually breaking in took too long and probably left scratches on the knob. I didn't stop to check.

The center of Tatum's desk was empty, the calendar pad showing only a slight indent left by his laptop. *Damn.* I started on the files in the credenza. A whistled "Born in the USA" in the hall, a rattle at the door as the guard checked the lock, and I dropped to my knees behind the desk. I held my breath until the off-key notes faded in the distance, then resumed my search. The paper files were useless, normal school administration stuff. The desk drawers were locked, and I couldn't risk scratching the wood. Wasted effort, getting into the office.

I stood with my ear against the door for a long minute before easing it open. The hall was empty. I made my way back to the lab without incident to find Carmen pale and pacing.

"Piece of cake," I said. I dropped the master key ring on her desk and stripped off my latex gloves, tucking them into the middle of a jacket stuffed in my backpack. The flash drive stayed in my pocket. Security might check my bag on the way out, but they wouldn't search me. Not that they'd necessarily alert on the flash drive since I was coming out of the computer lab. No sense taking any more chances. I crammed my textbooks on top of the jacket and left Carmen to lock up. "See you at the Trolley Stop in half-an-hour."

"I have to pick up Bruce first." Carmen tried for defiant and failed. She just looked anxious.

I shrugged off the guilt again. "Whatever. I'll be there."

An hour later she showed up. I'd finished my one margarita, since I was driving, and nursed a Red Bull. With Patrice's files to search through, I was facing a late night.

"Where's Bruce?"

"He dropped me off. He's in some kind of video poker tournament at the Cyber Café tonight," Carmen said. "I told him you'd take me home." She leaned in on her elbows so the bartender could hear her over the din. "Blue Moon, draft."

He filled a pilsner, stuck an orange slice on the rim, and set it in front of her. "Two dollars, ladies' night."

"Put it on my tab," I told him. We edged away from the bar to an empty table near the front window.

"Thanks again for helping," I said.

"Why're they watching me?" Carmen wiped the sweat off the side of the glass in even rows, top to bottom, all the way around. A deep frown made the stud in her eyebrow stand at attention against her white face.

The guilt I'd been fighting hit me again. "Tatum and Patrice?" I was stalling. She wasn't talking about the guys at the next table, even though they were checking us out. Ladies' night groupies on the prowl.

Carmen didn't even notice. My idiot question earned me a sharp look of reproof, and I caved.

"I never thought they'd connect us," I said. "New Year's Eve was a fluke."

"So should I worry?"

"They can't fire you, too. Somebody's got to run the lab, and we know Patrice isn't capable."

Her frown turned to panic. "I can't lose this job. I've got rent, and a car payment, and Bruce wants Ago boots for his birthday. They're six hundred dollars." Carmen gulped her beer, swallowing the words.

"Bruce." Contempt tinged my voice.

"I can't lose this job, not now."

"You won't." I hoped I was right.

The next open mic singer cranked his amp so conversation was impossible. I bought Carmen another beer, and we sat surrounded by angry white boy music. The fifteen-minute limit on each performer was there because of guys like him. He was followed by an acoustic blues duo, quiet and smooth, so we could talk.

"I know you don't like Bruce much, but he likes you," Carmen said.

"Sure he does." Another sharp look. "Sorry, okay, thanks. What makes you think he likes me?"

"He told me to tell you he recognized Tatum when we saw him New Year's. Sees him at the Cyber Café all the time."

I stopped mangling the empty Red Bull can and frowned at her. "That's hardly Tatum's style."

"Why not? He likes casinos, you said so yourself. The café's just a local version."

"Borderline illegal local version." I dropped the can on a passing server's empty tray. The euphemistically named Internet cafés were often fronts for online gambling, something paternalistic politicians frown on. With the city's persistent, but vague, threats of shutting them down, only big-money campaign donors with convoluted ties to café ownership behind the scenes kept things humming.

I mulled over the revelation. "Tatum a player?"

"Not in Bruce's circle, I guess. I dunno." Carmen's words were starting to slur. Always was a cheap date.

"C'mon, you need to go home." I flung an arm over her shoulder and steered her toward the door. "Sorry guys, this one's mine," I told the gang at the next table, just to enjoy the disappointed looks. Take my fun where I can.

———

Patrice's files were a disappointment. Apparently, Tatum's playing it pretty close with the new server, not even sharing his private partition with her. Her emails reeked of a growing desperation, not only about their relationship, which any fool except Patrice could tell is completely one-sided, but something else. Cryptic, which is odd for her. Never known her to do subterfuge well, except for the day she fired me. Maybe she's learning from him.

I need those server files.

When I finally crashed, my dreams had me chasing first Patrice, then Tatum, through the school as the fluorescent lights overhead flickered out one by one when I passed by. He disappeared into the computer lab, locking the door behind him with a huge combination pad I couldn't break. Mocking laughter seeped under the door to echo in the hallway, growing louder till it woke me up. So much for sleep.

Good thing my Tuesday classes were all in the afternoon, my head felt like cotton candy. I headed for the bookstore to put in a few hours of mindless sorting before going to campus. When I called Carmen, her voicemail picked up. I waited for her rambling message to finish before saying, "Hey, wanted to make sure you were okay. Call me." Thirty seconds later as I parked the car, she rang back.

"I was in the bathroom," she said. "For the third time."

"You only had two drinks, girl."

The silence stretched so long I checked to make sure the call hadn't dropped.

"It's not the beer." Carmen's sigh was almost as long as the silence had been. "I think I'm pregnant."

Good thing I was parked. "Ah, damn. Does Bruce know?"

"Not yet. I just did the stick test thing. Those can be wrong, can't they?"

"I suppose." I didn't want to kill her hopes. Reality would do that soon enough.

She sighed again. "I'm kidding myself, I know."

"Do you want me to go to the clinic with you? Find out for sure?"

"Thanks, but I'll handle it. Talk to you later."

I sat in the car for a long time, weighing Carmen's current problems with my own. Life has a way of putting things into perspective. The parking patrol mini-cart slowed down next to me, checking the meter I had yet to feed. A few quarters dropped into the slot satisfied the officer, and she moved on to the next offender.

Inside the store, Matthew and Sammy had their heads together over a watch. A guy I didn't recognize slouched away from me.

"S'ok, Georgio. She's my daughter," Matthew said. He mumbled a few words to Sammy, who nodded. "How about seventy-five till payday?"

"Hopin' for at least a hunnert," Georgio said.

Matthew and Sammy exchanged looks. "A hundred, and we'll wait till the end of the month. Will that help?" Matthew asked.

Georgio peeked in my direction.

I grabbed a stack of books and moved away to escape his suspicious glare, staying out of sight till the deal was done. When the bell jangled over the door, I went back to the counter. "You don't usually do loans in the front window."

"Yeah, well, Georgio's claustrophobic." Matthew slipped the watch into a brown envelope. "Passed out on me one time in back, so we stay here."

When he turned toward the office, I handed him the lock picks. "I'm done with my research on these, thanks."

Matthew's look told me I wasn't fooling anyone, but he took the case without calling me on it. "Mind the store. I'll be a few minutes." Sammy trailed him to the office, and they closed the door.

Carmen's predicament deflated my enthusiasm for payback over my relatively petty issues with Patrice and Tatum. I puttered around dusting the stacks, reshelving books left on the side tables, trying not to think too much. Traffic was light. When I'd cleaned and organized all I could, I curled up in the wing back with a copy of Montaigne's *Essays*, catching up on homework. English Lit wasn't in my computer science curriculum, but I had room for electives. If I couldn't fit in a philosophy course, I went with literature.

Matthew emerged from the office just before I left for class. No time for conversation, which was probably a good thing. I'm sure Carmen didn't want her news spread too far yet, and I don't know if I could've kept from telling him.

After class, I stopped in the computer lab. Carmen had left early, said she didn't feel well. Her phone went to voicemail again. I hoped she'd made it to the clinic so she'd know for sure what she was up against. I was halfway to her place to check before I realized if she was telling Bruce about his impending fatherhood, they wouldn't want company. I detoured for home.

Dinner was quick. It was Zigana's yoga night, and she left me to clean up. The apartment was too quiet to muffle the thoughts buzzing through my brain. I took my laptop down to Dino's coffee shop, logged into the public wi-fi, and attacked the school server. My frustration spilled over and I got reckless, hitting the firewall too hard too many times. It threw up an alert, and the system locked me out for twenty-four hours.

Damn.

As punishment, I forced myself to focus on the senior project I needed to complete by the end of the term in order to graduate. Usually, I wait till the last minute with assignments like that, telling myself—and Zigana—I work better on a deadline. I'd chosen computer forensic investigations for the capstone paper, unashamedly using my run-in with the Feds as a case study. School administration knew, no sense hiding it. I'd show how I'd learned my lesson, been rehabilitated and all, maybe earn a few sympathy points. Or not, if Tatum ended up on the review committee. Two lattés and a four-page outline later, I called it quits. Exhaustion overrode the caffeine, and I made up for the sleep lost the night before.

My one early-morning class was on Wednesday, an eight-o'clock two-hour lecture on Cisco firewalls, followed by lab time. I looked for Carmen's car, but it wasn't in her usual spot. I left another voicemail and set my phone to vibrate. A white-shirted nerd complete with a pocket protector manned the front desk at the computer lab. My replacement, I'd imagine. He hesitated when I handed him my ID and signed the log.

I waited, hand outstretched, for him to return it. "What?"

His pasty features flushed. "Nothing. Take the workstation front row center."

Keeping an eye on me, how cute.

For the next two hours, I played by the rules. Stuck to my student account, followed the assigned labs while Raymond, I heard someone call him, hovered near my desk every chance he got. He freaked a bit when he saw the hacker textbook I intentionally left next to the keyboard. I hid my grin and ignored him.

Carmen still wasn't in when I logged off to leave for lunch shortly after noon. I didn't ask Raymond where she was, no sense giving him the connection. I checked my phone while I picked at the cafeteria's daily special of chili-cheese fries. Missed a call from Carmen while I was in the lab, but no message. I tried one more time. "Tag, you're it," I said after the beep. I followed up with a text. She didn't respond.

When my afternoon lit class was over, I headed for the Oregon District. Wednesdays are my night to work the bookstore so Matthew can take Sammy to AA. It's an open meeting night, one where family and friends hang around to learn how to help without fostering co-dependency. Matthew is Sammy's only support, other than his sponsor. I try, now that we're on speaking terms, but it's not the same as someone who's known him forever. My role is behind the scenes, manning the desk whenever Sammy needs Matthew. Better than closing up shop whenever there's a crisis like they had done before I showed up.

Besides, Wednesday nights were my idea. Matthew never stayed open past six until I convinced him evenings would bring in new customers. We settled on one mid-week night and Friday, when the art district attracted foot traffic. Saturdays were more the party crowd, so that was pointless. But January is slow anytime, day or night. I spent four hours alternately pacing the aisles worrying about everything and parked in a corner trying to calm my brain with meditation. Neither one helped much.

Matthew showed up around eight-thirty. "Thought you'd have given up by now."

"Sign says open till nine, I stay till nine." I'd only taken one business class, but I knew if we advertised hours but didn't follow them, we risked permanently losing any customer who showed up to find a locked door. It was a running debate, kept us occupied.

"Just wanted to check my email," he said, pulling up a stool and logging in. The store computer is the only one Matthew would spring for, where he can tap the free public network for 'net access.

I swiped a rag over some non-existent dust and closed out the register while he surfed. He slid over to give me room at the cash drawer while he scrolled through his messages. I tried to keep my eyes off the screen, not wanting to blatantly pry. He switched to news headlines, and I lost interest.

"Hey." He stopped my hand in the middle of locking the money bag. "Isn't this your friend?"

A *Dayton Daily News* headline read, "Pedestrian critical after colliding with bus." My eyes locked onto the victim's name: Carmen Lowery. A two-paragraph story offered little in the way of substance. Apparently, she had been distracted, on her cell phone witnesses said, and stepped off the curb as the bus pulled in. Grandview Medical Center. Updates as available.

Matthew squeezed my arm. My face told him everything. "Go," he said.

I went.

Thanks to rampant confusion over HIPAA, hospitals won't tell you anything if you're not family. So I lied. The desk was happy to send "Carmen's sister" to the right ward.

I found her mom and stepdad in one corner of the netbook-sized waiting room, her father, Victor and his latest girlfriend in the other. A real sister I'd met a few times, Gigi, shuttled back and forth between them. I flagged her down, and after she took a second to focus, she hugged me.

"Thanks for coming."

"What happened?"

She pulled me away from the parental units before answering. "Stepped off the curb into the bus, I guess. Bruce said he tried to grab her."

"Bruce was there?" Bastard didn't even call me.

Gigi scanned the room. "He was here a minute ago, making sure Dad knew it wasn't his fault, must have went for a smoke."

I dismissed thoughts of torturing Bruce for now. "How's she doing?"

"She's still unconscious. Doctors aren't calling it a coma yet, say she's in shock, with a bad concussion." Her eyes filled. "Maybe worse. They were going to do an MRI, but we haven't heard anything."

I held off asking about the baby since I didn't know if Carmen had told her.

After introducing myself to Victor for like the third time, I sat down near Carmen's mother. "Mrs. Hamilton, I'm so sorry."

She stiffened and pulled away. "What are you doing here?" I was surprised at the venom in her look. She hasn't liked me much since Carmen came home from a pub crawl on her twenty-first birthday with the eyebrow stud. Blames me for corrupting her baby. If Carmen was laid up too long, Mommy Dear would find out about a few more piercings and a whole lot of ink. My one tattoo's a souvenir from a weak moment with Rake, and I keep it covered. Zigana wouldn't be much happier than Carmen's mother.

"Miles, I thought you asked the desk to make sure we weren't disturbed," she said to her husband. "It's bad enough that boy is here, but I won't have Carmen's ghoulish companions creating more drama."

I retreated into my leather jacket and black *AYBABTU* hacker t-shirt, taking in the jeans and scuffed knee-high boots. Dark clothes and a little eyeliner made me ghoulish? *Who knew?*

Miles took over. "Thank you for your concern, but Tabitha's pretty upset right now. I'm sure you understand," he said to me. He patted his wife's arm. "I'll just go have a word with the doctor, see how things are progressing." He motioned with his head, and I followed him into the hall. Gigi took his seat next to her mother.

We made it to the elevator lobby before Miles stopped. "I'm surprised you're here," he said.

"Why wouldn't I be? Carmen's my best friend."

"I suppose her injuries must overshadow your fight with her." He pressed the down button.

It took a second for his words to register. "Fight? With Carmen? Did she tell you that?"

"Bruce mentioned it." Miles frowned. "Such an odd young man. I'll never understand what she sees in him."

"Bruce mentioned it."

"That's why he tried to take her cell phone. He said you were harassing her."

The elevator door opened, and he waved me inside. I obeyed automatically, stunned by Bruce's accusation. Miles pushed the ground floor button and stepped back into the hall. "Don't come back."

The doors slid shut before I could respond.

Miles had clout, I'll give him that. Over the next two days, hospital security ran me off three times. I stopped when I read the news follow-up saying Carmen died of her injuries.

I never got to say goodbye.

Bruce was holed up somewhere, avoiding their apartment. Neighbors probably warned him off after I beat on the door loudly enough to drag them into the hallway to complain. I only knew his friends by first name, and his family was all out of state or I'd have stalked them, too. I parked outside the Cyber Café for a few nights hoping to spot him. No luck.

I conned the mortuary into telling me when and where Carmen would be buried since the obituary said services were private. I left my car outside Woodland Cemetery and walked across half the two hundred acres to stand behind a tree out of sight until Miles and Tabitha left in a stretch limo. Gigi stayed behind with Victor and his girlfriend, and Bruce.

I thought he was going to bolt when he saw me, but Gigi clung to his arm. She didn't hug me this time.

"Can't you leave us alone?" Her voice shrilled through the cold afternoon air. She pulled Bruce closer. "Tell her what Carmen said. Tell her to go away!"

"Please, do tell, Bruce." I folded my arms to hide my clenched fists and waited.

He fixed his gaze on my left shoulder and mumbled something to her, his words dashed away by a frigid gust.

Victor hung back to watch, the girlfriend whispering in his ear as she bounced up and down on her toes. Probably forgot who I was already.

Gigi prodded Bruce. "Go on, tell her."

He cleared his throat. "Carmen wanted you to leave her alone."

"Says you."

His face reddened. It wasn't from the cold. "Yeah, says me. We talked. Carmen said you were in trouble at work, tried to get her involved in some illegal shit. She didn't like it."

"Funny she never said anything to me." I pinned him with a stare, watched him squirm.

"Why would I make it up?"

"Why indeed." I turned to Gigi. "You believe his crap?"

She slid a half-step behind him. "I know you got a record."

"So's Bruce. Possession, a little shoplifting."

Gigi gasped and jerked away from him. His eyes finally met mine. They were cold, hateful.

"Did the supposed conversation take place before or after she told you about the baby?" I asked.

Gigi's shriek caught Victor's attention. He stepped back into the mix, grabbing Gigi's arm to keep her from attacking me.

"Carmen wasn't pregnant. She'd have told me!" Gigi's anger mixed with fresh tears. She buried her face in her father's shoulder.

He patted her head. "Guess your mother didn't tell you, huh?" She raised a startled face. "The doctor told us at the hospital, right after the accident. It's part of the reason she bled so much, I guess."

Gigi turned on Bruce. "You knew, didn't you? And you didn't tell me."

He hung his head and didn't answer. For a long minute the only sounds in the cemetery were the tolling bell from the stone chapel at the entrance and Gigi's sobs.

I gestured to get Bruce's attention. "We'll have this out later, you and I." Ignoring his angry glare, I turned my back on the sad tableau and left them to their grief. At least they had someone to share it.

That evening, Zigana and I shared a private wake service at Glen Helen Nature Preserve. The protected acres on the edge of Yellow Springs are a haven for lost souls who need to reconnect with nature and the universe. I go there regularly. Zigana and I braved the frigid January flurries with a few enclosed candle jars and a clutch of flowers. Carmen wasn't a big outdoors person, but she appreciated the Glen almost as much as I do. The honest-to-god yellow spring exudes an unmatched serenity, even in winter. Zigana claims to see its aura.

We found a sheltered spot near a downed maple tree across from the springs, and after fighting a stiff breeze to light the candles, huddled together to meditate on a blanket thrown over a boulder. I wrapped a second blanket over our shoulders, blocking out the chill. The musky candle scent Carmen favored swirled with the odor of decaying undergrowth and added to my gloom. We whispered quiet memories of Carmen, her ready smile, the way she laughed at a joke five minutes after it was told, her loyalty. I left a handful of dried sunflowers in a rock crevice near the springs where Carmen had scrawled her initials on our first visit. It wasn't the time or place to talk about how she died, or about Bruce's accusations. That came later, when we returned to the apartment to warm up with spiced rum.

"Why do you suppose Bruce told Carmen's family you had a fight?" Zigana broke the silence. We'd celebrated Carmen's life, mourned her death. Now it was time to find answers.

I sighed, as reluctant as Zigana to break the quiet moment, before reaching for the lamp. Kaleidoscope rays glimmered through the stained-glass shade and bathed the room in soft color that didn't quite reach the corners. We talked late into the night without illuminating the problem any more than the lamp did the edges of darkness in our little world, then went to bed, but not to sleep.

The next morning, Matthew echoed Zigana. "What possessed Bruce to tell Carmen's family you had a fight?"

Why did Bruce say that? I bit my lip, holding back a flood of useless recrimination, and forced a smile. "I don't know, but I'll find out. Soon as I pin him down." I told him how Bruce had been avoiding his usual hangouts.

"He's a regular at the Cyber Café?" Matthew squinted in thought. "Let me make a few calls." He disappeared into the office.

I'd been in isolation for the week since Carmen's funeral, even skipped more classes than I could afford to. Zigana had finally kicked me out of the house.

I sorted through another estate sale box, discarded the unusable volumes, and tried not to think. When Sammy arrived with the morning coffee, he handed me a cup without a word, patted my shoulder awkwardly, and joined Matthew. Paperwork and a handful of customers occupied me until lunch. The office remained closed. I ordered Chinese food for three to be delivered and left them alone.

Matthew emerged only when the smell of Szechuan seeped through the door. He looked pleased. Sammy trailed behind him, grinning.

"Tonight, after Sammy's meeting, we're going on maneuvers," Matthew said. "You can't come."

"Beg your pardon?" I stopped dishing out food. "You haven't learned not to tell me 'can't'? And where do you think you're going?"

"You need to stay here, get ready for when we come back."

I finished filling the plates while waiting for him to elaborate. He bit into an eggroll without filling me in. "And?"

Sammy chuckled at my irritation. "I can skip the meeting, ya know. This'll be good therapy."

"All right you two." I pulled back the food that wasn't already in their mouths and set it behind me on the counter. "Talk, or you don't eat."

They giggled like schoolboys while they outlined their plan to stake out the Cyber Café until Bruce showed up, then hijack him and bring him back to the store.

"There's a tournament tonight he's signed up for, starts at ten" Matthew said. "When he shows, we'll be waiting." He reached for his plate.

Sammy waggled his fingers at me. I returned their food.

"You know that's kidnapping," I told Matthew.

He shrugged. "Really think someone like Bruce is going to call the cops? Besides, Sammy here will say he came willingly, to apologize to you."

I choked on a grain of rice. "Apologize? Like that's going to happen."

Sammy handed me a bottle of water. "Maybe not, but at least you can get some answers. Matthew told me what he said about you and your friend. S'not right."

While I downed the water, I nodded my thanks for the drink and for the sentiment. "How do you know he'll be there?"

"Couple of my customers are regulars at the Café, too, that's why they end up here most months." Matthew scooped up the last bite from his plate and wiped his chin with a paper napkin. "Bruce is pretty well known there. Seems to have an in with the bosses."

I puzzled over the plan, not convinced they'd be able to carry it out, but certain I couldn't talk them out of it. Maybe it was worth a shot.

Matthew spent the afternoon prepping the office for our visit from Bruce. "Can't have him out here in front of the windows now, can we?" He was enjoying the prospect far too much.

"Sure, never let me in the office, but roll out the red carpet for him." I got caught up in the adrenaline rush, glad to think about something other than Carmen's death. It was there, lurking, but now I had a concrete plan of action to deal with it.

He laughed and tossed me the broom. "C'mon, you can help."

The office was bigger than I expected. Wooden shelves overflowing with books and odd memorabilia lined two walls plus half of the third, where a small window sat just above eye-level. File cabinets flanked a desk under the window. On the wall next to the door an old horse-hair chaise faced a couple of elaborately carved wooden side chairs on top of a faded Oriental rug. A side table between the chairs held an antique lamp with a red fringe shade. Cozy, if you like bordellos.

Matthew shifted a cardboard box from the floor to an empty spot on one of the lower shelves. Dust bunnies drifted across the floor from underneath. I tackled the bare wood while he unloaded another box sitting on the desk. A stack of magazines on top of the file cabinet went into the bottom drawer.

"So why are we cleaning for this idiot?" I asked.

"Making sure everything's out of reach," Matthew said. "Don't want any of my customers' stuff damaged."

We moved a dozen or so tagged items from the shelf near the chaise to the few remaining bare shelves across the room. For the final move, Sammy helped swap the chaise with the chairs, pinning a single seat in the corner next to the table. I moved the lamp out of reach.

At five-thirty, Matthew insisted we close the store for an hour to eat a real meal. If bar food counts. We hit the Dublin Pub for bangers and mash with a Guinness chaser, I was back at the counter by six-thirty, and they left for Sammy's AA meeting. Silence closed in, and with it, thoughts of Carmen.

She'd been working in the computer lab for six months when I started half-way through her freshman year. With my earlier credits from Sinclair College and a few correspondence courses the probation office set me up with, I was a junior at twenty-two to her nineteen. We hit it off when I talked back to Patrice, politely, in ways Carmen admired.

"Aren't you afraid you'll make her mad?" she had asked after I pointed out the flaws in Patrice's latest security directive.

"She made too much noise in the press when she hired me to admit it was a bad idea." I shredded the draft document and sat down to write a protocol with teeth. "Patrice doesn't know a memory chip from a video card. She needs me."

My hacking skills fascinated Carmen, and even though I had to watch what I tapped so the Feds stayed off my back, I taught her a few things. She learned fast. In the eighteen months we worked together, she'd learned to decipher hash codes, trace an IP address, and was just starting to get the hang of social engineering along with the confidence to pull it off, when....

I mentally slammed the door. I needed my wits intact to deal with Bruce in a couple of hours. Emotion would only cloud my head. I found a book on body language and forced myself to review some tells to watch for when it was time to ask questions. *But what questions?* Other than why he'd lied to Carmen's folks, what did I need to know? I found a legal pad in Matthew's file cabinet and started a list, like an if-then-else flowchart.

Why did he lie? If because he's an idiot, then the conversation is over. Else....

What did he hope to gain? If revenge because he knew I tried to get Carmen to dump him, then the conversation is over, again. Else....

If...what if? What else could there be?

I threw my pen across the room. Now who's the idiot? Think outside the box, and avoid getting trapped in another one. What did he have to gain by making me look bad?

As if she were sitting next to me, Carmen's words from our last evening together broke into my scattered thoughts.

"Bruce told me to tell you he recognized Tatum when we saw him New Year's. Sees him at the Cyber Café all the time."

If Tatum were behind all this, then....

I retrieved the pen and started a new list.

By the time I was ready to lock up for the night, I had three sheets of scribbled notes, diagrams, and question marks. Matthew called a little after nine to let me know they were at the Café waiting for Bruce. I shook layers of dust off the seldom-used blinds over the front windows before pulling them tight and bolting the door. With only the light from the office and back hall, the store took on a shadowy gloom that made me shiver. Zigana would say it was an omen. I unlatched the dead bolt on the alley entrance, leaving the doorknob lock fastened until Matthew and Sammy arrived with Bruce. After rearranging the chairs and lamp for the third time, I perched on the edge of the desk and waited. And waited. Not even the tick-tick of the big clock up front, usually a calming reassurance when I was here alone, took the edge off my jitters.

What the hell's the matter with me? It's just Bruce.

Nine forty-five. Ten. By ten-fifteen, I was ready to burst. Furious pounding on the back door brought me to my feet. I twisted the lock, and the door flew open. Matthew and Sammy pushed past me, dragging Bruce between them. He was unconscious.

"What happened?" I fought to keep the panic out of my voice as they dumped him on the chaise.

"I belted him," Sammy said with more than a hint of pride.

"You what?"

Matthew went into the bathroom and came back with wad of wet paper towels. "Here."

I backed away from his outstretched hand. "What do you want me to do with that?"

"Wipe his face, wake him up. He's not dead."

I took the towels and swiped in Bruce's general direction, sort of making contact, until he groaned in protest. I tossed the papers in the wastebasket and propped myself against the file cabinet, frowning at the room in general. "What the hell happened?" I asked again.

Matthew flopped into the desk chair and ran a hand through his hair, adding to its unruliness. "I'm not sure. He got into the truck no problem after we strong-armed him a little. Sammy kept an eye on him while I drove. I checked over my shoulder for traffic, and Bruce shoved me against the door. Then, I don't know." He looked to Sammy for an explanation.

"He went for the keys," Sammy said. "What was I s'posed to do?"

Bruce groaned again and sat upright, falling back against the tufted horsehair. A red welt darkened his right cheek. He squinted at us through a fast-swelling eyelid, first me, then Matthew, and finally Sammy. "Pretty good punch for an old guy," he muttered as he fingered the bruise.

Matthew stopped Sammy's retort. "We just wanted to talk to you. Why'd you try to wreck the truck?"

"What was I supposed to think, two guys grab me in a parking lot." Bruce focused on Matthew again. "Didn't recognize you till I saw her," he said, jerking his head in my direction. The sudden move brought out another groan.

"Coffee help?" Matthew asked.

Bruce nodded, moving more carefully. "Unless you got a shot of tequila."

"Coffee it is."

"I got it." Sammy left.

"What'd you want to talk about so bad?" Bruce ignored me.

Matthew looked to me, and I waved him on.

"Sorry to hear about your girlfriend," he said.

Bruce grunted a lame thanks.

"Why'd you tell the family she was fighting with Fatál?"

"Cause she was."

I bit back a response. Since they were chatting like old friends, might as well let Matthew handle things.

"Funny, Fatál didn't know there was a problem," Matthew said. He waited a beat. No response. "Why'd you take Carmen's phone?"

"She didn't want to talk to her." Bruce shifted his gaze to me for a split second, and he flinched at my scowl.

Matthew leaned forward, elbows resting on his knees, to bring his face even with Bruce. "Why are you lying to us?"

Bruce scooted across the chaise to put as much distance between him and Matthew as he could. I decided it was time to up the pressure. I moved into the empty chair at Bruce's elbow, startling him.

"I'm betting she had something on Tatum that you didn't want me to know," I said, watching for a reaction. He didn't disappoint. The bruise on his face vanished into the slow flush that spread to his forehead.

Matthew sat back in surprise. When he'd left to snag Bruce, I'd been convinced it all had something to do with the pregnancy. I pointed him to my notes on the desk and continued prodding Bruce.

"I'm betting once Tatum saw you with Carmen, and me, on New Year's, he decided to use you to cut off my pipeline through her to the lab. And you agreed." I fought to keep my voice even, letting the words sink in. "I wonder why."

A sputtering vehicle with a bad muffler chugged through the alley behind us, breaking the tense silence that hung in the room. I folded my arms over my chest and glowered at Bruce. And waited. Let him think the worst was going to happen. As Zigana taught me, a person's own imagination is worse than almost any reality.

Bruce shifted away, settling in halfway between Matthew and me, eyes averted while he fidgeted with the bruise. I studied his scrawny figure, trying to see him through Carmen's eyes. Barely my height, scrawny, mop of dirty blond hair trailing over the collar of his faded Puddle of Mud concert t-shirt. Oversized acid-wash jeans with a white Jockey underwear band sticking out the top. They didn't hang off his backside, but still not much of a fashion statement. He sported impressive gauges in both earlobes, probably double-zero or so, and a smattering of studs here and there. From what Carmen told me, I knew the creased leather jacket hid ink up both arms and across his back. She'd paid for most of it.

Snow melted into a puddle under his outstretched legs, trickling off the side zipper of his leather boots onto the rug. New footwear since I saw him last. My eyes narrowed.

"Nice kicks," I said, remembering Carmen's dismay at their cost. "Argo?"

Bruce jerked upright, pulling his feet back.

I took a stab. "Tatum must have handed you a chunk of change to scare Carmen away from me." His flush turned panic-pale.

"I don't know anybody named Tatum."

"Too late. Carmen told me a week ago you recognized him. Two days before her accident, in fact." I shifted in closer. "How'd he get to you?"

Matthew moved in on the other side. "From what I hear, Tatum's the debt collector for Cyber Café."

It was my turn to be surprised as Matthew continued.

"And he's not a patient man. How much you into them for?"

Bruce's eye shifted from me to Matthew and back again, growing anger mixing with the fright. "S'all your fault, bitch," he said to me. "You shoulda left her out of it."

"Out of what? What's Tatum hiding?" I asked.

Any answer was interrupted when Sammy pushed open the door with one foot, juggling a cardboard tray with four coffee cups. Bruce erupted from the chaise and knocked him aside. Hot coffee splashed on Matthew, who backed off with a yelp. Sammy collapsed on the floor at my feet. I stumbled over him trying to stop Bruce, but it was too late. He pushed through the back door and into the alley at a dead run. I made it to the door in time to see him cross Wayne Avenue headed toward the residential neighborhood behind the warehouse in the next block. I let him go.

———

Our imposed visit with Bruce kicked me from my doldrums. After his comments, I stopped thinking Carmen's death was an accident and started looking for answers. If I had in any way caused it, I owed her that much and more. First stop was security class, to keep my presence on campus legit. Two make-up lab sessions meant I could hang out in the computer lab all afternoon, no questions asked. In between exercises I searched the network, discreetly checking access routes, looking for blips in the system that always happen during an upgrade. Lucky I was in the middle of an actual assignment when Patrice showed up at my workstation. She was carrying a copier paper box.

"I was sorry to hear about Carmen. I always liked her." She motioned toward a stack of books next to the keyboard. "Mind if I set this down? It's stuff from her desk."

I slid my things aside and waited.

After an awkward moment, Patrice cleared her throat. "Anyway, Carmen's personal items. I left a message at her apartment, but no one's returned my call. Maybe you can give it to her folks?"

"They're not too fond of me right now, thanks to Bruce. You remember him, right? Tatum's friend."

Her eyes grew wary. "Carmen's boyfriend? What makes you think Dr. Tatum knows him?"

I swiveled around in my chair to face her directly. Meant I had to look up at her, but there wasn't room to stand. She had me blocked in. "He told me."

"Dr. Tatum?"

"Bruce."

"Bruce told you he knows Dr. Tatum."

I resisted an eyeroll. "Yes."

Patrice frowned into space, fingers drumming the box lid. She caught herself and jerked her hand back, tucking it into her pocket. "He must be mistaken."

"If you say so." I turned back to the computer, satisfied at the uncertainty I'd planted.

She hovered for another few seconds, watching over my shoulder. "You'll take the box?"

"Sure." I didn't look up until I heard her move away. When she was out of the lab, I shoved away from the desk and did some frowning of my own.

———

At home later, after dinner, I steeled myself and opened the box of Carmen's things. It was a rerun of what she'd collected for me, right down to the stuffed Y2K bug. I made a spot for that on my desk opposite the one she'd given me when I was fired and sorted through the other stuff. Coffee mug, a few pens, tattered copy of *The Hunger Games*, a wadded-up Dayton Dragons sweatshirt, and a folder of odd quotes and cartoons she liked to post over the desk. All perfectly innocent. *Wonder what else she might have had that didn't make it to the box?*

I tucked everything but the bug back into the box, folding the sweatshirt neatly on top, and replaced the lid. I debated calling Bruce about the stuff to harass him a bit more, but figured he wouldn't answer. Gigi didn't answer either. I left a message, not holding my breath that she'd call back. Need to work on that sixth-sense again. Less than an hour later, while I read a chapter on cryptology for the fourth time without focusing on the words, the phone buzzed.

"What do you mean you have Carmen's stuff?"

"Hello to you, too, Gigi. And it wasn't my idea. Patrice dumped it on me in the lab this afternoon."

"She should have called me."

"Take that up with her. She tried Bruce, and he couldn't be bothered."

I heard her relay my words to someone in the background, who responded with anger. "He's there, isn't he?"

"None of your business." Another muffled exchange before she continued. "Take the stuff to that bookstore where you work. I'll pick it up tomorrow."

"I won't be there till Saturday." Not true, but I couldn't resist putting her off.

Gigi's voice went up a notch. "Saturday then. And don't call me anymore." The line went dead.

I tossed my textbook onto the bed and considered everything Gigi hadn't said. Like why, if she didn't want to talk to me, she called back in the first place. And Bruce. Would she really take up with her dead sister's boyfriend that fast? *Cold.* Wish I could figure out what women see in him.

I spent Friday catching up on class work and the rest of my labs. Patrice stayed away, going so far as to detour into an empty conference room when she saw me in the hall. I considered making up an excuse to corner her there and decided to let it slide. I tried to tap into Carmen's school email account, checking for any last-minute messages. It was gone, deleted already, and she'd been dead less than a week.

Saturday was quiet at the bookstore. Sammy slunk around more dejected than usual, refusing to believe I didn't blame him for losing Bruce.

"Let him fix things," Matthew said when I commented on Sammy's mood.

"He can't bring Bruce back."

"I mean make him do penance. He was a good Catholic boy, years ago. It's in his blood."

I couldn't think of anything remotely useful that would satisfy Sammy's need for atonement. Until Gigi walked in.

"Where's Carmen's stuff?" she asked, ignoring my greeting.

I saw Bruce in the car out front and had an idea. "In the back, hang on." While I collected the box off the worktable, I called Sammy out of the office and whispered in his ear.

His face lit up. He nodded, lifted his jacket off the hook by the back door and slipped into the alley.

I stalled Gigi's departure to buy time for Sammy. "Not sure what Carmen kept at her desk, but this is all they gave me. You'll have to call Patrice and ask about her paycheck and stuff, and the school office for academic things."

"I know what to do." She grabbed the box without looking inside. "Now leave us alone."

I hung onto the box, suspending it between us like a buoy bobbing in stormy waters. "Don't you want to know why she died?"

"She died because a bus ran her down," Gigi said. She jerked the box free.

I cringed inwardly at her crudeness. "Bruce knows more than he's letting on."

"Leave Bruce alone." Her face reddened. "I heard what you did to him the other night. Should've called the police, but he doesn't want to make trouble."

Over her shoulder I saw Sammy pull up around the corner across the street in Matthew's faded yellow Chevy pick-up. "Of course he doesn't." I turned my back and let her leave.

On-location Gathering

"Physical security inspections"

While Sammy tailed Gigi and Bruce to find out where they were staying, I surfed Internet café locations in Dayton. I've had my own laptop since high school after convincing Zigana it was a requirement for class, so I've never needed to use a public facility like the cafés. Plus most of them have the reputation of being gambling joints more than the family video game centers they advertise. I found a few in the city, including the one where Tatum and Bruce hang out, and picked out the one that was closest without being in too-seedy a neighborhood. Google Maps' street view allowed me to check out the area while I strategized. I needed to get familiar with the general operation of these places before I hit the Cyber Café.

Catching up at school took all my time for the next week, but I rewarded myself with planning my reconnaissance adventure between assignments. After brunch with Zigana on Sunday, I headed back downtown. I drove past the address Sammy gave me for Gigi's new place and found her car at the curb. I was tempted to corner Bruce again, but decided he wasn't worth the effort at this point. "Tomorrow is another day," Matthew would say, channeling Scarlett.

A BP gas station down the street from the Internet café had an unlocked outside bathroom. It was cruddy and smelled like a long-abandoned locker room. I breathed in short, shallow bursts while swapping my black jeans and sweater for a long denim skirt, white blouse, and navy blue down jacket I had picked up at Goodwill. The skirt hid my boots, so I stuffed the old-lady Oxfords I'd found into my backpack with my clothes. A poofy stocking cap and black-framed reading glasses completed my transformation. I tossed the bag into the trunk of my Fiero, grabbed a red quilted shoulder bag that held my wallet and Android cell phone, and walked two blocks to the café.

For a room full of people and computers, it was eerily quiet. The lab at school hummed with quiet chatter and tinny music escaping from iPods. Not here. Everyone wore headphones and kept to themselves. The only sound came from fingers tapping a keyboard or clicking a mouse, with the occasional low cough or shuffling feet. Weird.

My quick glances around could be mistaken for nerves, I hoped. I tagged the security cameras, relieved to only find one at each exit. An empty cubicle in the corner near the windows gave me a view of the front door and just one customer close enough to see my screen. An interior door near the information desk held a tantalizing "Authorized Personnel Only" sign. I scooted up to the monitor and read the instructions taped to the wall. Payment first. Of course. I made a big deal of wiping down the equipment with an anti-bacterial towelette from my bag. I signed on using a pre-paid Visa card I'd picked up at BP, setting up the required user account with a throw-away email on Yahoo. Two-fingered typing with lots of pauses to look confused was a challenge. After checking the bogus account and sending an email to "Mom" about the dullest imaginary life I could think of, I played a couple of rounds of Slingo. When the guy in the next cubicle left, I brought up a command prompt to check the ipconfig for the system, snapped a picture of it with my Droid, and closed out the window. Three seconds, max. Another pass with the towelette to remove fingerprints and I was done.

Not that it did me much good. I infiltrated the café's network when I got home, no problem. Lousy security, but no real data, either. All the client information was stored in an off-site server. Same for the second Internet café I hit a few days later. But during a visit timed with Tatum's much-publicized trip to DC for a lobbying session, I found his Cyber Café used the same server. Now to exploit that link.

Cracking the server needed more credits than I'd accumulated in my hacking group. I spent a couple weeks racking up points by providing almost-legal services for shadowy clients who posted anonymous want ads. Snooping on girlfriends and bosses was the big thing, tracing email and credit card statements. Easy stuff. My biggest concern as always was staying under the radar. No sense having the Feds knocking on the door again. Earning enough credits to run the script derailed my schoolwork, and mid-terms loomed before I could stop renting out my talents. Finally, I started two cracks, one on the school system for Tatum's database, the other on the Café's server, before returning to neglected assignments.

Trying to study at home was pointless. Zigana's mood matched the cold grey weather of February. Business in the shop was non-existent. Her gentleman friend from New Year's Eve was eager for a commitment. He had yet to learn you don't push Zigana to do anything. As therapy, she tackled a way-too-early spring cleaning of the apartment to the accompaniment of ear-splitting Rolling Stones tunes. Fortunately, the buildings on either side of us weren't residential or angry neighbors would've beaten down the door.

"Hey!" I called twice and all but jumped up and down in front of her before catching her attention. "The base called. You're drowning out the C-5s. The pilots are complaining."

She tossed a sponge into a bucket propped on the window seat and collapsed into her chair. "Turn it down," she said, waving toward the stereo.

I obliged before parking on the loveseat. "You want to talk about it?"

"What?"

"Hank."

"No."

"Seems like a nice guy."

Zigana blew a puff of air at the window pane and drew patterns in the frost with her fingernail.

"You always yelled at me for doing that," I said. "And for bottling things up."

Her hand dropped into her lap. "Never have kids. They throw your words back at you." She pulled off her scarf and scrubbed at her head, tangling her dark hair. "Aren't you supposed to be at school or something?"

"I'm *supposed* to be studying for my next certification test, but the decibels had my desk dancing."

She smiled a little at that one.

"Hank's a nice guy," she said. "But…." Zigana ran a hand over her forehead.

"He's not Tobias," I finished for her.

After a long stretch of silence, she agreed quietly. "He's not Tobias."

I leaned forward and touched her knee. "No one is, 'Gana. But he makes you happy, when you let him."

"I don't need someone to make me happy. That's my responsibility."

"You know what I mean."

She sat up and faced me, her eyes sad. "I know what you mean. But I can't give him what he wants."

"It's been what, forty years? You avoided relationships while I was growing up, because of me. I bet you did the same thing when Harmony was little." I pushed back the hair she hid behind. "I don't think Tobias would mind."

Zigana jerked away like I'd stabbed her with my penknife. "You have no idea what Tobias would think. Leave it alone." She cranked up the music again before squeezing out the sponge and tackling the baseboards, slopping water on the hardwood floor in the process.

I stifled a sigh and went to find the mop. After cleaning up the mess behind Zigana's rigid back, I stashed the mop and made a pot of coffee. While it brewed, I studied the hand-lettered poem she'd hung in the kitchen for as long as I can remember, her careful calligraphy a deep red against a deckled ivory background. It was by one of the few known Gypsy poets, *Papusza*, or Doll, but in a language I couldn't read. Something about the regrets of passing youth, I remember Zigana telling me. One of her few visible concessions to the past. I set a mug of coffee on the mantle, planted a kiss on the back of her head, and left Zigana to her thoughts.

Matthew's mood wasn't much better when I arrived at the bookstore for my Wednesday night shift.

"You're late. Sammy's in the car already," he said by way of greeting.

"What's with you people? Is Mercury in retrograde or something?" I shoved my backpack under the counter. "I'm here. Go."

A welcome silence descended after he huffed out the door. I made a cursory pass through the store shelving misplaced books, flicking the duster over exposed surfaces and generally earning my meager salary. Four hours passed with nary a customer, but I read five chapters of Cisco and finished my senior project outline. My phone buzzed fifteen minutes before closing.

"Lock up and meet us at the Dublin Pub," Matthew said. "There's a Guinness here with your name on it." He ended the call before I could respond.

I never understood how Sammy could go from his AA meeting to a bar, but he didn't see a problem.

"I'm an alcoholic, not a hermit," he had told me when I asked him about the disconnect. "My friends are here. I'm here."

From the number of empties on the table when I arrived, Matthew had been drowning his bad mood. He stood to pull out my chair and wrap me in a hug before staggering back into his seat.

"Hope Sammy's driving you home," I said.

Sammy raised his glass of Canada Dry ginger ale. "Got it covered, Missy."

I picked at the remnants of cracker bread on the appetizer platter, careful to avoid the Reuben topping, and washed it down with the dark ale they had waiting for me. "So what'd you want?" I asked Matthew.

He squinted into his half-empty glass and said nothing. A local Irish trio finished setting up on the tiny stage at the front of the pub. The raucous chorus that opened their set allowed him to ignore me for several minutes before he asked, "Your grandmother's never going to forgive me, is she?"

I couldn't believe I'd heard him right. "Say what?"

Matthew drained his glass and shoved it across the tiny table. He shook his head at the server who motioned with one of the empties asking if he wanted another. He pointed at the ginger ale Sammy raised with two fingers in response. I waited until the server returned with their sodas to try again.

"You've been talking to Zigana?"

This time he nodded in response. "Tried to, anyway."

And here I thought she was upset over Hank. "About what?"

"Doesn't matter. She hung up on me. Twice."

He nursed the ginger ale in a brooding silence through the rest of the set while I tried to make sense of his efforts. Zigana had offered him no encouragement on New Year's and he never struck me as a masochist. When the trio took a break, I asked, "What was so important?"

"I thought maybe now, after everything." Matthew leaned his chair back on two legs, earning a glare from the bartender. The legs hit the floor with a dull thud. "Doesn't matter. Just wanted you to hear it from me, in case she said anything."

"She's not talking to me right now, either." I checked the time. "And if I don't get home soon, I'll really be in trouble."

"*Help!*" Matthew's phone squawked the Beatles' anthem. "Scuse me." He fumbled through his jacket for the inside pocket. When he saw the number on the screen, his bloodshot eyes widened. "It's Zigana." He disappeared onto the patio away from the noise leaving me to look to Sammy for answers.

Sammy shrugged. "I got nothin'."

I waited until the music started again before hunting for Matthew outside. He was huddled in the corner under an awning, shielded from the wind but still shivering.

"Hang on a sec," he said into the phone. He cradled it against his chest. "Tell Sammy to meet me in the car, okay? I'll talk to you tomorrow."

He left me standing in the cold.

Zigana was asleep when I got home. No note, no explanation for the night owl's uncharacteristic early bedtime. I banged around the kitchen making tea, hoping she'd appear to scold me for the noise. No dice. I brooded in my room, adding a splash of Jameson to my mug from the bottle Matthew had given me for Christmas. Back at my books, Cisco wasn't enough to distract me from my thoughts. No results yet from the latest cracking script. Television was full of reruns and college basketball play-offs. Finding a two-inch article in the *Dayton Daily News* crime log officially declaring Carmen's death an accident sealed my gloom.

I pulled Carmen's stuffed Y2K bug off the shelf over my desk. She'd drawn heavy outlines around the tufted white eyes and a yin-yang tattoo on one skinny blue arm, streaked the fuzzy coral hair with red and black marker, and added a large splotch on the side its nose. A wart, maybe? The unadorned mate staring down at me from the bookshelf accused me of neglect. I slammed the decorated bug on the arm of the chair, expecting the built-in glass-shattering tinkle to punctuate my mood. Nothing.

Of course.

I upended the bug, half-expecting to find genitalia sketched on the bottom. Clumsy black stitches held the seam together under a pointy lavender tail. My penknife sliced through them, and when they separated, a flash drive poked out from the pouch where the noisemaker had been.

Cisco, scripts, Matthew, and Zigana vanished in an adrenaline-rush of possibilities.

For all Carmen's good intentions, the files she saved were a mess. Most of them were logs of student activity in the lab, class notes, exercises—nothing of interest. The HR records offered fodder for rumor and speculation, but not much else. I set those aside for a lazy snow day. It took almost three hours of sorting, but eventually I reached the Heart of Gold—improbability at its finest. Tatum's automatic laptop back-ups, the new server links, everything. What I could only flail at, Carmen nailed blindfolded. The timestamp on the last file clutched at my chest. Less than twelve hours before her encounter with the bus.

Someone knew. Someone who didn't want anyone else to see what she had. Patrice? Too crass for her, even to satisfy lover-boy. It had to be Tatum.

My vision blurred from unshed tears as much as from exhaustion. I'd been up twenty-two hours and faced a critical test in less than six. I had to sleep. Another shot of Jameson followed by a hot shower dulled the circular pounding in my brain enough to close my eyes until an insistent tap on the door broke through the haze. I hit the alarm button to quiet the blare I'd slept through.

"You okay?" Zigana called from the hallway. "That thing's been beeping for fifteen minutes." We didn't go for the old necktie-on-the-doorknob routine, but we never walked in on a closed bedroom door, just in case.

"C'mon in." I pushed myself upright against the pillows as she entered the room.

"I brought coffee." She handed me the mug and sat down at the desk, not quite facing me. The gutted Y2K bug lay next to my laptop. She fingered the spilled stuffing. "Taking out your frustrations on helpless toys?"

After last night's secrets and avoidance, I couldn't resist a brute force attack. "Carmen left me a message from the grave."

Zigana dropped the fluff like it singed her hand. "Don't say things like that."

"That was low. I'm sorry. But she did, sort of." I pointed to the computer. "She copied all the files I need to find out what Tatum's up to." Zigana frowned at the blank screen. "Hit the space bar."

The rows of data didn't clear her confusion.

"She left everything on a flash drive hidden inside that goofy green animal," I told her. "I found it last night."

"That's one of those little rectangle things you carry around."

I groaned obligingly at her willful Luddite comment. "Yeah, those little rectangle things." I explained what Carmen's drive contained until Zigana's eyes glazed over, which didn't take long. No sense in pushing it past that point. She took the empty mug, and I rushed through a tepid shower to wash the cobwebs from my brain. For the rest of the day, classes would demand all my attention. So I thought.

The school lots were full when I finally worked my way downtown through the sleety, mushy morning. Some kind of home and garden show at the Dayton Convention Center ate up all the street parking. I ended up on the top floor of the parking garage across the street from campus, made it to class just as my philosophy instructor was closing the door. He never tolerated tardiness, especially on test day, and my apologetic smile didn't crack his displeasure. I slid into my seat and focused on calming breaths while he passed out the test booklets and bubble sheets. Old school.

The multiple-choice questions were lame, sprinkled with the usual assortment of ambiguous questions. When I was in the mood, I could take a few minutes to decipher the pattern of answers, but today I raced through on my wits and left hacking behind. The final essay took more effort. I filled two Blue Books with what I hoped were legible scribbles, expounding on the merits of Montaigne's work and comparing it to the later efforts of Emerson, another favorite of mine.

"Five more minutes," the instructor said.

I skimmed the last few paragraphs to make sure I'd hit the required summary points, tying everything together with the opening thesis, and signed my name at the bottom. My test was the last one to hit his desk.

After the emotional roller coaster of the previous day, and the late-night review of Carmen's files, I was spent. Fortunately, my next class wasn't until four. I had time to find a decent breakfast off-campus, figuring I could hole up at the bookstore to review in peace. The weather had cleared, so the walk back to my car was bearable. I tossed my backpack onto the passenger seat and slid behind the wheel. I was fumbling for the ignition when a hand tapping on the driver's window startled me. I dropped my keys. Instinct kicked in, and I hit the door lock with one hand while scooping up the keys with the other. When I turned to the window, I almost dropped them again.

Suits. Two of them. A dark sedan that screamed Feds was parked behind me.

"Ms. Wood? Agents Bratton and Reynolds, DHS. We'd like to talk to you." The vocal suit flashed a badge and an ID. Department of Homeland Security.

Not again.

I took a deep breath and considered my options. While running them down on my way to Canada was an attractive thought, I'd have to face Zigana's disapproval. I cracked the window.

"My PO has everything you should need." Pendleton would be livid, but let him deal with them. He was my keeper for another two weeks.

"Your PO doesn't have to know about this if you cooperate. Would you step out of the car, please?"

I tucked the keys into my right hand in the attack posture taught in any good self-defense class and unlocked the door. They moved back just enough to allow the door to open, catching it halfway and blocking the gap. I was trapped.

"What do you want?" I clutched my Droid in my left pocket, wondering if I could text blind.

Bratton spoke again. Reynolds just glowered. Reminded me of a dour Penn and Teller, although Reynolds was the tall one.

"What's your interest in the Cyber Café?" he asked.

I scrunched up my face, feigning deep thoughts. "Isn't that the strip bar on Franklin?"

Bratton didn't look amused. "We understand you've been harassing its clients, snooping around the premises. I'm sure your PO would disapprove. And if you're hacking again, the judge will disapprove you right back into prison."

"I never went to prison. Suspended sentence. Booking at the county hardly counts as jail time."

"Cut the crap." Reynolds' voice had none of the bland professionalism of his partner's. "You're interfering with a government investigation, and I'd have no compunction in taking you down now."

"Then do it." His posturing provoked me more than I liked. But I was tired, and hungry, and getting scared, no matter how much I fought letting it show. "If you've got a warrant, use it. If you have evidence, take it to my PO, or the judge. Don't harass me in a deserted parking garage over rumors."

Reynolds took a half-step in, backing me against the car. Bratton shouldered him back.

"There's no need to get worked up," he said. "We're doing you a favor by warning you off. Your friend's death was an accident. You need to let it go. And stay away from the Cyber Café."

I caught my breath and jerked my attention away from Reynolds. "What do you know about Carmen? Bruce put you up to this, didn't he? That asshole."

"If we could verify who made the call, we'd have your warrant," Reynolds said.

Bratton threw him a look that shut him down.

"At this point in time, our investigation into your activities does not rise to the level of cause for a warrant," Bratton said smoothly. "For your sake, I hope it never does. It'd be a shame to land on the judge's desk so close to the end of your term."

A beater car drove onto the parking level followed by a dark green Beemer and cruised past us, its occupants staring openly. The tinted windows of the BMW hid the driver, but it slowed down to watch as well. The agents pulled back to a respectful distance, releasing me from my awkward press against the door frame.

Bratton handed me a business card. "If you think of anything about the establishment in question that might be helpful, it would be in your best interest to share it with us immediately. Otherwise, keep your distance. Thank you for your cooperation."

I waited until they were in their car and pulling away before collapsing into the driver's seat. I closed the door, locking it again, and started the engine. Even with the heat cranked up full, I shivered. I checked my Droid. The red Record light flashed. I hit Stop, then Play.

"What's your interest in the Cyber Café?"

Bratton's voice crackled through the car. I leaned my head back, closed my eyes, and celebrated small victories.

The suits had hardly disappeared down the ramp in their Fedmobile when another vehicle pulled in at an angle, blocking me in against the hulking air conditioning units. I'd had enough of intimidating goons for the day and considered ramming my way out, but my Fiero was no match for the Escalade. I gritted my teeth and adjusted the rearview mirror to get a better look. Something about the SUV was familiar. No memory links prepared my tired brain for who opened the driver's door.

Tatum.

He stopped about ten feet from my car, arms akimbo, palms facing up.

"We need to talk." A damp breeze grabbed his words in a splatter of sudden raindrops and bounced them off the concrete abutments surrounding the garage.

"It's raining." I called through the window, stalling.

How'd he know I was here?

"No shit." He shrugged into his trench coat and pulled the collar up. "Your car or mine?"

I hesitated another few seconds before leaning over to unlock the passenger door. I pushed it open a few inches and scooted my backpack into what passed for a rear seat behind me.

Tatum slid into the car with another gust of wind and rain. He ignored the water dripping from his perfect blond hair and fixed me with a curious gaze.

"You need to stay away from those guys," he said.

"What guys?"

"Bratton and Reynolds, DHS." He nodded in the direction their car had gone.

"How did you know I was here?"

"Same way they did, I'd imagine. I tapped your phone's GPS."

My hand went to the Droid tucked back in my pocket, but I didn't bother recording. Tatum couldn't send me to prison.

"We all make mistakes. Even talented hackers like you," he said.

His easy smile raised the hair on my neck. "I understand how they could get into the GPS, but you?"

"A non-descript private school admin nobody like me?" He laughed. "You'd be surprised."

"You're pretty good on a computer, are you?"

"I'd better be. The government spent a lot of money training me."

"Air Force." I knew he was retired military, nothing unusual about that in Dayton. With Wright-Patterson Air Force Base dwarfing the city from the northeast, lots of troops retire and just stay put.

"Air Force Institute of Technology. I assume you know what that is?"

"More or less. Grad school for the troops, intelligence, special ops."

"Cyberwarfare. I wrote the AFIT training manual."

My eyes widened at Tatum's cavalier pronouncement of what the government preferred to deny. I shifted in my seat to face him better, studying his features with a new interest.

"And they let you retire?"

"Yeah, well, I like to play cards, and the brass decided it made me a security risk." His smile faded into a simmering anger. "At least one of them did, and he had enough pull to make things difficult."

A streetlamp in front of the car flickered on, chasing the shadows cast by rain. It brought him back from whatever memories nagged him.

"Enough people value my abilities to funnel special projects to me now and then. The school network is…convenient." A clap of thunder drowned out his words.

I flinched. Storms unnerve me.

He must have seen my discomfort. "This is going to take a while. There's a thermos of coffee in my car. Why don't we move over there?"

"No." My brain buzzed with the revelations of the afternoon. No way in hell I was getting in his car until I had answers.

"Okay, there's a Beaner's a few blocks over. Shouldn't be much business this time of day. I'll buy."

Tatum returned to the Escalade and led the way out of the garage to the coffee shop where Patrice had fired me. I considered bolting when we hit street level, but my curiosity wouldn't allow it. I made sure to get to the counter before he did though and bought my own coffee. A quick text to Matthew offered a little security before Tatum joined me at a table away from the bustle.

I started the conversation, determined to reassert control in a situation I didn't understand. "You said you like to play cards. Blackjack?" I guessed, remembering his casino jaunts with Patrice.

"Blackjack's for simpletons," he said. "I prefer poker."

"And that makes you a security risk how?"

"The military thinks it leaves me open to blackmail, like they used to claim with homosexuality. Stupid on both counts, but that's the way it is." He dropped an ice cube into his coffee and watched it dissolve before taking a sip. "But you don't really want to hear about my gambling issues, do you?"

"Depends. Why'd you track me down?"

"Same reason DHS did, probably. Warn you off the Cyber Café."

"So you're hiding from them, and you all want me out of the way. Like Carmen."

"I'm sorry about your friend. That should never have happened."

"You don't think it was an accident?"

He pursed his lips in thought. "I hope it was, but I can't be sure. I told you, I handle special projects. The Cyber Café's one of them, for reasons I can't explain. When you started poking around at school, I had to get you to stop. Firing didn't work." He warded off my indignation with a raised hand. "I know, you needed the job. Sorry."

"Why didn't you just ask? I'd have listened."

"Would you?"

I flushed. "Probably not. But you could've asked."

"Anything I could have said would have stoked your curiosity. I know how hackers think."

"But Carmen wasn't a hacker. She was no threat to you. And now she's gone." Frustration and anger fused to push tears to the surface. I was losing my grip. "I need food." I bought a sausage roll and ate in silence while he talked.

"After I saw you on New Year's, I realized Carmen was funneling information. Bruce I knew from the Café. He's into them pretty heavy, so I told him I'd erase his debt if he'd convince her to stay away from you." He swirled the last of his coffee before downing it. "I never expected her to end up dead."

"So it wasn't an accident." The sandwich lodged in my stomach like a bowling ball, but at least the rumbling stopped.

Tatum shrugged. "I don't know. Bruce says it was. But we both know he's less than reliable. I'm not sure that makes him a killer, though."

I mulled over the possibilities. "You're right. He's an idiot, but I don't really think he'd murder. Although with the baby, maybe it seemed like a two-fer."

"What baby?"

Tatum's face tightened as I told him about Carmen's pregnancy. "I didn't know." His voice was hoarse. He shoved away from the table to refill his coffee cup and came back composed. "I'm assuming Bruce was less than thrilled."

"No kidding." I steered the conversation away from Carmen. "So what's got DHS and your nameless employers so interested in a gambling den?"

"It's more than a gambling den, although it does attract some interesting clientele. It's also a very powerful server network. It doesn't take a hacker to imagine the possibilities there."

"You're a military hacker? A white hat."

"We'll go with gray hat." His low laugh brought back my chills. "The white one got pretty grimy during my years in the service, but we can't talk about that."

"So, what can we talk about? You tracked me down for something."

He lounged back. "When I found out DHS was onto you, I needed to run interference. They can be pretty heavy-handed."

"Paranoid, you mean."

"That, too. But until I knew what they had, I wanted to make sure you weren't being fingered for something I did."

"Big of you." I snorted. "Like what?"

His smile was enigmatic.

"I know, I know, you can't tell me. So why'd you come after me?"

"I thought I'd catch them, stop them in their tracks. But I was too late."

"Why would they listen to a retired Air Force hacker?"

"They'd listen to that hacker's commander-in-chief."

The implication stopped *me* in my tracks. "What the hell are you saying?"

"I'm not saying anything, remember?"

No matter how I wheedled and finessed, using my best social engineering skills, he refused to answer further. I tried a different tack.

"What about Patrice?"

Tatum straightened. "What about her?"

"Is she in on the big secret?"

"Leave her out of this. She doesn't know anything."

"Got that right."

His eyes narrowed. "I know you blame her for firing you, but I told you that was my fault."

I studied the riddle that was Tatum, not sure I trusted him. Patrice was a chink in his armor. His tense stare kept me from telling him about how she asked me to spy on him. Save that ammo for another day.

"I'm supposed to believe you showed up in the garage to what, protect me from the Feds?" I stacked my empty dishes and brushed a few crumbs off the table. "Thanks, I guess. What's in it for you?"

His posture relaxed. "Like I said, I need you to back off the Café, too, that's all. For once, DHS and I are on the same page. They just don't realize we're in different books." He grinned at his own joke.

It was time to be magnanimous. I didn't need physical access to the Café any longer. I had all his files. And access to the network remotely, if I really wanted it.

"Okay, fine. I'll stay away. No sense jeopardizing the end of my sentence. I need to be off paper and to graduate in June so I can get on with my life. The Feds have caused me enough trouble."

"Good." He stood to face me as I zipped my coat. "If they bother you again, let me know. Call my cell." He scribbled a number on his business card and handed it to me. "And give Patrice a break. She was only protecting me."

Sure she was. "Whatever. I don't work there anymore so it doesn't matter." I started for the door.

"Let me know if you need extra time with graduation requirements or anything. I'll take care of it."

I kept walking. And I disengaged the GPS on my Droid.

The bookstore was too quiet to contain my churning emotions. Matthew and Sammy were holed up in the office. Normal enough, but today I imagined they were avoiding me after the scene at the DubPub last night. I dragged an old Nordic-Trac exercise machine out of the storeroom. One of Matthew's clients had never reclaimed it, and he kept insisting he'd start exercising some day.

I spent a furious half-hour on the machine trying to discharge pent-up frustrations. Matthew would be pleased the equipment he got stuck with found a good use, if he ever came out of the damn office.

Probably brooding over the lack of customers, like Zigana always did this time of year.

It was February for crying out loud, what did they expect? No one in their right mind slogged through southwest Ohio winters for shopping unless it was for food or beer. Or school.

Blew that philosophy test for sure.

The four o'clock Cisco test wouldn't be much better, what with constantly changing specs and upgrades.

Did I even study the right version this time?

With her contacts in the school bookstore, Carmen had always helped order my texts. Not this time. And never again.

I slammed the door on my mental whirlwind, forcing myself to breathe through the physical and emotional pain as I pushed harder and faster on the Nordic-Trac. The clanging bell over the door signaled a customer twenty minutes later. I eased to a stop, wiped my face with an old sweatshirt, and returned to the counter.

It was Gigi. She looked decidedly uncomfortable, pacing in the front window. She stopped when I came up, but didn't look at me.

"Bruce wants to talk to you," she said to my stocking feet. Boots don't work so well on a Nordic-Trac.

I stifled a groan and closed my eyes for a second, glad she wasn't looking at my face. "Where is he?"

"Not around that old guy. His eye still hurts. I think he's got permanent damage, but he won't go to the doctor."

"He'll get over it."

Her face reddened. She even stamped her foot. "Why are you so mean to him? He never did anything to you."

My anger found a target. "He took advantage of my best friend, knocked her up, maybe shoved her under a bus, and took up with her sister the next day. I'd say I have cause."

Gigi found her target as well. She slapped me, hard.

I didn't flinch. I deserved it.

"You bitch! I told him this was a mistake." Her screams brought Matthew and Sammy running.

"What the hell's going on out here?" The splotch on my cheek was like a red flag to Matthew. He turned on Gigi. "Get the hell out of my store."

I grabbed his arm before he shoved her out the door. "No, it's my fault. Gigi, I shouldn't have said that."

"Damn right you shouldn't." She jerked away from Matthew. "He wants to do you a favor for some bizarre reason, and you insult him again. I don't know why I bothered." She turned to leave, pulling back when Sammy inched around Matthew to block her path. "Stay away from me, old man. I have Mace."

"Everybody calm down." I fought to keep my voice reasonable. "Guys, go back to the office, I can handle this." At Matthew's doubting frown, I added, "Really, I'm fine. Go."

He cocked his head at Sammy and after a warning glare at Gigi, they left us alone.

"What does Bruce want?"

Gigi hugged her shoulder bag closer. "Says he wants to warn you, so you don't end up like Carmen. I don't know what he means," she said, cutting off my question. "Says to meet him at their apartment tonight."

"He still has the old place since he moved in with you?"

"How did you...the lease is up. He's moving his stuff out tonight. Come or don't come. I don't care."

The rumbling in my gut was back. I calculated the hours for my cert test and a stop for real food. "Seven-ish?"

"Make it nine, he works until eight-thirty."

My surprise must have been obvious. She threw back her shoulders and scowled. I swear she almost stuck out her tongue at me.

"Yes, he has a job, a good one. I'll tell him you'll be there at nine."

The bell clanged again and she was gone.

I collapsed onto the stool and cradled my head in my arms on top of the counter. Three strikes for the day and I was out. A minute later, Matthew laid a gentle hand on my shoulder. One look at my tear-streaked face derailed whatever he intended to say. He led me to the chaise in the office where I curled into a ball and buried my head. As he pulled a quilt off the shelf and covered me with it, I mumbled, "I have a test at four."

"Shhh. I'll wake you in plenty of time." He flicked off the lights and left me in quiet, if not peace.

The smell of fresh coffee roused me an hour later. Sammy stood next to the chaise holding a cup and looking sheepish.

"Matthew says you need to wake up, he's got food."

I scrubbed at my face, wincing when I touched Gigi's handprint.

"She hit you because of me?" he asked.

"She hit me because of me." I accepted the coffee and swallowed half of the steaming liquid before scooting off the chaise and following him to the worktable.

We ate in silence, shoveling down burgers and fries from the deli in the next block. I jumped when the clock chimed the quarter-hour.

"Damn, gotta go." I washed down the last bite with the rest of the coffee.

"Sammy's going to drive you to school and bring you back," Matthew said. "No arguments."

It was easier to agree, and I didn't have the energy to fight. I needed all the strength I could muster for the test.

———————

"You don't have to wait, it'll take a couple hours," I told Sammy when we pulled up in front of the entrance.

"I'm going to an AA meeting at the library. I'll be back here by six." He patted my shoulder. "Break a leg, Missy."

I brushed back more emotional tears and managed a smile. "Six it is."

Setting aside the upheavals of the day and concentrating on access control lists and firewall configurations for two hours proved to be good therapy. It wasn't my best showing on paper, but I scored high enough to earn the second of four required certifications that passed for the final exam. Two more and I'd have the Cisco credentials I needed to get hired after graduation. When I climbed into Matthew's truck next to Sammy at six o'clock, my smile was genuine. His face lit up in response, and we drove back to the bookstore wrangling over the upcoming NCAA basketball play-offs.

I took the guys for drinks at the Trolley Stop to thank them. We drove separately so I could meet Bruce. It was karaoke night, and the place rocked with too-loud canned music and bad singers. With the Presidents' Day holiday on Monday, I was done with school until Tuesday and I wanted to celebrate something, anything. I kept the events of the day to myself for the evening, needing to process everything internally before sharing it with Matthew. Or Zigana. After my one Guinness, I switched to ginger ale with Sammy.

"Speaking of Zigana," I said, pointing my glass at Matthew.

"Were we?"

"What's up with the phone call?"

"Did you ask her?"

"I'm asking you."

He ignored me and nudged Sammy. "Your favorite song's on the list up there. Show us what you can do."

Sammy balked until he spotted "Born to be Wild" on the neon playlist displayed next to the stage. "Well, maybe one song." He joined the line of giggling co-eds and drunk frat boys at the sign-up sheet.

"A biker song, really?" I laughed.

"He had a nice Harley Sportster before he enlisted." Matthew took a long pull of his beer. "His dad sold it two weeks after he shipped overseas." He waited until the latest screecher was done abusing Queen's "Bohemian Rhapsody" before he said, "I didn't want to talk in front of Sammy. He's afraid of Zigana."

"He's never met her."

"Heard me grouse about her enough in the past, and your 'Gypsy grandma' spiel spooked him plenty." He grinned at me. "Guess you come by it honest."

"So what'd she want?"

"I think she wants me to do penance, after I told you it'd help Sammy." He snorted. "That one came back to bite me."

"After all these years?" I realized as I said it that the passing of time wouldn't matter to Zigana. Her personal brand of karmic Catholicism didn't have a statute of limitations. "And?"

"And what?"

"What does she want you to do?"

He shrugged and drained his glass, holding it up to signal the server for a refill. "Not sure yet, says she'll let me know."

"You going to let her string you along?"

"For now."

Sammy took the mic, and we gave him our attention as he strutted and wailed. "Born to be wild…."

"Never want to die," Matthew said, finishing the stanza under his breath.

I clinked his refilled glass with my ginger ale.

Threat Modeling

"Identify and categorize primary and secondary assets, threats, and threat communities; Map threat communities against primary and secondary assets"

Refusing Matthew's offer to join me at the meeting with Bruce didn't sound like such a good idea after I arrived and found him alone. I'd counted on Gigi as a buffer, if nothing else, all the while planning to stay out of arm's reach. Carmen's old apartment was nearly empty, half-a-dozen cardboard boxes scattered among the dust bunnies and litter in the living room. What had passed for furniture — a sagging futon, packing crate table, couple of plastic lawn chairs — was gone. The counter separating the kitchen area overflowed with heaps of dirty dishes and crumpled cereal boxes. A clean space on the floor outlined the missing entertainment center that had held Bruce's 42-inch flat screen. A gift from Carmen, of course. Not that she could afford it, but if it made him happy, she burned up the plastic and worried about payments later.

Wonder who pays them off now that she's gone?

Bruce didn't say anything when he answered my knock, just went back to wadding up a stack of t-shirts and tossing them into a box. I watched him for a few minutes, waiting. I could be patient.

When the last of the clothing was packed, more or less, he pointed to a pile of books in the corner. "You want any of those? They're Carmen's."

I almost said, "No use for books?" but decided antagonizing him was a bad idea. "Got another box?"

"In the closet. Tape's on the counter."

I assembled the box and loaded the books without checking the titles. They were Carmen's. That was enough. He stuffed the cereal boxes into a green trash bag and loaded the dishes into a laundry basket. By then my patience was spent.

"I didn't come here to help you move."

He paused half a beat as he taped the box of t-shirts closed. "You need to stay away from Tatum. He's dangerous."

"Why do you care?"

"I don't." He looked at me for the first time since I'd arrived. "But Carmen did."

I caught my breath.

"I know you don't like me much. I don't particularly like you. Always telling Carmen I was no good, trying to split us up." He stacked the boxes next to the door and balanced the basket of dishes on top. "None of your damn business. Neither is Tatum." He hiked himself onto the counter and slumped there like a gargoyle, swinging his legs and leaving black marks on the paneling with his fancy boots. "But she liked you. And whether you believe me or not, I'm sorry she's gone. I'm warning you for her sake."

I crossed my arms over my chest and stared at his haggard face. I almost believed him. Almost. Until those boots clattered against the paneling again.

"He paid you to keep her away from me."

"Says who?"

"Says Tatum."

His legs stilled mid-swing. He squinted at me, head lowered. I could see his mind racing. He scooted off the counter and leaned against it, matching my pose. "Can't image what he'd talk to you for, but he lies. A lot."

We stood facing each other for a long minute. He must have reached a decision of some kind, because he pushed himself away from the counter and raised his head. I was surprised to see that when he stood up straight, he was taller than me.

"Look, Tatum's not a nice guy. You know that. Carmen told me you two talked about what he was up to with what's-her-name Pat something—your boss—after hours. But that's not all. He's the collector for the guys who own the Cyber Café, and a bunch of other places."

Shades of Matthew's gangster films. "You mean he twists arms and breaks knees like in the movies?"

"No, asshole, he's smarter than that." Bruce looked disgusted. "You're a hacker. This is the twenty-first century. When the high-rollers want into the big games, they have to turn over credit card numbers, bank accounts, passwords. If they don't settle up fast enough to suit the owners, Tatum taps the accounts and takes what they owe, plus a shitload of interest. They can't report it to the cops because their kind of gambling's illegal."

I frowned. The list of names and numbers in the database made sense now. I watched Bruce watching me and tried to decide who to trust: the deadbeat in front of me or the smooth talker who knew how to hack my phone's GPS and track me down in the parking garage.

"If all that's true, why warn me? I'm not a gambler," I said.

"He's dangerous."

"You said that."

He shuffled his feet and said nothing, an internal battle playing shadows across his face.

"Why do you think he's dangerous?" I asked.

"I'm pretty sure he killed Carmen."

The room spun. I dropped to the floor, cross-legged, and stared at him. "If you have proof...the police said it was an accident, based on your testimony I'd imagine."

"Yeah, well." He slid down the front of the counter and sat facing me. "You were right about the boots. He paid me a thousand bucks to keep Carmen away from you. I used every excuse I could think of, took her cell phone, made up those threats Gigi told you about." He hung his head. "I couldn't believe it when the bus...after she died, I was afraid he'd frame me for it." Bruce fixed his eyes on me, terror lurking in their depths. "He still might, 'specially if he knew I was talking to you."

I held his gaze for a long minute, searching for answers. When nothing overrode the fear and confusion that gripped him, I rolled to my knees and stood up. The living room was barely big enough to pace in. I stopped by the front window and peeked at the night sky through a missing mini-blind slat. Maybe the stars held a clue. Zigana said they did. From the fourth floor, I had a view of the city that could have been beautiful on a different night. After the day I'd been through, I saw only the dirty grimness, the empty buildings and littered alleys. An SUV inched down the side street next to the apartment complex, no headlights. It passed under a streetlamp and I froze.

An Escalade.

The answers I needed arrived in a flood.

"Okay, Bruce my new buddy, here's what we're going to do." I grabbed a scrap of paper off the floor and a stubby miniature-golf pencil from the counter. Words flowed as fast as the thoughts formulated, and I scribbled while I talked.

Bruce listened, jaw slack, brow furrowed as the plan unfolded from my brain. I tore the paper in half and handed both pieces to him. "You'll need a throwaway email, like this one that I use. Know what that is?"

That pricked his not inconsiderable male ego. He stood to face me, posturing. "How many you want? I got three."

"One will do."

He snatched the pencil and scrawled the address.

I stuffed the note in my pocket before picking up the books and balancing the box on my hip. "Now you're going to throw me out of the building. Loudly."

"Huh?"

"I think Tatum's outside."

His face blanched. He shook himself and raised his chin. "Then get the hell out of my apartment."

"Not here, downstairs where he might see you." *Idiot.* I suppressed the tagline. "I'll email you this weekend after I figure things out."

Bruce followed me out the door and clattered down the four flights of stairs at my heels. His heavy steps earned more than one insult from behind closed doors, but he didn't seem to notice, or care. I stopped at the main entrance, out of sight of the street.

"Ready?"

He nodded.

"Make it good." I kicked open the door and stumbled onto the sidewalk. "I'm going already, you bastard. Get your hands off me." Anxiety added a realistic edge to my angry roar.

The shove he aimed at my back was harder than necessary. I tripped over the stoop, righting myself before I hit the ground.

"Go on, bitch. And don't come back. Told you once, I told you a thousand times, you're nothin' but trouble." His overacting echoed off brick walls and faded into the neighboring gloom. He posed in the lighted doorway, arm outstretched, pointing like some impervious overlord from his damn role-playing games.

Adrenaline fueled one final dig. "She was too good for you, you know. Bastard." I stashed the box in the Fiero's miniature trunk and accelerated away from the curb, tires spinning. Love that rear-wheel drive for effect.

I kept an eye on the rearview mirror until I hit US 35 east out of the city. Too early for the bar crowd, so traffic was light. If Tatum tried to follow me now, his arrogance would tip me off. As I approached my exit at I-675 north, a thought struck with such a jolt I almost missed the ramp. I checked my phone. The GPS was still off.

How did he find me?

The rest of the drive passed in a blur. "Who's driving your car?" my psychology-cum-philosophy prof always asked. Lucky for me whoever or whatever lurked in my brain knew the way home. I coasted into my reserved spot in the alley behind the shop and waited a thirty-count before getting out to. No one drove past. I slipped in the back door. A staircase led from the workroom to our living quarters overhead. The street remained empty for the full minute I stood at the base of the stairs. Pale beams from the streetlamp illuminated the showroom, flickering off the glass and metal display cases, and creating an eerie backdrop for my unsettled nerves. Tatum knew where we lived, but I was home now, with Zigana. If he wasn't the good guy he tried to portray earlier, he had no idea what he was up against.

Gray hat my ass.

I hoisted the box of Carmen's books again and headed up the stairs.

———

Exhaustion got me through the night. After the nightmares faded, I slept dreamlessly until the sun was high enough to shine through the peaked window onto the bed. Bathroom stop first, then I hit the laptop to call in reinforcements using one of my bogus email accounts. When I staggered into the shop, coffee mug in hand, Zigana was bent over her wires and beads.

She peeked at me over the task light and, apparently satisfied that I was alive, said, "You locked the door."

"Oops."

While the street-level doors were secured at night, the upstairs locks were a different matter. In my state of heightened paranoia, before going to bed I'd locked every door and double-checked windows we hadn't opened in years. I'd forgotten she had a date with Hank at the Little Art movie theater.

"You had your keys, right?" I pulled a stool from under the counter and slouched next to her. She looked at me and waited, her brow furrowed, as I scanned the shop. Her patient attention squashed my apprehension. A long slurp of coffee fortified my nerves. I started with the ambush by DHS, replayed the scene with Tatum, glossed over my breakdown at the bookstore, and ended with Bruce.

She stopped working when I got to the part about Tatum, but she didn't interrupt. Our role-playing outside Carmen's apartment made her smile, a bit grimly, but a smile at least. She shook her head when I held up the coffee pot to refill my mug and returned to her beads.

"So now what?" she asked when I sat down again.

I checked the time. "TK should be here any minute. I need his services."

"Sex is great therapy, but how's that going to help?"

"Not those services." I made a face at her and she laughed. "He's going to sweep the house and cars for bugs."

Her hands stilled. "Really think that's necessary? Tatum's a computer geek, not a spy."

"I don't know what he is." I got up to answer TK's knock at the back door. "But I intend to find out."

While TK did his thing upstairs, I walked down to the gas station to buy a Cricket pre-pay cell phone. I used it to call Matthew at the store.

"Write this number down." After he had my burner phone number, I hit the high points of my meeting with Bruce and told him about TK's work. "When he's done here, I'll bring him to the store."

"Don't bother," Matthew said. "Sammy can handle it. I'll see he has the equipment."

"Our Sammy?"

"Long story, call me when you're done there. We'll have dinner tonight."

TK finished the living quarters and started on the shop while I took time to shower and change. I met him in the workroom, damp hair clinging to my forehead, but feeling more human. Zigana always taught me to take care of myself first. Then I can handle whatever else the universe throws my way. The situation with Tatum and DHS threw me off kilter, and I needed to regain control.

"No mics or cameras in the building," TK said. He pointed to two small components on the card table. "Found those on the cars."

I examined one of the gadgets, recognizing it from units I'd seen online. "Tracking. Shit. What kind of range?"

He shrugged. "Can't say for sure. Depends on the receiver as much as the transmitter. I'll do some checking."

I tossed the device up and down a few times, considering its implications, and my options.

TK packed up his gear. "Got another job in Huber. Nice to see you again, Zigana," he called through the doorway.

"What do I owe you?" I asked.

"She took care of it." He threw me the smile that made our in-kind trades so enticing and left.

I called Matthew to let him know what TK had found and to finalize dinner plans.

"We'll come out to Peach's," he said, naming the lone Yellow Springs sports bar. "Bring Zigana if you want."

I tucked that odd request away to puzzle over another time, but agreed.

My next course of business was a deep-scan of my computers. I ran every check I could think of and a few new ones I found online. Not surprisingly, the desktop was clean. I stay on top of that one because I use it as a proxy server. The laptop I tend to neglect. It's with me all the time for school, and I get careless. The usual background scans handle most things, but any time I visit a hacker site, I have to expect an attack of some kind. It's what we do, just to prove we can.

To combat Tatum's skill level, I would need a better firewall and encryption. I run Windows for most stuff because of college, but I also have a virtual machine OS that uses Linux. Better for hacking. That latest Cisco certification I'd earned came in handy for something other than a piece of paper as I set up a firewall designed to keep any intruder at bay. I hope.

Life caught up with me, and I crashed for two hours before it was time to meet Matthew and Sammy. And life had more surprises. Zigana agreed to join us. We shared the lumpy bench seat against the wall near the patio door at Peach's while the guys sat across from us. Their plastic chairs rocked almost as much as the table did on the rough tile. Music blared from the CD juke box across the room, and one of the four televisions overhead escaped the mute setting. A typical Friday night crowd talked over the noise, adding to the din. When the overworked server made it to our table, we ordered drinks and appetizers and settled in to wait. Peach's isn't known for speedy service, especially on the weekend, but it makes up for it in friendliness and decent food.

With Matthew and Zigana facing each other again, I expected awkward. Instead, Zigana turned on more charm than I'd seen in years.

Even Sammy relaxed. She coaxed him to try hummus from the pita chip platter and laughed when he grimaced.

"Tastes like wallpaper paste," he said, rinsing his mouth with ginger ale.

"You make a habit of eating wallpaper paste?" She handed him a chip with a dollop of *tzatziki*. "Try this one." The Greek yogurt dip was more to his liking, and he licked his fingers in appreciation.

I kicked Matthew under the table. We shared an amused glance at their antics, and dinner passed in a haze of alcohol and the comfort of bar food. I lost track of how many Guinness refills the server brought. Zigana and Matthew shared hesitant memories of happier days with Harmony, and I basked in the unexpected emotional warmth. *My family to the rescue.* When the band launched into its warm-up chords, making further conversation impossible, we settled the tab and headed out into the cold night air. Matthew was parked around the corner in front of the post office.

I stopped him before he unlocked the truck. "We never talked about Tatum."

He looked to Zigana. She took a deep breath and nodded at him.

"Come back to the apartment. I'll make coffee," she said. She looped her arm with Sammy's and led him down the street.

I looked at Matthew and shrugged. He held out his arm. I matched Zigana's pose and we followed.

Matthew's concern echoed Zigana's when I showed him the trackers TK had found on our cars. He tossed one to Sammy, who leaned closer to the pole lamp for a better look.

"LiveWire brand," Sammy said in a matter-of-fact voice I didn't recognize. "Cheap, but you can track it with your smartphone." He fixed me with a steady, clear gaze, a stranger in a familiar face. "If you disable it, you'll tip them off. Right now they just think you parked the car. I can show you how to block the signal."

"I thought about that. Wait, you can?" My amazement, and the extra Guinness, set Matthew off in a fit of laughter. Zigana's indignant glare as she passed out coffee calmed him fast.

"Sorry, I wasn't laughing at you, really," he said, choking back another spasm. "But that look! I told you Sammy could handle it."

Sammy exchanged the tracker for a coffee mug, and his face resumed its normal bland expression. "I was Army, Special Ops. Could tell you lots of things, but then I'd have to kill you."

"He could, too." Matthew said. "Bruce's lucky all he got was a black eye."

I studied Sammy with a new respect before cringing at the thought. "You killed people?"

"It was war, Missy. That's what soldiers do."

My crude question, and Sammy's subdued response, left a pall over the room. I was embarrassed at my insensitivity. Sammy was embarrassed at his answer. Zigana, bless her, rescued us both.

"So, you said we can block those things." She settled next to him on the loveseat, angled to meet his now troubled eyes. "Help us out here, Sammy."

He looked to Matthew, who nodded encouragement. After a gulp of coffee, he set the mug on the side table. Face and voice switched again, and the professional Sammy gave us a lesson in GPS radio frequencies. He talked for a good fifteen minutes, holding even non-techie Zigana's attention. Matthew looked on like a proud parent watching his only son win the National Spelling Bee. When I realized I coveted that look directed at me, my embarrassment returned. I mulled the chaos my emotions had become and missed the end of Sammy's lecture.

"You okay, Missy?"

"Sure, yeah, okay. You'll help me find a blocker? I'd appreciate it." I caught myself overcompensating and backed off. No sense spreading the discomfiture.

"I'll reinstall these tracking units before we leave. Come to the bookstore tomorrow. We'll take the truck from there." Our meek Sammy turned to Matthew. "If that's okay with you."

Matthew grinned. "Sounds good to me."

"Then what?" Zigana asked. Her quiet words held an undercurrent of anxiety.

My untouched coffee was as cold as the shiver that ran through my body. "I'll let you know when I figure that out."

The visit to Sammy's supplier the next morning was quick and painless, except to my bank account. Spy gadgets don't come cheap. The guy's stash filled the basement of a non-descript two-story in an older neighborhood on the north side of Dayton. Good thing Special Ops Sammy was there to handle the transaction. I know computers, not GPS frequencies and radio signals. When we left with our purchase, old Sammy slumped into the truck and handed me the keys.

"You drive, Missy. I'm beat." He leaned back and closed his eyes.

Sammy's emotional battle added another puzzle to the mix. Zigana called it *naswalemos*, the sickness. "I could maybe help him, if he'd let me," she'd said last night after the men left.

"I doubt if he would. The Gypsy thing scares him pretty good."

"Of course, he's *gajo*."

As if that explained everything.

My own emotional disarray affected my sense of direction on the way back to the bookstore. I pulled up to a stop sign, debating which way to go, when I noticed the street name. Stanley Avenue. I took a deep breath and mentally reached out to those Romani spirits Zigana warned against.

I turned left. Houses became sparser the longer I drove, more empty land and fewer cars. I slowed to check the patchy numbers perched at odd angles along the roadway. Distant memory from past library research gave me the number to look for. I found it, faded and peeling from a battered mailbox, in front of an old farmhouse. Levi and Matilda's Gypsy homestead. Several additions had been tacked on over the years, and cracked vinyl siding covered the original brick. The barn I'd seen in pictures at the library's archives was gone, leaving a patch of weeds overtaking what remained of the stone foundation. I cruised by slowly, checking for signs of life. It looked empty, so I backed up and pulled into the drive. I turned off the truck and sat staring at the house. Beside me, Sammy snored gently.

I lost track of time as the stillness calmed my churning thoughts. Gypsies take care of family, and I felt Matilda's presence span the generations, across some divide I could only dimly imagine, and touch my soul. Zigana would freak, but it eased my fears, this connection with the past. Bigger men than Tatum had tried, still try, to run off the Romani. I'm part of the new breed, grafted to the discipline of the traditional *tabor* by the DNA of Toby and Matthew. Romani loyalty, our desire for independence and justice, merged with the knowledge of millennia and the tools of technology, made me stronger.

And when pushed, more dangerous.

After a while, I dug in my pocket for a handful of coins. A bedraggled Rose of Sharon near the back stoop made a decent makeshift altar. I scattered the money and sent a few words of thanks to the universe, to Levi and Matilda, before starting the truck and driving away.

It was nearly lunchtime when we made it back to the store. I hit the Arby's drive-thru at the corner before dropping Sammy off with a bag of food and a hug as I switched vehicles.

"Tell Matthew thanks for the use of the truck. I'll call him later." The less time the GPS tracker on my car sat at the bookstore, the better I'd feel, but I wasn't ready to activate the blocking device.

"Wait until you really need it," Sammy warned again.

I waved an acknowledgment and headed home to Zigana.

Except for my shift at the bookstore, I stayed close to home for the full three-day weekend. I insisted on working my regular hours. My funds were all but gone, and I refused Matthew's offer to pay me for personal time off.

"Your partner would say that sets a bad precedent," I said when he tried to send me home.

"My partner's not my kind of businessperson if she puts profit over compassion." But he let me stay. Probably wanted to keep an eye on me anyway.

Sammy had reinstalled the tracking unit on our cars to avoid tipping Tatum off, adding an unobtrusive mounting bracket around each for the blocking device we bought. It was little more than a glorified Faraday cage, designed to block radio transmissions. I could slap it over the tracker myself in only a few minutes. I tried to explain it all to Zigana. As usual when it comes to anything technical, she blew me off.

"Do what you need to, tell me what I need to know to not screw it up. Nothing more."

For a smart, independent woman, she sure has her blind spots. I guess we all do.

The rest of the day I holed up outlining and discarding plans to take Tatum down. I made a list of his possible motivations for running me off. Bruce said he had access to clients' bank accounts, so he was probably skimming. I needed to know who those clients were. Maybe he was into a little blackmail, too.

Unfortunately, with fewer than three weeks left till I was off paper, I couldn't afford to antagonize DHS. They could still come after me, but it would be harder to make a case if I was careful. I checked my credit card balance and started another list, this one of the hardware I needed to set up a more secure, anonymous network with no traceable links. Most of the software was open source, but I'd need to add to my chatroom balance to access some of the more questionable programs. Add those hours to the to-do list.

I also had to be pragmatic. I needed to graduate. If I tipped Tatum off, he could make that impossible. And if I didn't keep up my class work and finish the final Cisco certification the job offer hinged on, I'd be practicing, "Would you like fries with that?"

"You know that's not going to happen." Zigana said during dinner prep Sunday night. "You've always got a home here, and I can use you in the shop."

"Hank would love that. Bet he's counting the days till he can stay here instead of taking you to his place all the time." I leaned over the bubbling pot on the stove and inhaled the spicy scent of white bean chili. "Did you add extra cumin?"

She swatted me away with a wooden spoon. "Of course I did. Go make the salad."

I dug romaine and spinach out of the crisper drawer and started chopping carrots and peppers from the veggie bin. "You know he doesn't like me."

"Who?"

Her studied nonchalance wouldn't fool anyone, especially me.

"Hank, goof." I pointed the knife at her. "I cramp his style."

"He doesn't have a style. And don't wave that thing at me." The oven timer beeped. She nudged me aside to remove a pan of cornbread. "Get the cooling rack." I tried three different cupboards while she stood holding the hot dish, tapping her foot. "Under the range. How long have you lived here?"

"You know I don't bake." I set the rack on the counter and returned to the salad.

"You hardly cook at all." She opened a bottle of wine while the cornbread cooled enough to cut. "Even after I taught you how."

"My stuff's never as good as yours. Why should I try to compete?" I scooped the last of the veggies into a wooden bowl and doused them with vinaigrette.

Zigana ladled chili into ironstone bowls. As we ate, she tried the nonchalance thing again. "I'm not seeing Hank anymore."

Considering her deliberate lack of emotion, buttering my third slab of cornbread gave me time to mull over a response. Since she didn't volunteer anything else, I went with, "Your choice or his?"

"Mine, his, doesn't matter. It was fun while it lasted, I guess." She toyed with her salad. "He wants a wife."

"Live-in housekeeper, you mean." I'd seen the way he took Zigana's attentions as his due, never lifting a finger to return the favor. I'm surprised she had put up with him as long as she did. "You do what you want. As long as it's not because of me."

"It's not always about you."

"And here I believed you when you told me I was special."

Her smile rewarded my lame attempt at humor. "So how do you propose taking down Tatum without creating more problems?"

I wasn't satisfied with her explanation about Hank, but apparently she was done with the topic. "First, I have to figure out why he's worried about me, find out what he's hiding in the school network."

"Those are the files Carmen left you?"

"I think so. Bruce says he's a collector for the gambling clubs, so they may be client lists. He might be running a little blackmail business on the side and he's afraid I'll expose him to his bosses. They probably wouldn't take too kindly to that."

"What about the military thing? Is he really still connected?"

"Maybe." I sopped up the last of my chili with a chunk of cornbread. "I have an idea how to test his pull at DHS and throw off his suspicions at the same time. If it works."

"Let's see if it will." Zigana cleared the dishes while I bagged the bread and topped off the wine glasses.

When she brought out the Tarot deck, I balked. "Do we have to? You know whatever you turn up makes me second guess myself."

She was adamant. In her mind, Tarot held all the answers, if we only interpret them correctly. Her expectant look left no room for argument. I swallowed my objections and sat down across from her. After shuffling the cards thoroughly, she lit a candle and positioned it at her right hand, midway between us, next to the stacked cards.

"Cut the deck," she said.

I complied with deliberate movements so as not to let my impatience show.

She reassembled the deck and began dealing the cards across the table.

"Ten of Wands," she said. "Your energy is going in the wrong direction."

Let the second-guessing begin.

She flipped up the next card.

"Six of Cups. You're stuck on something from your past. If you get past it, you'll likely find success." She tapped the card twice to get my attention. "Like I keep telling you, leave the past alone."

I stifled a sigh at the ambiguous vagueness of her comments. Zigana glared at me and turned up the next card.

"High Priestess. You're hiding something, maybe from others, maybe from yourself. Open up. Listen to your intuition, and don't be afraid to share your feelings."

She smiled at the fourth card. "This is your relationship paradigm. Temperance. Good resolutions for problems and people that plague you."

The fifth and final card brought a frown. "Seven of Cups, in your finance paradigm. You could be misusing your talents, squandering your life. Money may not be the root of all evil, but it can certainly cause lots of problems."

As usual, Zigana's Tarot predictions shook me, even though I scoff at them. And as usual, I didn't let on. She means well. In my mind, Tarot is too much like astrology, which we also disagree on. Depending on who does the interpretation, and who receives it, the same cards can mean wildly different things. I held more confidence in the power of suggestion.

Unfortunately, *her* suggestions unsettled my resolve. I'd hoped to spend the rest of the evening deciphering Tatum's files. *So much for that.* The thought of misused talents and bad energy ruined my concentration, so I let Zigana talk me into joining her for another activity I don't appreciate as much as she does: gallery openings. Since she joined the Yellow Springs Arts Council, she goes to every single exhibit in town, and there are lots. Which is fine. I like art as much as the next person.

Okay, maybe not. I don't mind an occasional museum trip, but I prefer artifacts, and even surrealism to abstract splashes of color. Jackson Pollack leaves me cold, and too much of the stuff Zigana promotes is right up there with his best, or worst. It's all in perspective, she says. My perspective is I have to recognize at least something on the canvas. Dali I can stare at for hours.

But I went, largely to atone for lingering doubts about the breakup with Hank, certain it was my fault, guilty at my relief that it was over. Which reminded me.

"I was surprised you joined us at Peach's Friday." We were halfway between galleries, one exhibit down, one more to go. Felt I'd earned the right to pry a bit. "Matthew said a while back he thought you wanted him to do penance. Does that mean he's in the clear?"

She stumbled slightly. "Damn boots." She leaned on my arm to check the left heel, avoiding my question in the process. There was nothing wrong with her footwear. A display in the front window of an art shop gave her the next distraction. She pointed out the work of the latest and greatest phenom I'd never heard of. Her enthusiasm for the intricate paper cuttings mounted in tiny shadow boxes was more than a little over the top, but I listened. I let her give me the fifty-cent bio of the artist as we made our way to the gallery at the Arts Council building, reserving personal questions until we got home.

———

When we were back in the apartment, I made tea, cut the pan of brownies she'd left cooling on the counter, and joined her in the living room.

This time a program brochure she'd picked up at the gallery absorbed her attention. I snatched it away and waved it out of reach.

"Stop ignoring me."

"I'm not ignoring you." She studied the depths of her tea. "Okay, maybe I am. What was the question again?"

I flung the brochure back at her like a Frisbee.

She laughed when I missed, then her face grew sad. "Matthew's not doing penance. I just had to work it all out in my head before I could let him into my life. Our life." She met my worried gaze and burst out laughing again. "Oh, stop. You look like my grandmother."

My surprise must have shown. She went to her room, and I heard her rummage through the dresser. She emerged with a mosaic box similar to the one Harmony had left for me. She cradled it on her lap, staring at nothing for several minutes. I didn't rush her.

A deep breath, straightened shoulders, and she opened the lid. The same musky scent I'd noticed from my box wafted into the room. Zigana flipped through a small stack of photos and handed me a faded sepia print. A gnarled old woman with a wrinkled frown sat frozen in time, framed by a patterned scarf covering most of her dark hair. It draped over her shoulders, revealing little of the dress underneath.

Crooked hands clutched the scarf's fringe. For all the dourness of her expression, the eyes were lively, mischievous. I guessed the frown was intentional, mugging for the camera. They reflected Zigana's features. And my own.

"Huldah, my mother's mother," Zigana said.

"My great-great-grandmother." I counted off the generations, hardly believing what I was hearing. Or seeing.

"Supposedly Queen Matilda was her great-great-great aunt." She ticked off the greats on her fingers.

The picture and connections made our Gypsy heritage more real. I'd half-believed it was a family myth. "Why now?"

Zigana gave a rueful grin. "Something Matthew said about your needing connections beyond him and me. Made sense at the time. I'll probably regret it later." She held out her hand, silently demanding the picture's return. It disappeared into the stack and she returned the box to her room.

"When did he say that?" I asked when she was back in her chair.

I could see the wheels turning while she debated how to respond. My frown returned. I wiped it away before she could notice.

"We talked," she said around bites of a brownie.

"I gathered that. When?" The phone call at the Dublin Pub came to mind. "Last Wednesday, when we were at the Pub."

"Sure, right." She rushed on. "Anyway, I decided maybe you needed to know something about our family. As the oldest females, from Matilda all the way down to me, Harmony, and you, it's our duty to carry on the traditions. And that sixth-sense you want to ignore."

"I don't ignore it, just keeping it real." Her digressions confused me. I tried to piece all the new information together and came up short. "So where does Matthew fit into all that?"

"When I'm gone, I don't want you to feel like an orphan." She bit her lip. "Don't read too much into it, okay? Harmony saw something in him, even if I never understood what. And he's your father, no escaping blood. Let's leave it at that." Zigana carried her cup to the sink. "Cover the brownies when you're done, will you? I'm going to bed. It's been a long day."

For the second time in recent memory, the night owl disappeared into her room early, leaving me to wonder what else she was avoiding.

Since I'd spent most of the day on much-needed family time instead of foiling Tatum, I plowed through my latest checklist until nearly three in the morning. A few hours in the hacker chatroom building up my credits so I could acquire the right software. An hour sorting the database files from Carmen's flash drive into groups by the fields that I now realized were bank account or credit card numbers, and another hour identifying the institution each represented. Not difficult, only tedious. Banks use a standard routing number from the Federal Reserve which is easily tracked. Master Card, Visa, AmEx, Discover all have set number formats. If I'd been paying attention to that data instead of the name and doc fields, I'd have picked up on that sooner. My bad.

Tatum had collected financial data on one hundred eighty-seven gambling clients, with a combined six-hundred-twelve account numbers. Each client had at least one bank and two or three credit cards listed, including an interesting assortment of offshore institutions. Those would be fun to hack.

Because I knew DHS lurked much too close, I spread out my online activities. One wireless network for general information searches. Another through a series of ghost proxies for the chatrooms, and a third to check email and stuff. Might as well make the Feds work for a living.

When I got tired of looking at account numbers, I did some research on the tracking units TK had found on our cars. Too basic for DHS. Besides, they weren't the ones who showed up at Carmen's apartment. Had to be Tatum.

When I couldn't focus on the monitor any longer, I shut everything down and sprawled across the bed to think. Carmen's Y2K bug stared at me from the shelf next to its now-modified partner. Mine didn't have the dash of Goth hers did, but I'd added navy eyelashes, henna tracings on the lime green hands, and a gold tooth. My final touch, the Romani *hai'she'li* in clumsy calligraphy, adorned the wide green belly. *I swear.*

For however long, for whatever sacrifice, even if it meant school and the job and everything, I'd find out the truth about Carmen's death.

If Bruce was right, Tatum had a debt to pay. I'd be only too happy to collect.

Like I said, we're not vigilantes, Zigana and me. We're law-abiding citizens, mostly, content to let the authorities deal with the bad guys. Sometimes they need a little help is all. The middle-school bully who found himself at the wrong and painful end of his own practical joke that back-fired in front of the entire class. The perv hanging out in the park whose license plate mysteriously expired two months early, giving the cops probable cause to pull him over and find his stash of kiddie porn. The booster club treasurer with the extravagant purchases who caught the auditor's attention after a vacation picture lifted from her private Facebook feed showed up on the group's home page. Little things. If karma needs a push, I'll provide the momentum.

I swear.

Vulnerability Analysis

"Discovering flaws in systems and applications which can be leveraged by an attacker"

With only two weeks until Mardi Gras, Zigana and I spent Presidents' Day tearing down the last of the holiday décor and getting ready for spring. She decked out the shop in feathers and beads, added a few glittery masks she had brought back from New Orleans, and transformed the silver and white snow castle of winter to an almost garish purple and green and gold wonderland. Almost. For all the glitz, Zigana has great taste. If I tried to throw together the stuff she did, it would look like a nauseated flea market. That's why I'm just the labor. She goes all out with the decorating, and her shop is known for the displays. Brings people in just to see what she comes up with every season. More traffic in the store, more sales. She may not like technology, but she knows retail.

After the last gauzy banner was in place, and the umpteenth balloon filled with helium and tacked in bunches rising from each corner shelf, I left Zigana to jewelry making and went shopping. Tom's Market prides itself on local, organic produce: butternut squash, onions, spinach, fresh tomatoes. Everything else I needed I could find in the pantry at home. I chopped and diced, simmered and baked the afternoon away. When Zigana came upstairs at five-thirty, I was ready.

"Sit." I poured us each a glass of wine and set a plate of spinach salad in front of her. One more quick stir of the pot, releasing enticing aromas of cumin, cinnamon, and garlic, and I joined her at the table.

Her eyes glinted in amusement. "Proving me wrong, are you?"

"Proving you right." I held out my glass in a toast. "It's good I don't forget those traditions."

When the salad plates were empty, I dished up mounds of couscous and ladled spicy Moroccan stew on top. A dash of fresh cilantro, a dollop of Greek yogurt, and we were content to eat in silence, savoring the clash of flavors and textures that worked as well on the plate as Zigana's designs did in the store. She swallowed a bite of *naan* bread and leaned back with a satisfied sigh.

"Nice to come up to a home-cooked meal once in a while. Thanks."

"I should do it more often. No reason you need to wait on me." I scraped the plates and filled the dishwasher. "There's cherry cobbler for later."

"What happened to the brownies?" She topped off the wine glasses before settling in the living room.

"It was a late night, they didn't survive." I stretched out across the loveseat and propped my legs on the arm. "Should probably think about getting back to the pool before I can't fit into my clothes. Is our Wellness Center membership still active?" I'd been on the swim team in high school. It was the only exercise I'd tolerate. Gaunt Park's outdoor pool was fine in summer. In February, I had to find other venues. After high school, Zigana had tried to convince me to join her at Curves women's fitness studio, but torture apparatus for pay is not my idea of fun. I'll stick with swimming.

"Where do you think I go three mornings a week?" She sorted through a stack of CDs next to the stereo before selecting one and loading it in. Quiet strains of Billy Joel's *Fantasies and Delusions* piano concerto floated through the air. We relaxed into our own thoughts and let the music soothe. The last gentle notes of the disc faded away before either of us spoke.

"Your probation's up soon, isn't it?" she asked.

The question caught me off guard. "Ash Wednesday, oddly enough. Why do you ask?"

"Do you have to go back to court or anything?"

"Just sign off with Pendleton, I think. I'll call him tomorrow to be sure." I swung my legs off the cushions and sat up. "Why do you ask?"

"Trying to get a calendar straight in my head. And you're done with school when?"

"April 29. Graduation's May 8. And I'll be twenty-five on May 13, how's that for stacking the mileposts. Want me to write it all down?"

"Don't be a smartass. I was just wondering if maybe you should hold off on teaching Tatum and Patrice a lesson until things calm down a little."

"You mean when I can't screw up my life any worse."

"That too." She tossed a throw pillow at me. "I'm on overload these days is all, worrying too much."

I relaxed. "Sounds like you need a good reboot and defrag." I threw the pillow back. "Sure Hank's out of the picture?"

She collected the glasses. "Moving on. I want to check on this last batch of Merlot. The temperature gauge is being weird, and I don't want the wine ruined."

"Need me to take a look?"

"Even overloaded, I know how you hate basements. I can handle it. Thanks again for cooking."

Try as she might, Zigana couldn't cure my lingering terror of a basement. At our old house in north Dayton, it had been more of the creepy cellar of horror movies, damp and musty, full of cobwebs and shadows. I was eight years old when the neighbor kid talked me down there on a dare, then turned out the light and locked me in, alone. Three hours passed before Zigana came home from the shop to hear muffled sobs. My terrified screams had long since faded into hoarse whimpering when she found me. Tonight's offer to help her took a concerted effort. I was glad she refused.

I puttered around the kitchen for a bit, washing a few pans the dishwasher couldn't handle, folding the placemats and batik napkins just so, and making sure I returned all the utensils to their proper place. Zigana's very particular about her kitchen. I don't point it out to her, but that's one of the reasons I don't cook much. In anticipation of another late night, I checked my stash of Red Bull. One can.

"Hey, I'm going down to Speedway. Need anything?" I called to Zigana from the top of the basement stairs. My head knew her wine galley was nothing like the old cellar. My heart didn't buy it.

"No, I'm good. Let me know when you get back." Her voice floated up along with the smell of fermenting grapes and an assortment of spices.

I bundled up against the February wind and locked the door behind me. Didn't usually bother when I was only walking to the next corner, but Tatum had me on edge. No way I'd put Zigana at risk. I emptied the Speedway cooler of five cans of Red Bull.

"Got a Speedy Rewards card?" the clerk asked, not looking at me.

A hand clamped onto my shoulder and I yelped. That got her attention.

"Damn, Bruce, what are you doing here?" I shook off his hand and told the clerk, "S'okay, he's a friend." I took my change and the plastic bag bulging with cans. Bruce followed me out the door.

"Didn't mean to scare you," he said.

"You shouldn't be here." I led him around the corner toward Keith's Alley, away from the glare of the overhead lights.

"You didn't answer your phone, or my email."

"I turned the phone off, told you that. And I said I'd email when I knew what I was doing." I checked the street for cars. For Tatum. "What are you driving?"

He pointed to a green Honda on the side street. "I was coming to your place when I saw you go into the gas station."

I crossed to the car. "Hold this." I handed him the bag of Red Bull and got down on one knee to peer under the bumper. Nothing.

"What the hell?" Bruce took a step back.

I brushed the snow off my pant leg. "Tatum put a tracking device on my car. Looks like you're clean."

His eyes widened. He jerked around like he expected Tatum to jump out of the shadows. "It's Gigi's car. She'll kill me if I get her mixed up in this."

"Calm down." I grabbed my bag. "I said you're clean. But you shouldn't be here. Go home."

"He cornered me at the Café last night."

It seemed risky standing on the street corner together, so I took him back to the apartment. I unlocked the back door to the shop and hollered down to Zigana. "I'm back, with Bruce. We'll be in the kitchen."

"Okay." I heard the question in her voice. "I'll be up in a minute."

Back upstairs I put on a pot of coffee and stashed the Red Bull. "You need cream for your coffee?"

"Rather have the Red Bull," he said.

Figures. *There goes my supply.* I handed him a can. "What'd Tatum want?"

"Work stuff. Sorry to hear about Carmen, which he already told me last week. Had me carry a load of boxes to the storeroom, and when nobody else was around, asked if I'd heard from you." He popped the can and took a swig. Must have forgotten what he was saying, because it got quiet.

"And?" I restrained my swinging leg from kicking the words loose.

He focused on me again, and I realized his eyes were more than a little dilated.

"Oh," he said. "I told him what you said, that you just picked up stuff you left at Carmen's, tried to start a fight, and I threw you out." He chortled. "Thought that was pretty funny he did." Bruce took another swig.

"What are you on?" I leaned closer and sniffed. Reminded me of Matthew's back room after hours. "Weed. You idiot. How's Gigi like that while you're driving her car?" Zigana's footsteps sounded on the stairs. "Pull yourself together. 'Gana doesn't appreciate drugs in the house." What adults did to their bodies was personal business. Bring it into her home, it was Zigana's.

He sat up straight and rubbed a hand across his face, followed by a half-hearted effort to smooth his wild hair.

"Stop fussing. I said pull yourself together, not act like a dork."

"Who's a dork?" Zigana caught the last of my hiss as she came into the kitchen. "Hello, Bruce." She unloaded a case of wine bottles onto the table. "I was sorry to hear about Carmen."

"Me, too. I mean, thanks." He stumbled a bit getting to his feet. "I'd better go. You'll send me that email?"

"I'll walk you to your car." I pulled my coat back on and ushered him out the door under Zigana's suspicious frown. "Be right back," I told her.

I joined Bruce in the car for a few minutes to evaluate his condition. No signs of paraphernalia. "When was your last hit?"

He slumped in the seat. "Back in the apartment. God, you're worse than my mother."

I handed him another Red Bull I'd brought along, hoping the extra caffeine and sugar would counteract the pot. My stash was down to four cans.

"Did you turn off the GPS on your phone like I told you?" Much as I wanted to part company, I needed to be sure he was safe.

"Nah, Gigi likes to play *Pokemon Go*." His earlier fear gave way to chemically-enhanced braggadocio. "Besides, it's you he's after, not me. I see him at the Café every day. We're pals."

"As long as he can use you."

His eyes darkened, but only for a moment. "Nah, we're cool. He trusts me."

"About as far as he can throw you," I muttered.

"Back off. I said I'd help take him down for Carmen's sake, not yours."

"You really think he had something to do with her...accident?"

Bruce squirmed in the seat, refusing to look at me. "I dunno, maybe. Maybe not. Your hacking sure made him nervous, so maybe." He crushed the empty can and tossed it over his shoulder into the back seat. "Maybe."

I opened the door and climbed out. "Just be careful, okay? And don't come back out here. I don't know what he's up to yet, but I don't trust him. And he knows it."

"Email me when you figure something out."

The awning over the pharmacy sheltered me from the wind as I watched him drive away. Either he was still working for Tatum or he was dumber than I thought. I regretted telling him about finding the tracker. His sudden appearance in town after I told him to keep his distance had thrown me off guard. I wouldn't underestimate him again.

The short, post-holiday week sped by with no more from Bruce…or Tatum. I spent the following weekend helping Matthew with inventory and slogging through Tatum's documents. The pieces were coming together, just too slowly for my liking.

After dinner Monday, Zigana said, "Dmitra's coming tonight. Got your escape plan in place?"

Given my preoccupation with Tatum, I'd lost track of the dates. Zigana's pal Dmitra came over every month, fourth Monday like clockwork, for a mani-pedi spa night, filling the apartment with acetones, acetates, shellac, and I don't know what all. The fumes give me an instant migraine. Usually, I would spend the evening with Carmen, returning home only after the odors dissipated.

Carmen.

An inward flinch, a stab of loss I tried hard to ignore. Headache or no, I had work to do, for her.

I retreated to my room, shoved a towel in the crack under the door, and fired up the computers. A new flow chart on the white board hung on the back of the door gave me a visual to help connect the dots. Tatum. Cyber Café. DHS. My notes listed an innocuous corporate name as the owners of the Café. I started a list of details I needed to investigate, beginning with who the faces were behind the names. Added a cursory check on the DHS guys Bratton and Reynolds when it occurred to me I'd believed their veiled threats far too readily.

And Patrice, where did she fit in? As I puzzled over her seemingly clueless behavior, I found myself imitating her annoying habit of finger drumming. I yanked my hands away from the desk and sat on them for a few minutes while I thought. Zigana had said Patrice spoke at Council about fracking—not an easy subject for a layman to understand. Even if she was from Arkansas where they've dealt with the problem longer than we have in Yellow Springs, her involvement as a spokesperson didn't fit with the Patrice I knew. *Unless she had something personal to gain.* I added a background check on her to my list. Then a stop at Dayton Police Department for a copy of Carmen's accident report since my efforts to get one online had failed.

And then there was school.

I pulled the Glen Helen wall calendar down and counted the weeks. Eight weeks left in the semester if I counted cram week. Senior project due to my advisor in six, exams two weeks later. It seemed like a long time, but when I checked the workload, I knew it would be tight. I'd ignored my final project, doing little more than scribble an outline and make a list of references. Add the research paper for Lit, the final Cisco exams which required heavy study themselves, and I was in for a beating. Plus I still needed to work. Good thing my tuition and fees were paid. Living expenses were minimal. Much as I hated to ask, I knew Zigana would let me slide on my half of the rent if necessary.

I popped open a can of Red Bull and frowned. The calendar, flow chart, and list taunted me. Time to replenish my beverage stash again.

———

I was awake when the alarm went off next morning, restless dreams disrupting the few hours of sleep I'd managed after sorting the database. A stack of printouts with all the files organized four different ways: by financial institution, by what appeared to be a client number, by date, and by an odd field I'd yet to identify. It held a string of alpha-numeric characters – not a hash that I could decipher, but some kind of personal code. Add that to the list of things to suck up my time.

At school, I parked on the street since I only had one morning class. A planned visit to the courthouse and the police department before afternoon lab meant I'd be in and out of the garage. No sense paying twice.

Tatum intercepted me at the entrance to the computer science building, interrupting my contemplation. Really should start paying attention to my surroundings. He held the door open, exuding all the charm he possessed in such overwhelming measure.

I scooted past him with a nod of thanks. He followed me up the stairs even though his office in the computer lab was on the first floor. I clutched my backpack tighter and stopped outside the classroom. "Did you need something?"

"Wanted to make sure DHS wasn't giving you any more problems." He waited till another student dodged around us. "I was serious about helping with that, don't forget."

"I won't." I motioned toward the lecture hall. "I'm late. Rather not give the prof an excuse to dock me."

"Of course not. Go." He pulled the door open with a flourish and waved me through.

I tried to slip into a seat in the back row unnoticed. No dice.

The professor launched into his usual tirade about tardiness. He must have spotted Tatum behind me because his expression flipped. "Glad you could join us, Ms. Wood. Chapter twelve, please. Routers and switches."

My after-class visit to the courthouse for corporate records was less than helpful. Two levels of shell companies held shares in the Café, one of them out-of-state. I got copies of what I could, hoping my friend Phil, a third-year law student, could make sense of it all. The police department wasn't much better. They turned over the basic report of Carmen's accident no problem—for the proper fee of course. I paid cash, trying not to cringe at my dwindling funds. For the investigator's notes, I'd have to wait the standard seven-to-ten business days, and they'd come snail-mail. The signed request form meant I was leaving a paper trail. *Damn.*

All the bureaucracy took longer than anticipated. The computer lab was full when I arrived, and I got stuck in the last row where all the outdated machines were on rotation out the door.

Wonderful.

At least I wasn't front-and-center where Raymond-the-nerd could keep an eye on me. I plugged in my headphones to shut out the normally comforting bustle of my surroundings so I could concentrate on the assignment. I barreled through the required labs and video lecture in record time. Hope some of the information stuck. I bundled up for the sprint across campus to the English department and headed for the door.

Patrice waited for me in the hall outside the lab. Raymond must have been watching after all and tipped her off.

"Do you have a minute?" she asked.

"Not really."

"This won't take long." She stepped aside and ushered me into her office.

Curiosity overrode my hesitation. She closed the door and moved behind the desk. "Have a seat."

I remained standing. "I have Lit in ten minutes."

She pursed her lips, shuffled some papers on her desk. When she started the finger drumming, my patience vanished.

"Look, I have to go."

"Why were you talking to Dr. Tatum?"

Ah. She must have seen us together. A stream of interesting responses ran through my mind. I played it straight, sort of.

"He apologized for any trouble because I lost my job, then my best friend. Even offered to help if he could. Wasn't that great of him?"

Patrice paled and sucked in a breath. I almost felt sorry for her.

Almost.

"Help you? How?"

I shrugged, hiking my backpack higher on my shoulder. "Dunno, just said he felt bad. Told me to call him if I needed anything." I watched the emotions play across her face and wished I had a camera to record them. Jealousy, anger, fear. "Anything else?"

She shook her head slightly and pulled into professional mode. "No, that's all. You can go."

I bit back a grin and left.

———

On my way home after class, I dropped off the corporate paperwork at Phil's place in Beavercreek. He was immersed in law review edits, but assured me his roommate, a first-year law student studying contracts, would appreciate the exercise. Knowing the workload 1Ls carry, I doubted that. I left a six-pack of Corona as payment and gave him my secondary email for contact. When he questioned my insistence on secrecy, I hedged.

"Trust me on this, it's a long story. We'll save it for your graduation party."

From the doubtful look on his face, my answer didn't come close to satisfying him. But we had enough history that he didn't push.

———

Zigana had dinner ready when I got home shortly after six. She waited until the plates were empty and we were into our second glass of wine to drop the third shocker of my day.

"Your probation officer called. He's not very happy with you right now." Her eyes were worried.

Pendleton. Forgot that item on my to-do list for the day.

"Says you're not returning his calls or his email."

Damn. "I didn't expect him to be checking up on me this late in the game. I only gave you and Matthew the burner number before I turned off my phone. Should I call him now?"

"No, he said he'd be unavailable tonight except for an emergency." She cleared the table while I loaded the dishwasher. "He wants you in his office tomorrow at eight-thirty, no excuses."

"Did he say why? I'm not due to check in until Friday."

Her worry lines deepened. "Something about you stirring up trouble when you should know better. He wouldn't tell me any more than that."

Zigana went off to a committee meeting, and I holed up in my room with schoolwork. Lack of sleep caught up with me, even after my last can of Red Bull, and by midnight I was comatose. Sometime in the early morning hours when exhaustion wore off, frenetic dreams returned. Questions about Pendleton's sudden interest in me buzzed through router-and-switching configurations, mixed in with a dash of Hemingway and Chandler. For the second morning in a row, I turned off the alarm before it rang.

As Zigana had said, Pendleton was not happy with me. I made sure to be on time, and unlike my last visit, he didn't keep me waiting. He spent the first five minutes chastising me for not appreciating the "opportunity" Patrice offered by hiring me with a criminal record and the next five giving me grief for turning off my phone and ignoring his email. I let him rant. Nothing I could say to any of his complaints would make a difference. They were all true, as far as they went.

Eventually he realized I wasn't fighting back. My out-of-character meekness seemed to confuse him. "What do you have to say for yourself?"

I took a deep breath, crossed my fingers in my jacket pocket, and breathed a silent apology to Carmen. "My best friend died a few weeks ago. I guess I just lost it, kind of went into hiding."

That set him back. "Who was that?" He flipped through his file looking for my list of contacts.

"Carmen Lowery. It was on the news, at least a couple times. She was hit by a bus."

The bluster went out of his posture. His tone softened. "I saw the report, but I didn't make the connection."

I slouched a bit further in the chair, playing the emotional female to the hilt. "It's been pretty rough." A slight catch in my voice accented the role.

He cleared his throat and pulled away. "Well, yeah, I'd imagine. I'm sorry for your loss. But what's this about harassing Dr. Tatum?"

"All I can figure is Patrice saw him talking to me at school yesterday. First time I'd seen him since Carmen died, and he wanted to express his sympathy is all. You can call and ask him." I kept my head lowered and peeked at him to gauge his reaction. "She's got a thing for Tatum, probably jealous he was talking to me."

"Don't go there," he said, relief echoing in his voice as we moved back to safer ground. "Whatever there is between those two is none of your business. You've got seven days left on my watch. Let's try to get through it with no more problems."

We set a time for the final paperwork meeting and he kicked me loose. "Turn on your damn phone," he said before closing the door on me. I waved it at him with a nod and left.

I sat in the car for a bit waiting for my pulse to return to normal and considered my options. Since the phone was on, I made the call.

"Tatum," he answered after one ring.

"You said to call if I needed help."

A pause. "Hang on."

I heard a muffled exchange followed by the closing of a door.

"I'm glad you called," he said. "What's DHS want now?"

"It's not DHS. It's your girlfriend." The anger I'd hidden from Pendleton spilled over.

"Patrice? What happened?"

I filled him on the summons to her office and subsequent call to Pendleton. "I can't have her giving my PO second thoughts about ending supervision. His report carries all the weight with the judge."

He didn't hesitate. "I'll take care of it."

A dead line punctuated his words and left me with more possibilities to consider.

After a quick call to Zigana to reassure her I wasn't locked up somewhere, I spent the hours before class immersed in the library reference section collecting the required hard-copy sources for my senior project. I grabbed a salad in the cafeteria before Lit and then wasted half of it. Little sleep. No appetite. I was losing it.

I found an empty lecture hall and sat in the dark for thirty minutes, brooding and trying to make sense of the shambles my life had become. For all my efforts to be independent, to make sure no one worried about me or had to deal with my problems, I had a dead best friend because she tried to help, a fretting grandmother because she *couldn't* help, and a father chomping at the bit to fix everything for his little girl. But I wasn't his little girl, never had been, really, and he knew it. The disconnect only made things worse. All the times he hadn't been around to take care of things when I was growing up made him more determined to come to my rescue now. But this was beyond his movie-hero fantasies. I had to get my head straight, find a solution on my own, and stop making things worse by bungling through what I didn't understand. The answers were out there, in Tatum's files, in the Café's servers, maybe both. I just needed to find them.

For the next week, I played the saint. Work, school, home, no hacking, nothing to give Pendleton or DHS reason to think twice about letting my supervision expire. I stocked books for Matthew. I sold jewelry for Zigana. I read and took notes and ran practice tests for Cisco. Patrice passed me in the hall of the computer building one afternoon. I concentrated on an out-of-date flyer for a New Year's Eve kegger on the bulletin board, and when I finished reading it for the third time, she was gone.

By the following Tuesday night when I left the bookstore after my late shift, with fewer than twelve hours to go before signing off with Pendleton, my nerves screamed from pent-up tension. Matthew pulled up next to me in the alley behind the store while I scraped frost from the Fiero's windshield.

"Leave your car," he said. "Sammy's got a table for us at the DubPub."

A few drinks sounded like the perfect remedy, but I shook my head. "Zigana's expecting me."

He leaned over and pushed open the door of the truck. "She's with Sammy."

I didn't really believe him until I saw them together in the booth along the wall. Phil was there, too, and TK. A string of black and silver balloons floated from the chair tacked onto the end of the table. For the first time in longer than I could remember, I had to fight back tears. Even Carmen's death hadn't pushed me over the edge. It's not a luxury I allow myself to indulge in. Zigana smiled at me from where she sat wedged between the wall and Sammy, eyes glistening to match my own.

Matthew took charge. "Knock it the hell off, you two, this is a party." He made sure everyone had a fresh drink before offering a toast. "To the end of past mistakes, and the beginning of new tomorrows."

"Here, here," echoed around the table.

I downed the shot of Jameson he set in front of me, letting the burn of the whiskey singe away the thought that flashed through my mind.

And to new mistakes yet to be made.

Pendleton ignored my bloodshot eyes the next morning when I showed up to sign the papers terminating supervision. A blank signature line labeled "Judge" mocked me from the bottom of the page. He caught where my finger pointed and chuckled.

"Don't worry, he'll sign it. I haven't given him any reason not to. The prosecutor signed off last week."

"Last week?" I stuck the pen back in the holder on his desk. "Before or after you raked me over the coals?"

"Before, although you had me second-guessing myself for a few days. I'm a pretty good judge of character, and I didn't think you'd be dumb enough to screw up so late in the game."

"Gee, thanks."

He laughed again. "I'd say it's been a pleasure, but I know you don't look at it quite that way." Seriousness replaced the joviality. "If you play your cards right, you can petition for expungement in another few years. Check into that. No sense having a specious felony conviction follow you around forever. You're a better person than that."

I flushed at the unexpected compliment. He shook my hand, and I held on for a second longer than necessary.

"Thank you, Joe, for everything," I said, using his first name for the only time in our almost five years together.

He tilted his head in acknowledgment. "You're welcome, Fatál. Take care of yourself."

———

Zigana was in a mood when I got home, storming around the kitchen, slamming pans and utensils, muttering to herself. I stood out of range for a few minutes, waiting for a lull in the action.

She finally spotted me. "What are you staring at?"

"Wondering if I need body armor to come in, is all."

She just glared.

I sidled up to her and wrapped my arm around her shoulder. "Pendleton sends his love, says he'll miss you."

Her face cleared. "You're officially done with all that? Good." She returned the hug. "Now turn me loose, the sauce is scorching."

"So are you by the sound of it. What's up?"

"Remember that notebook Jocelyn found on her driveway after some sleaze tried to buy drilling rights on their farm?" She didn't wait for an answer, anger spilling her words out in a rush. "The oil company media brigade says we planted the notebook and 'found' it to make them look bad. As if they need any help."

When she dumped the tomato sauce over a plate of pasta and tossed the empty pan into the sink, I knew she was pissed. She usually treats cookware gently, like the craft tools she insists they are. I guided her to a chair and stuck a wine glass in her hand.

"Let me finish up. You talk."

The notebook had caused a ruckus in the Yellow Springs activist community. Supposedly it outlined the drilling company's "nefarious" plans to mislead landowners into signing over drilling rights. This was the fracking threat Patrice had spoken against. Pages in the notebook offered ways for a spokesperson to derail objections by denying anecdotal evidence and the growing scientific support against their methods.

"They're trying to baffle 'em with bullshit, Jocelyn says." Silver and stoneware clanged as Zigana arranged the stack I sat on the table.

I cringed at the noise, knowing that after she calmed down, she'd regret any chips or cracks. But I let her rant. Springers don't need much in the way of hard evidence. The mention of oil companies and drilling had been enough to set off the hardcore tree-huggers in town who ran home-based solar grids and rooftop wind turbines. And Zigana.

We were half-way through dinner before she ran out of steam and I could ask, "Have you seen the notebook?"

"Just the cover and a few pages. Jocelyn scanned a couple of the worst paragraphs and packed the original in a plastic bag like they do on *CSI*. She even wore gloves, so they could test for fingerprints." Zigana shoved her plate away. "Not that they will. Our worthless state rep agreed to forward it to the Attorney General's office when we threatened to go to the media, but the oil companies spend a boatload of cash every election. We don't expect any kind of real investigation."

"Give them a chance. Maybe they'll surprise you and do the right thing for a change."

Her glare returned.

I cleared the table, hiding my skeptical eye roll behind her back. "So what happens now?"

"We're meeting at Jocelyn's tonight to decide." She checked the time and stood up. "I really wanted to be here with you to celebrate."

"Don't worry about me. We celebrated last night. I still have the headache to prove it." I squeezed her shoulder. "I need to study anyway. Go to your meeting."

A comfortable silence settled over the apartment after she left. Instead of heading straight for the computer, I poured another glass of wine and curled up in the front window seat. A frigid March wind left Xenia Avenue deserted. Scattered snowflakes drifted past me onto the pavement two stories below, coating the street and sidewalk with a glistening carpet. I felt truly free for the first time since the Feds had showed up at the door of Rake's apartment and he'd turned on me. Tatum loomed, and Carmen hovered, but I could handle those problems on my terms. Last night's celebration had released the anxiety I'd harbored while I was afraid to breathe too loudly, to move the wrong way, to jeopardize my final release. That chapter was over.

I returned to Tatum's database files and my notes with a renewed sense of clarity and control. While Zigana was out, I racked up a few extra credits on the usergroup so I could download the updated hacker software I needed for my laptop. I drew up a calendar of the days remaining in the semester and blocked out class and lab time, study hours, and work. In what little time was left, I scheduled each item on my list.

Match the names on the Café roster with Tatum's files and run backgrounds: check.

Review the police report on Carmen's accident, which had finally arrived in the mail yesterday: check.

Track down any witnesses, other than Bruce: check.

Which reminded me, he expected an email. I logged into the throwaway account. Three more messages from him in the past twenty-four hours, and the latest one came from his regular email. After mentally cursing him out, I replied to that email with a cryptic "I've found something, give me another day" comment to see what I could shake loose. If he was in cahoots with Tatum, that should move up the food chain pretty rapidly. If not, I had other plans for Tatum.

The door slammed downstairs.

"Fatál! You in? Jocelyn sent pastries."

"Be right down." I closed out my PCs before joining her in the kitchen. One thing any hacker knows is an online computer is a vulnerable computer. Except for the uninterrupted times needed to run a hack or when I was at the keyboard, my computers stayed off.

In the kitchen, Zigana leaned against the counter, arms folded across her chest, waiting for the tea water to heat. The furrows in her brow would be permanent soon if she didn't lighten up.

"How was your meeting?" I scooped one of Jocelyn's famous cinnamon nut buns off the plate on the table.

"Patrice was there."

I gasped, choked, and coughed up a few crumbs. She handed me a napkin.

"She acted like we were old friends." The tea kettle's shrill whistle interrupted. While the leaves steeped, we sat down facing each other, pastries forgotten.

I'd been shocked into silence, my mind racing.

Zigana's account of the gathering was brief. In the heated hunger for a fight over the mysterious notebook, calmer heads had prevailed. The group agreed to give the Attorney General's office a chance to investigate. A few of those in attendance who had more science expertise would continue their studies of the potential hazards of fracking, gathering evidence for future battles.

"Patrice didn't have much to offer other than a few comments from her experiences in Arkansas. But that was like ten years ago, when no one but the experts knew what fracking was."

"She mention me?"

"Not a word." Zigana pushed the plate toward me. I finished the bun I'd started on, with hot tea to wash down the crumbs, but I didn't taste it. She picked at a pastry and left me to my thoughts.

From Patrice's behavior at school earlier in the week, it was obvious Tatum had told her to leave me alone. It was too soon for my email to Bruce to have filtered down, so her appearance in town could be unrelated. Maybe she really did care about fracking and that's all there was to it.

Or maybe not.

We debated the possibilities until the tea pot was empty. By then it was late, even for Zigana. Sleep beckoned.

I spent fifteen minutes meditating before climbing into bed. It calmed my brain and allowed me a few hours of rest before the what-ifs crept in and shook up the neurons.

What if Tatum sent Patrice to Yellow Springs to check on me—on Zigana? I already had to deal with guilt that my hacking may have led to Carmen's death. I couldn't have 'Gana drawn into the mix. I had to be more careful, to warn her. Not that she would listen.

What if Patrice had come here on her own to intimidate me, a jealous female clinging to her man? A woman scorned is an unpredictable threat. I'm a hacker. I think like one, like Tatum does. Patrice is a mystery on too many levels. "Keep your friends close, your enemies closer," Sun Tzu says in *The Art of War*. Or maybe it was Michael Corleone in *The Godfather*. Matthew would know.

What if Tatum was using Bruce to get to me like he did with Carmen? Bruce is clueless enough to let himself be duped again. At least he acts like he is.

Whirling possibilities left me staring into the dark while time inched from four to five o'clock. Muffled chimes from the living room mantel clock sealed a decision. I used the nightlight on my phone to jot a note, releasing the thoughts from my brain to the page, and rolled over to bury my head in the pillow. Now I could sleep.

To bolster my reclaimed discipline, I spent the weekend at home studying my notes and fine-tuning details instead of acting rashly. It was Zigana's turn to supply the weekly Yellow Springs peace vigil contingent with coffee and hot chocolate on Saturday, so I minded the shop while she walked the two blocks down and back. Some of the demonstrators have probably been gathering at the corner of Xenia Avenue and Limestone Street since the Vietnam War. Delivering warm drinks kept the half-dozen hardy souls from freezing to death in the sharp cold. She never said anything, but it also allowed Zigana to join the effort for at least a few minutes without feeling guilty for ignoring business. Not that I had many customers to attend to while she was gone, but it gave me a chance to fine-tune my plans.

Exploitation

"Focus solely on establishing access to a system or resource by bypassing security restrictions"

I waited until Monday to take action. Figured that gave Bruce time to alert Tatum I'd "found something," if he wanted to. During the drive downtown, I called Bruce and let him spout off for a minute because I'd ignored him. When he ran out of expletives, I loosed the first round. "I know I promised to find out who killed Carmen, if anybody did, but DHS is watching me. I have to back off."

"Thought you were off paper, so they couldn't touch you." He sounded cautious, fishing.

I'd never told him when my probation was up, and Carmen had never remembered my termination date. Patrice had the information in my school records. By default, so did Tatum.

Now Bruce?

"Yeah, well, whatever they're looking for at the Café has them pretty wired. If they get paranoid enough, anyone who gets in their way is suspect. I can't take that chance. Carmen would understand."

I could almost hear the wheels turning. I passed a steel-hauler and two tenth-of-a-mile markers before he answered.

"Makes sense, I guess. Anyway, I probably overreacted, thinking Tatum did anything. Not his style. He just wanted you to back off." Bruce's relief was evident. I was ready to chalk him up as a puppet and move on until he said, "Carmen always was a klutz. I told her to watch out for the guy with crutches or she'd trip."

I slammed on the brakes. The driver behind me laid on the horn and flipped me off as he skidded around my Fiero. "What guy with crutches?" I hollered over the blare, steering onto the shoulder before the steel-hauler caught up and used me as a speed bump. I'd read the police report several times, noted the witnesses—all three of them—and no one had mentioned crutches. Not that they mentioned much else, either. Funny how no one sees anything when there's a chance they'd have to testify.

"I don't know, just a guy we saw on the street before the accident."

His renewed caution brought me back to the bigger picture, to the plan being implemented. I was supposed to ease his suspicions, not heighten them. I drew a deep breath and focused on calming my voice.

"Sorry, semi tried to run me off the road. Anyway, the police did their thing, decided it was an accident, so I guess we have to let it go at that. As for Tatum, I can't take any chances he'll keep me from graduating. Best to leave it to DHS to track down whatever he's up to, and hope they leave me alone."

"Good. I mean, sure. I understand. Carmen wouldn't want you to get in any trouble because of her."

"That means a lot, that you understand Carmen and all." I could live with being magnanimous if it kept him off balance. After mentally adding *crutches* to my list for the week, I crossed off *confuse Bruce*. Next up: *poke Patrice*. I checked for traffic and merged back onto the highway. "See you around."

———

Classes and an advisor's meeting on my senior capstone occupied the morning. My advisor acted sufficiently impressed with the scope of my paper, urged me not to leave it to the last week of the semester, and didn't mention Carmen's death. Doubt he even knew. Basically, he did his job, nothing more. I grabbed a sandwich in the cafeteria before heading for the computer lab.

Patrice ducked into her office when she spotted me in the hall. I let it go until I'd finished three hours of practice tests and another hour of research. Let her stew. On my way out of the building, I knocked on her closed door.

"Got a minute?" I didn't let her object, dropping my backpack on one side chair and settling into another like we were due for a chat. "Zigana said she saw you at Jocelyn's last week."

"Who?" She halted the paper shuffle that marked our infrequent meetings. She frowned, puzzled, whether at the name or the topic, I couldn't be sure.

"My grandmother, at the thing about fracking in Yellow Springs. Said you were a big help with your input on what happened in Arkansas and all."

"It's an important issue." The lines on her face smoothed. This she could handle. "Zigana's your grandmother? I didn't know."

Patrice doesn't lie well.

"Yeah, she raised me. We still live together there in town where you saw us New Year's."

"Of course, that's where I've seen her before. She's a...distinctive character."

I chortled like the air-headed co-ed she wanted to see me as, sharing a private moment with a gal pal. "You could say that. People aren't usually that kind, especially when she's throwing Gypsy curses at them."

Her eyes widened. "Curses?"

I waved dismissively. "Carry over from her mother. I'm only a quarter Gypsy, so I don't believe that stuff. Zigana though, it's in her blood." I laughed again and related a playground bully story from my younger days. "She's very protective of her friends and family." I let that sink in for a beat longer before skipping on. "Sounds like Tatum, sorry *Dr.* Tatum, forgives me for hacking in the lab. Any chance I could get my job back for the rest of the semester?"

"What do you mean?" She strained to follow my sudden change. "You talked to Der...Dr. Tatum again?"

I let her ponder, watched the finger drumming creep in again until she caught herself.

"He mentioned it in passing," I said. "When he offered to help if I needed anything for school."

Back to the paper shuffle. "We're at full staff, and the semester's almost over. I'll keep you in mind if something opens up." She threw her shoulders up, back in administrator mode. "Anything else? I'm very busy with the accreditation committee."

I popped out of my seat and grabbed my bag. "Nope, just thought I'd ask. Thanks for your time."

"Close the door on your way out."

As I did, grinning once my back was turned, I mentally checked off my list. Patrice had been duly poked.

For the rest of the week, when I wasn't working or in school, I concentrated on tracking down information on Carmen's accident. I started with the investigating officer, a silver-haired veteran named Jackson McQueen, to follow-up on Bruce's crutches guy. It took three days to untangle his patrol schedule, and a round of phone tag to get him to agree to meet me at Ohio Coffee Company on his lunch break. By then it was Friday. I waited nearly an hour before he showed. His partner was a red-haired female who barely made the height requirement, but she was built like a linebacker. I wouldn't want to tangle with her. She sat in the next booth and half-turned away from us.

I started in on McQueen, hoping to appeal to his sympathies. "Like I said on the phone, Carmen was my friend. Her boyfriend's an ass, keeps wanting to blame me for the accident, and that's kinda hard to live with."

His partner snorted behind me. "Oh, you're good. But the puppy dog eyes don't suit you."

I snapped upright and turned around to meet her amused gaze over the arm stretched across the bench behind me. Her teasing smirk stemmed my irritation. "If you want to join this conversation, you may as well sit at the same table."

She scooped up her coffee and bagel and squeezed in next to McQueen. "Haskins," she said, extending her hand in greeting.

"You always speak for your partner?" I asked.

McQueen leaned back, hands raised, and let us work it out.

"Only when the women try to play on his male ego." She cupped her face in her hands and made an exaggerated pout. "Please, Mr. Officer-sir, you're so big and strong. A poor defenseless female like me needs a manly man like you to protect me." She widened her eyes and batted her lashes in a moue that would do the Kardashian sisters proud, then crossed her eyes and laughed. "You'll get a lot further if you give it to him, and me, straight."

I couldn't help it. I liked her. I looked to McQueen.

He shrugged. "You heard the lady. And I use that term loosely, with all due respect." The final words came out in grunt as she elbowed him in the side.

My sixth-sense told me I could trust them. "I'm not so sure Carmen's death was an accident. Convince me."

McQueen sat up. "No one ever suggested it was otherwise. Why're you suspicious?"

"Like I said, her boyfriend's an ass."

"That's Bruce Walker," Haskins said.

I nodded. "Right after it happened, he lied to her family, said she was upset because we'd had a fight and that's why she stepped off the curb in front of the bus." I swallowed the lump in my throat caused by such a bald statement. "Why would he say that if there wasn't something else going on?"

"Maybe that's what she told him," McQueen said. "We never got a chance to talk to her."

"Two things, for starters." Haskins stepped in. "And both come down to motive. One, why do you think he would lie, if he did? You must have some idea if you're so convinced. Two, if it wasn't an accident, who had a reason to push her, and what was it? You think he did?"

Her perceptive directness told me she was no ordinary street cop. I was stuck. If I told them Tatum paid Bruce to keep Carmen away from me, she'd want to know why. Any answer would lead to more uncomfortable questions about my own motives. And my hacking. I went with the safest diversion I could think of.

"She was pregnant. And I doubt he was happy about it."

"So you think he did it," Haskins said again.

I propped my elbows on the table and dug suddenly-cold fingers into my temples. They were patient. Good interrogation technique, waiting out the silence.

"A part of me can't believe he'd do that to Carmen," I said after a long minute. "But he's an idiot as well as an ass. Maybe he thought she'd only get hurt a little, lose the baby, and he'd be off the hook."

"In case you haven't heard, abortion's legal in this state," McQueen said.

I slumped against the back of the booth and avoided their scrutiny. Snow fell again, thick heavy flakes clinging to pedestrians and cars alike, masking the grime of Ludlow Street. Carmen hated snow. I knew that about her. But I didn't know how she felt about abortion. *Odd.* For all we shared, we never got to important things like philosophy of life and death. Now we never would.

"I want to believe it was an accident," I said in a voice so low they had to lean in to hear me. "Convince me. Please."

I'll say this for Dayton's finest, they spent their entire lunch break and then some going over each item on the report, every statement, adding commentary here and there about witness demeanor that the bare facts couldn't cover. Nowhere in their notes was there anything about a man on crutches. I asked.

Nearly an hour later, their portable radios squawked. "Paul-42, 10-51, accident with injuries, Third and Jefferson. Medics dispatched."

"Paul-42, en route." Haskins answered as she scooted out of the booth.

McQueen scrawled a number on the back of a business card. He dropped it on the table and joined her. "Call us if you think of anything specific," he said. "We can always reopen the case."

He'd given me cell numbers for both of them. I tucked the card into my wallet next to the one from DHS, doubting my personal motives now, and wondering how I could pull off the plan I'd convinced myself was foolproof.

Or if I should.

If I was only after revenge, I'd screw up my own karma while doing nothing to nudge Tatum's. For all her talk, Zigana also made sure I understood the difference between justice and vengeance. The universe is wiser than we'll ever be. "Think it all the way through," she'd said many times. "Are you prepared to deal with whatever the worst is that could happen? That's what you have to be ready for." Expose the bad stuff so the authorities can do their job, fine. Push karma too hard because you think you know better, and she'll bite you in the ass. Bad karma comes from bad actions—and choices.

Zigana's words had come back to haunt me when I interfered with Sammy's coffee scam. I'd jumped into that one not knowing the whole story. *Can't afford to make the same mistake again.* Life is rarely as straightforward as it appears at first glance, and I needed to understand Bruce better, plus find out the truth about Tatum's dealings. I had to fill in those missing pieces before I knew in what direction, and how hard, to push.

I regretted my visit with Patrice. Other than firing me, at Tatum's urging, she'd done nothing to harm me. Gave me the job in the first place, and I'd riled her up to make myself feel better. So petty. And so not wise.

Brooding over my imprudent tendencies colored the rest of the day. I cut off a tailgater on the drive home. I snapped at Zigana and slammed the bedroom door hard enough to rattle the walls. The headboard creaked when I jammed the pillows against it and propped myself up on it with my knees. I ignored her call to dinner and moped in the growing darkness until she tapped on the door. If she hadn't let herself in without waiting for an invitation, I'd have ignored that, too.

"What's got you all wound up? I thought your plans were all coming together." She curled up on the end of the bed at my feet.

"Yeah, well, you thought wrong." Her pained expression broke through my self-loathing. I leaned forward into a cross-legged pose and laid a hand on her knee. "I'm sorry 'Gana. You didn't deserve that."

She patted my hand. "What happened?"

I told her about my meeting with the officers, how their insistence on motives for anyone who would kill Carmen forced me to confront my own motives. "I couldn't tell them about Tatum, not yet. They'd either call DHS to see what's up or lock me up for hacking in the first place. And what if he didn't have anything to do with it? Bruce isn't the most reliable witness. He could just as easily have been keeping me away from Carmen while he talked her into an abortion, not because of anything Tatum said."

"I thought you said Tatum paid him."

"Doesn't mean Bruce didn't collect for doing what he wanted to anyway. Be just like him to screw Tatum over, too." I linked my hands over my head and stretched. "Thing is, I can't go at this like I have been. It's not about me. I'm not seeing the whole picture, and until I do, I'm messing with people's lives for selfish reasons." I collapsed back into a slouch. "The same thing I've been accusing them of doing. And I hate hypocrites, especially when it's me."

She gathered me into a hug. "You're not a hypocrite, you're confused. Give yourself time, and you'll figure it all out. Then if anybody needs to be held accountable, you'll be able to call them out in good conscience."

I leaned my head on her shoulder and sucked in her emotional strength. If she believed in me, maybe I wasn't so bad.

Eventually she nudged me away and stood up, groaning. "Damn muscles locked already. Getting old and decrepit."

I swung my legs off the bed and matched her wince. "So what's my excuse?" Our shared laughter lightened the room more than the desk lamp I flicked on. "Did I miss dinner?"

"Yes and no. Matthew called while I was cooking. He and Sammy have a buddy playing at Peach's tonight, and they want us to join them. I put the soup in the fridge. It'll be better tomorrow, anyway."

"I didn't hear the phone." I stepped into the bathroom to run a brush through my hair.

"He called my cell."

I stopped mid-stroke. "Since when does he have your cell?" I could see her face in the mirror. I swear she blushed.

"When you turned yours off, I made sure he had my number in case he needed to find you."

Except I'd given him the burner number for that very reason.

"I'll meet you downstairs. I want to change my blouse," she said on her way out the door, gone before I could ask more questions.

We made it to Peach's with ten minutes to spare before the kitchen closed. The last-minute rush made for a long wait until food appeared. Matthew and Sammy showed up a few minutes later with a younger guy in tow.

"We ordered an extra plate of nachos in case you guys didn't eat," Zigana said after introductions were made.

She scooted over to make room for Sammy on the bench next to her, Matthew across the table. I was stuck facing the new guy, Adam West.

"Yeah, don't go there," he said when I smothered a laugh. "My folks had a juvenile sense of humor."

The Friday night crowd was already lubed and raucous, ready to party, when the band started warming up.

"I didn't know Matt had a daughter." Adam raised his voice to be heard.

Suspicious me, I noticed Matthew gave all his attention to Sammy and Zigana rather than chatting with his friend. "Did he put you up to this?"

"What?" Adam's feigned innocence confirmed my fears. "My dad's in the band."

My doubt must have been obvious, because when the server arrived with drinks, Adam held a whispered conversation with Matthew. Matthew shrugged and refused to look my way.

Adam turned back to me. "It's no big deal. I graduated in January and moved back to Dayton last week. None of my friends are here anymore. Matt thought we might get along."

"Sure 'Matt' did." The sour look I directed at Matthew was wasted. "Did he also tell you I'm a felon?"

"As a matter of fact, he did. But he never said you were a prickly bitch."

If I hadn't seen laughter in his eyes, I'd have been offended. Instead, I found myself flushing.

"He didn't ask me to marry you, just have a drink and say hello." Adam tapped my glass with his. "Hello."

I sipped my beer and considered the number of times I'd overreacted in the past month. He was right. I squashed my annoyance and tried to be civil. "How long have you known him?"

"Matt? He went to school with Mom at Belmont, so most of my life."

"So you know Sammy, too," I guessed.

"Not so much. He's a couple years older. Mom was a year or two behind Matt, I think. They dated for a few months his senior year and stayed friends after he graduated."

I'd barely gotten used to the idea of Matthew and Harmony, much less him and another woman. Adam's revelation reminded me how much I didn't know about Matthew's past. The band interrupted my musings when they launched into their first set.

"Which one's your dad?" I asked.

Adam cocked one ear toward me to hear over the volume. "What?"

I pointed to the band, then to Adam, and mouthed a silent question.

"Oh," he said. "The drummer."

"You play?"

He shook his head. "Nope, trombone in high school is all."

Competing with the din required too much effort. I kicked Matthew under the table, and after he rewarded me with a sheepish grin, we settled back to listen. Adam's dad the drummer was good. Made up for the off-key lead singer. Play loud enough, with sufficient energy, and the audience doesn't care so much. Appreciative tipsy females danced in the narrow aisle near the raised bandstand, outdoing each other in an effort to attract the musicians' attention. Peach's isn't big enough for a real dance floor, but that didn't stop them. I wonder what it is about women and guitar players. And drummers. A petite redhead had her eye on Adam's dad, grinding a little harder whenever he looked her way. Which was often.

I studied the man behind the Zildjian cymbals and drum set, covertly comparing him to the guy across the table from me. Even in the funky lighting I could see the resemblance. Dusty blond hair, wide cheekbones, sculpted eyes. I'm a sucker for well-shaped eyes, windows of the soul and all. First thing I notice. If Adam aged as well as his father, in another thirty years some woman—or guy—would be very grateful.

A loaded platter of chicken nachos pulled me away from what could prove to be a dangerous line of thinking. I hadn't been in a serious relationship since Rake. After he bolted, his lousy behavior even made me think twice when a lesbian friend asked for chance. Love her to death, but I'm not bi-curious enough to make that work long-term. TK's usually around when I have an urge to bed someone. Now he's got a girlfriend who doesn't appreciate our agreement much. We hadn't been together in months, which made Adam look better than he should have.

Or so I told myself while I worked my way through food and another beer. By the time the band took their first break, I needed one, too. I excused myself and dodged a server on the way to the ladies' room.

When I got back, Adam's dad was in my seat, the redhead perched on his knee. Even more startling, Matthew and Sammy had switched places. Zigana's head practically rested on Matthew's shoulder as he whispered in her ear. *What the hell?*

I stood next to Sammy, arms crossed, and waited for them to notice me. Zigana finally did, and jerked away from Matthew. He just grinned.

"How're you and Adam getting along?" he asked.

My alcohol-induced mellowness vanished. "We'll talk about that later, you and me. What's with you two?" I indicated Zigana with a chin thrust.

I went too far with the tone.

Zigana returned the attitude with a chin tilt of her own. "None of your business." Her eyes locked mine, and I backed down.

Sammy offered his seat since mine was taken. I shook my head. "I need some air." I slipped onto the patio where the smokers gathered, even in the chilly dampness of early March, and flopped into a chair upwind with my back to the door.

Zigana and Matthew?

My overworked brain couldn't make sense of it. I lost myself in winter dripping into spring off the Glen Helen trees across the street. In a few weeks, the ground might be dry enough I could hike there again. An escape into the woods usually cleared the mental cobwebs. I needed to visit the spring where we had held the memorial for Carmen, talk to her. I'd rarely asked her advice when she was alive. She was more the little sister drinking in my questionable wisdom. *Maybe I should have listened more.*

A burst of music escaped as the door to the bar opened and closed. Sounded like the band was back at work. My jacket appeared dangling over my shoulder.

"You'll need this." Adam held it open while I slipped my arms in.

"Thanks."

He pulled up a chair, propped his feet on another one, and sat quietly with me. He let me break the silence when I was ready.

"You ever hike at Glen Helen?"

"Once or twice," he said. "I prefer John Bryan, or Clifton Gorge. More challenging." The state parks shared borders with the Glen Helen Nature Preserve. It was hard to tell where one ended and the next took over.

Another stretch of quiet. The smokers all escaped back into the heat, leaving us alone.

"Where'd you go to school?" I asked.

"Antioch Los Angeles."

I squinted at him through the dim glare of twinkle lights. "With McGregor, I mean Antioch Midwest, right there in town?"

"They don't have an MFA program."

"You got an MFA?" Now he had my attention. Computers are my passion, but literature runs a close second. While I crammed as many electives into my tech-oriented schedule as I could, in my next life I'd get a Master of Fine Arts, too. And a doctorate in philosophical literature. His education and experience in LA left me feeling provincial. I'd never been further west than Chicago. I peppered Adam with questions about his classes, the city, his favorite authors. He liked Chaucer. I preferred Montaigne. He was a fan of David Foster Wallace whose post-modern tragic-hero persona usually left me cold.

During a lull in the conversation, Adam blew on his hands and rubbed them together to generate heat. "Stimulating as this is, any chance we could continue the discussion inside?"

I realized I was shivering, even with the jacket. "Awfully loud in there, but you're right. At least it's warm."

He held the door open for me, earning muttered complaints from patrons within range of the cold gust. "So we'll have dinner somewhere quieter."

I stumbled on the jamb. "I already ate."

"I didn't mean tonight. It's almost eleven. Maybe Sunday? Unless you're into blue laws."

He was teasing me again. Annoying, but I liked it. Which was even more annoying.

Another round of drinks waited on the table. It pushed me over my usual limit of two a night. I didn't care. A sneaking giddiness needed taming.

Or encouraging.

The volume in the bar seemed to jump up a notch with each set the band played. This was the third, and conversation was all but impossible. I caught Zigana's eye and motioned to the door. She checked her watch.

"At the break?" she asked.

Good thing I could lip-read. I nodded. She leaned in to tell Sammy and Matthew, and I turned away. Still not sure what to make of all that, not sure I wanted to know.

"We're leaving at the break," I said to Adam. "Sammy's driving, right?"

"My car's outside, but this is only number two." He raised his glass to punctuate. "And I'll hang around till the band's done and have some coffee. Stay long enough to meet Dad, will you?"

"What's with Dad and the redhead? If you don't mind my asking."

She was drinking at the bar now instead of dancing, but sitting at an angle so she could always see the drummer.

Adam waved her over. She hopped off the stool and worked her way through the crowd while he talked. "Jennifer's hoping to be the third Mrs. West."

Before I could get an explanation, she dropped down to her knees and propped her elbows on the table.

"You must be Fatál, did I say that right? Missed you earlier. They sound good tonight, don't they? Bobby's new cymbals are awesome. Took him forever to find the ones he wanted. And tuning! Did you know cymbals have to be tuned? I didn't. Had to have a special tool and everything. Bobby's good at that kind of stuff though, you know? It's really his band, even though Larry fronts. Just because he can sing a little. Bobby sings better, but he'd rather play."

Adam broke in. "Breathe, Jenny."

She giggled. "Sorry. One too many Jaeger shots. It's Patty's birthday. We're celebrating." She pointed to her dancing partner from earlier who was cuddled up to a tall guy at the bar.

"Twenty-nine?" I asked. Never thought she'd hear me.

"Aren't you sweet? Nope, the big four-oh. I hit mine last month. Patty made sure I didn't kill myself, so it's my turn to get her through it. That's what friends are for, huh?"

A drum flourish ended the set. "Oops, gotta go. Bobby needs a drink. Nice to meet you." She sashayed back through the crowd to the bar.

I crossed my eyes, sucked in my cheeks, and held my breath. Adam laughed.

"Damn." I exhaled loudly. "Number three, huh?"

"Mom was number one, when they were eighteen. Lasted about three years. They stayed friends because of me, which was nice, I guess.

Number two is better left to history." He stood up to greet his dad with a hug before making the introductions.

"You look like your mother," Bobby said as we shook hands.

I froze. "You knew Harmony?"

"Matt brought her to the divorce party after I split with Adam's mom. I tried to hit on her, but she only had eyes for him."

"Dad, please." Adam shuffled his feet and frowned.

"At your divorce party." I looked to Adam. He half-shrugged an apology.

Zigana appeared at my elbow. "Ready? We'll meet you out front." She smiled politely to Bobby and Jennifer and left.

"I don't think she likes me much," Bobby said.

"Can you blame her?" Adam said. "You hit on her, too."

My gasp was lost in Bobby's laughter. "Yeah, well, she's a good-looking lady." He pulled Jennifer close. "All in fun, huh, babe? I can still look."

"Okay, we're done." Adam threw an exasperated look at his dad, which was ignored. He took my arm. "C'mon, I'll walk you outside."

I stopped in the lobby. "Don't go outside again. It's too cold."

He nodded his head toward the bandstand where Bobby and Jennifer were in a clinch to a song blaring from the juke box. "If that didn't turn you off to West men entirely, I'll call you tomorrow about dinner Sunday."

I grabbed the pen off the hostess stand and jotted my number on his palm. "Good night."

Zigana huddled with Matthew and Sammy in the parking lot, arguing and trying to stay warm. "No, we can't all fit in the pickup. We can walk."

Matthew turned to me for support.

"Leave it," I said. "We'll walk." I linked arms with Zigana and started up the street. Before we made it half a block, Sammy pulled up in the truck with Matthew in the passenger seat and trailed us home. He waited until we unlocked and stepped into the stairwell before tapping the horn and cruising away.

"Tea?" I asked Zigana when we reached the kitchen. An explanation of the evening would be nice, too, if I could get her to talk.

"Bed. Are you at the bookstore in the morning?" She closed her bedroom door on my reply, her "See you when you get back" slipping out before the gentle click of the knob.

Restless sleep didn't help my mood. Zigana had never shut me out as much as she had in the past month. I was still cranky when I got to the bookstore as Sammy arrived with the morning coffee. His cheerful greeting grated. I took the cup he offered and grunted something close to thank you.

One eyebrow went up. "Okay then, Missy. I'll be in the back."

I slouched on the stool by the register and brooded, crumbling a bagel I'd brought from home. Something had to give. When I drained the coffee and tossed the cup in the wastebasket, I mentally tossed my mood with it. *Stop avoiding, start dealing.*

"Hey." I tapped on the office door where Matthew and Sammy were working. "Got a minute?"

Sammy opened the door. "I'll go mind the store," he said, brushing past me.

"Not necessary," I said to his back.

"Let him go. He's embarrassed." Matthew had his feet propped on the desk, balancing his chair on two legs. He looked as rough as I felt.

"What'd I do to embarrass him?" I laid back on the chaise and used the stains on the ceiling for a quick Rorschach test. They all reminded me of food. *Guess I should have eaten the bagel.*

"It's not always about you."

"People keep saying that." I rolled over onto my side to face him. "So what's bugging him?"

"He's kind of hooked on Zigana, and that's all I'm going to say." He held up his hands to ward off my astonished exclamation. "Not my story. He said I could tell you that much, but I'm not saying any more."

"And who are you, Cyrano? Is that why you and 'Gana had your heads together?" Of all the scenarios running through my head, I'd missed that pairing. I realized with a rush of relief I'd been afraid there was something brewing between Matthew and Zigana. Too weird to contemplate, and proved how bizarre my imagination could be. This I could handle. Maybe.

He dropped his head back and closed his eyes. "What'd you think of Adam?"

"About that." I swung my legs off the chaise and glared at him. "Matchmaking. Seriously? Do I look that desperate?"

"Too involved in that crap with Tatum maybe to realize you don't have a life."

"I have a life." My indignation rang hollow.

Matthew opened one eye long enough to say, "Yeah, right."

"I have as much of a life as you do."

"I'm almost fifty, we're on a different measuring stick here." The raised chair legs hit the floor. "And this time, it *is* about you. You work here. You work for your grandmother. You go to school. Since Carmen died, you've been even more isolated. When was the last time you went out with someone your own age? On a date, maybe?" He ran his hands through his hair. "So yeah, I was matchmaking. I'm your father. Kinda thought I might see grandkids of my own some day."

Guilt replaced my irritation at his plaintive tone. Maybe he'd learned Zigana's emotional manipulation better than I thought. Before I could absorb it all, Sammy burst through the door.

"Tatum's here."

I stepped in front of Matthew to stop his charge for the door.

"This is my battle, for now." I squeezed his arm. "Go with me on this."

A box of books from the worktable offered a delaying tactic and a barrier as I meandered to the front counter, carrying it in front of me like a shield. Tatum stood relaxed, hands in his pockets, studying the shelf of new releases by the register. He didn't acknowledge my presence until I said, "Not your usual hang-out, Dr. Tatum."

"And Patrice's office isn't supposed to be yours." He waited until I emptied the box, slowly. "Would you like to explain why you asked for help, then sabotaged my efforts to keep her off your back?"

"Seemed like a good idea at the time. Visiting her, I mean." I stacked the box under the register and took refuge on the stool behind the counter, sorting newspapers. Matthew and Sammy hovered in the stacks, just out of sight. "It was a bad day. I couldn't make rent. Since she fired me, I took my pissy mood out on her."

"You knew it would upset her."

I shrugged. "Reasonable assumption. Maybe not the wisest move, but like I said, it was a bad day."

I locked onto his stare with all the composure I could muster and waited him out. He broke first.

"Which one's your father?" He gestured toward the men hovering behind me.

I stiffened. "How…what makes you think that?"

"Patrice must have mentioned it." He smirked. "And you just confirmed it."

Only Patrice doesn't know about Matthew. And his comment confirmed my suspicions about Bruce. Which meant Tatum probably knew I'd found the tracking devices. *Damn.*

"Why are you here?" I tried to remember what else I'd been stupid enough to share with Bruce.

"You're not answering your phone."

"Technical difficulties. You could've talked to me at the lab Monday."

"And risk getting Patrice riled up again? No thanks. She's hard enough to handle on a good day." He flipped through a First Edition of *True Grit* displayed on the counter.

"And do you? Handle her, that is."

He dropped the book. "I told you, leave her out of this. Because of your earlier misunderstanding with her, I offered to make sure you got through school, to run interference with DHS if they hassled you. That's it. Anything else is none of your business."

Misunderstanding. It pushed my timeline up, but I decided to drop the bombshell I'd held in reserve. I wanted to shake his defense of Patrice, see where it led. "You know this all started because she had me spying on you."

I followed Tatum's glance down the aisle, looking for Matthew and Sammy. "They know all about it," I said, followed by a slow deep breath. *Might as well go all the way.* "But I'm sure Bruce told you that already." From my perch on the stool, I could see his fists clench at his sides before he flexed his fingers with a rigid determination that showed in his face.

"You keep insinuating I have some personal connection to Bruce. He's an employee at the Café. We certainly don't socialize. As for Patrice, you're fishing and it's not wise. I can only control so much of what happens." He tapped the cover of *True Grit.* "Did you see the remake with what's-his-name Damon as the Texas Ranger? He got off lucky." Tatum fixed me with a stare again, his eyes cold. "Never underestimate the striking power of a viper."

This time I caved. "Since you asked, did you want to meet Matthew?" At the sound of his name, he and Sammy appeared from where they'd been lurking in the stacks.

Tatum's enigmatic smile held a tinge of acid. "Not really."

I didn't exhale until his Escalade pulled away from the curb.

"Damn it!" I pitched a newspaper across the room. It slid down the wall behind the coffee table.

Matthew slapped the "Back in fifteen minutes" sign into the front window and locked the door. He led me back to the office and pulled out the Jameson.

"Drink." When I tried to refuse, he said, "Half a shot is all. Drink."

The burn cleared my head and stoked the anger simmering in my chest. "I let him get to me." I collapsed onto the chaise. The ceiling stains morphed into ominous mushroom clouds.

"You think his threat was serious?" Sammy hovered at my side.

"Not with us as witnesses." Matthew stowed the bottle back in his desk. "But he can still cause trouble."

"How so?"

I spoke around the crooked elbow hiding my face. "He's president of the college. He can make sure I don't graduate. I don't graduate, I don't get the job. I don't get the job, you're stuck with me here forever." A peek at Sammy, and I added, "Got space in your apartment for a roomie?"

They were smart enough to stop talking at that point. We sat in silence until a tapping at the front door roused Matthew.

"Should be UPS," he said. "I need to get that."

"Go. I'll be out in a minute to help unpack." I waited till they were gone before sitting up. No sense letting them see the tear stains.

———

When I got home, I avoided Zigana and stumbled into bed, pulling the blankets over my head. It was dead quiet when I woke. And dark. Three-thirty in the morning. I'd slept through dinner and then some. A covered tray sat in the pool of light under the desk lamp when I flicked it on. Zigana's stealth visit left a thermal dish of stew and a chunk of sourdough. I didn't think I was hungry until I took the first bite. After twenty hours of no food, I scarfed down everything in two minutes flat. When I stacked the dishes back on the tray, I found her note.

Matthew told me what happened.

Still not entirely comfortable with their blossoming relationship, whatever it was, but at least I didn't have to relive the visit with Tatum for her. There was a voicemail from Adam, left after midnight, with a lot of background noise. Something about his mother, and Florida, and the Cincinnati airport.

"I'll call when I'm back in town," is all I heard clearly. I shelved the annoying pang of disappointment with my burgeoning gloom and headed for the bathroom.

A shower and time with a toothbrush made me feel almost human. As I wiped spit off my chin, I lectured myself in the mirror. Out loud. "Knock it the hell off. You're better than Tatum is. And smarter. Now get your shit together and keep your promise to Carmen."

I moved the tray of dishes to the kitchen and brought back a mug of tea and a Red Bull. First things first. I popped the can and downed it while shredding the old timeline. My to-do list still made sense, mostly, but I had to focus, not let Tatum and Patrice push my buttons. Five weeks till the end of school. *I can do this.*

When the laptop booted, I started a new timeline. At the top of the page, in 36-point dark red Gothic Bold, I typed the broken English hacker meme: *AYBABTU* – All your base are belong to us.

You're mine, Tatum.

For the next week, I avoided Tatum and Patrice. I stayed out of the computer lab until they were gone for the day, catching up on my assignments during evening hours. I checked out all the reference books I could for my senior project and did the research at home or online. In and around studying, I visited each of the witnesses from Carmen's accident. It's harder for people to say no, or to lie, when face-to-face. The first two added nothing new to what they gave McQueen and Haskins at the scene. Number three, a retiree from Waynesville, was harder to pin down. I made the 35-minute drive south on Sunday afternoon and found her working in a shop on Main Street. Reminded me of Zigana's place, only more cluttered with mass merchandise trinkets instead of handmade arts and crafts.

The woman began fussing with the inventory as soon as I asked about Carmen. "She was your friend? I'm sorry, that must be tough. But I told the officers everything I could." She was short enough I could see gray streaks and roots showing through her bleach job when she ran a nervous hand through her hair.

"I understand, and I appreciate your agreeing to talk to me. Her boyfriend, the guy who was with Carmen when she fell, did you see him?"

"Sure, he had a hold of her arm when they passed me in the middle of the block. Tall kid, saggy pants." She shook her head in disgust. "I never understood why they do that. Do you girls really find that attractive?"

"Not me. How did she fall if Bruce had her arm?"

"It looked like he tried to steer around the guy on crutches at the corner, and she jerked away. I guess that's when she fell. There was another guy blocking my view, so I didn't actually see it happen." She shuddered. "Glad of that. I'd have had nightmares for sure."

"You saw the guy on crutches?" My sudden intensity got her attention.

"Well, yeah, didn't I tell that to the police? I mean, I saw him, but I didn't see him, if you know what I mean."

"What *do* you mean?"

"I saw him from behind is all. He was there at the corner, kind of wobbling around. The boyfriend stepped between him and her, and she pulled away. I saw a cell phone fly over her head into the street, so I guess that's what I had my eye on when it happened." She squinted at me. "I didn't mention that?"

"If you did, it's not in the report." I fumbled through my wallet for McQueen's business card. "Could you call the officer and tell him, please?"

She stepped away. "Oh, I don't think that's necessary. Like I said, I really didn't see anything happen. There was another guy, the one who was closer, that I saw the officers talking to after, and then the cell phone, and all." She busied herself with dusting an already-clean shelf. "I'm sure if he was important, they talked to him already."

No amount of cajoling convinced her. A pair of shoppers entered the store and she turned her back on me. The conversation was over.

On the way home, I called McQueen's cell. It went to voicemail. I tried Haskins. She answered on the first ring. I gave her the details, careful to keep any I-told-you-so out of my voice.

"The lady from Waynesville, huh? Okay, got it. We'll follow up with her Monday." A muffled background exchange, then she said, "Make that Tuesday. We're in court tomorrow."

"You'll let me know if you find him?"

"We'll be in touch."

She hung up on me.

I made it home in time for dinner with Zigana before hitting the books. Cisco couldn't hold my attention for long. Finding the mysterious crutches-man had me pumped. A few hours with Tatum's database files, and I made some interesting conclusions.

Like Bruce said, Tatum collected debts for the Café. *What a guy.* A quick calculation showed that in the last six months covered by the data, he'd pulled down an extra twenty-five thousand over and above the base debt amount owed the Café. *Interest? Finder's fee?*

A separate file on the drive contained what appeared to be a log of correspondence with some of them, linked to emails on an alternate account. I set up a hack to get the password. Comparing the client IDs from the second file with the collection list was even more interesting. I'd cracked the code on the IDs earlier and knew some of them were big shots around town, business execs, politicians, a few preachers. Those who merited personal emails also owed the most money—and had the most to lose if their vice became public. They were the clients padding Tatum's private bank account to the tune of another fifty thousand.

Blackmail.

I checked the time before tapping Tatum's school email. One-thirty Monday morning. Not likely he'd be online and notice a visitor. I was in and out in only a few minutes, downloading the recent contacts and emails, appending them to the files I'd collected for Patrice. Only one name appeared in both this account and in the client list, Khan37, the name I'd flagged weeks earlier. A cursory attempt to track it to a real person before Carmen's death had come up empty. Now I tried harder. I started a second hack to break into the Khan37 account. While it ran, I searched Tatum's documents list for anything related to the user name. Eight files were linked to the ID, all encrypted. I was running out of credits in my usergroup and of bandwidth in an increasingly fuzzy brain. Five hours till class and another Cisco exam. I left the hacks running and forced myself to review the test prep one last time before falling into bed.

At least I passed the exam. Only one more Cisco hurdle before I earn my certification. Tatum couldn't stop that from happening. If I had to come up with a way to test at an independent facility somewhere besides the school, Cisco wouldn't care. My biggest concern was my senior capstone. If he decided to make things difficult, he could drop a dime on the review committee. Without credit for all that work, I wouldn't graduate. Two weeks and a bonus weekend before the project deadline. Time to buy a little insurance.

I made the call from the burner phone while standing in the school's main lobby so I could see everyone within earshot. It took so long for the DHS secretary to put me through I almost hung up.

"Bratton."

"We need to talk. Same place. One hour."

"Make it two. I'm in a meeting."

He was willing to come, I gave him the win on the time.

The black Fedmobile was parked on the garage roof when I pulled up in Matthew's truck. Easier to swap out vehicles at the bookstore than to install the tracking shield for a quick trip.

Bratton stood at his rear bumper, making me come to him. He left Reynolds scowling in the front seat.

"You had to bring him?" I nodded toward the car.

"Too damn cold to stand out here and chat." He opened the back door of the sedan. "Get in."

I noted the absence of inside door handles. Standard law enforcement practice, so the bad guys can't escape. "Not a chance, not back there."

He slammed the door and stared at me for a long minute. Apparently, his background check hadn't told him how stubborn I could be. He opened the driver's door. "Pat, get in back, will you?"

"What the hell?" Reynolds exploded out of the car, his fury directed at me as much as at his partner.

"Just do it." Bratton's sternness, and I'd bet seniority, won out. Reynolds climbed into the backseat and slid over to the driver's side. Bratton made an exaggerated bow toward the passenger door. "Ms. Wood."

When we were settled in the car, I skipped the niceties. "Tatum's skimming from his collection accounts at the Café."

"No shit." Reynolds' anger still simmered.

Bratton shifted to plant his back against the door, facing me full on. "We told you to stay away from there."

"I did. Stay away, that is." I took another big chance. "You know I don't need physical access to get information."

His eyes narrowed. "Just because your probation's up doesn't mean we can't haul you in for hacking."

"And if you had any evidence, you'd have done that already." The slight vibration from the Droid in my front jacket pocket reassured me Record was functioning. "Besides, I'm not after the Café, or their money. I want Tatum. I think he had a hand in my friend's death."

Bratton stopped Reynolds' retort with one raised finger. "Still think you know better than the local police?"

"I found a witness they missed."

"Now she's Nancy Drew." Sarcasm spilled over from the backseat.

I cracked open the door, preparing to leave. "Look, if you guys want to play good cop-bad cop, you need to work on your routine. If you don't want to hear what I've got, fine. I'll take Tatum down myself and hand him to you wrapped in a pretty red bow. Let you explain *that* to the big boss."

Bratton swallowed a grin and warned his partner off with a look. Reynolds sank into the backseat grumbling under his breath.

"So, Tatum's skimming," Bratton said to me. "We know that, and don't care so much. If the owners find out and handle it themselves, we turn it over to the locals and move on, which means less paperwork for us." He folded his arms. "What else've you got?"

"He's blackmailing some of the big-name clients." I'd prioritized the data I found, intending to dish it out in small enough chunks to keep them interested without giving away everything.

"Says you," Reynolds muttered.

Bratton wiped the surprise off his face and spoke carefully. "What makes you think that?"

I ignored Reynolds, encouraged by Bratton's sudden interest. "I found a stash of emails he exchanged with the high rollers. They're cryptic, but the numbers don't lie. Between the skimming and the blackmail, he pulled down about seventy-five thousand in six months."

"And where did you find this stash of emails? We've been through all the Café accounts," Bratton said.

For now, I'd give them one more piece, one that might save my ass. "He's using the school network as a ghost proxy."

That shut them both up. They listened without interrupting for the next ten minutes while I outlined Patrice's hacking request, the data files, and my subsequent firing. I neglected to mention the copies I held of everything I'd found. More insurance.

"So why are you telling us this?" Bratton asked when I stopped talking. "Doesn't it spoil your revenge fantasy if we get him and you don't?"

"I don't want revenge, I want justice." My words surprised him. Reynolds just snorted. "I don't give a damn what he does at the Café. Anybody dumb enough to get wrapped up in a mess like that deserves a shakedown. Hypocritical blowhards, most of them. But if he had anything to do with Carmen's death, because of me—" I caught my breath. "He has to be held accountable. You and the locals are the ones to take care of that. No matter what you think of me, I'm not a vigilante." I let that sink in before adding, "And I need to graduate, so I can get on with my life. He can prevent that if he finds out what I've got on him."

"So you want protection," Bratton said.

"I don't want to be responsible for another death, mine or anyone else's. If he had a hand in Carmen's accident, and if he thinks I might expose him, graduation could be the least of my worries."

Reynolds leaned forward and whispered in Bratton's ear. Eavesdropping's a hobby of mine, and it was a small car. I can put together whole thoughts from a few phrases. I feigned disinterest, studying my fingernails, hoping they'd forget I was there and talk louder, but Bratton was smart. All I got before he shut Reynolds up was "documents" and "Wright-Patt."

Bratton turned back to me. "You said the files are on the school server. Still have access?"

"As long as I'm a student in good standing." Get that plug in there, make sure they didn't jeopardize anything. "But I can't get into

Tatum's stuff anymore. He changed all his passwords. If I dig, it could tip him off."

He bought it. DHS must not be as familiar with my skills as they thought. "Okay, get us a copy of whatever you have, we'll take it from there."

Last thing I wanted to do was hand over my files. I stalled. "But he could still think it's me, if you start poking around."

Bratton's patronizing look set my teeth on edge. "We've got the best cybergeeks in the country in our office. He won't find out."

Yeah, right. "He already knows you're onto the Café."

Bratton frowned. This time he whispered to Reynolds, who hung in suspension over the back of the seat. All I caught was "Damn Walker." It was enough.

I fumbled for the door latch again. "I need to get back to school. You'll take care of Tatum and keep me out of it?"

"Send us the files." Bratton scrawled an address on a note pad attached to the dash. "It's a secure ftp site." He held onto the paper when I tried to take it from him. "And don't get any ideas about using it to hack us."

"Of course not." *Mind reader.* "I'll send them tonight after I get home."

Good thing my subconscious knows the way to the bookstore because I definitely wasn't in mental control of the truck. Everything the DHS guys said, and didn't say, buzzed through my head. Tatum was up to a whole lot more than a little get-rich-quick blackmail. The letterhead Bratton wrote the ftp link on showed he was Secret Service, merged into DHS in the 2003 agency realignment. Probably part of the hacker-nemesis Electronic Crimes Task Force.

And Bruce. Sounded like "Damn Walker" was playing a three-way con, trying to outmaneuver Tatum, DHS, *and* me. Bad move. The new intel was a worthy payoff for the calculated risk involved in contacting Bratton to begin with. I sent him the files I promised, more or less. I also squirreled away encrypted copies in three different cloud sites. Now that he had a hint of what information I'd gathered and how, there was a chance he'd use it against me and raid my equipment. I added digital files of our recorded conversations to the hidden stash, too, just in case.

Before I logged off, I checked my throw-away email. A message from Phil read, "Ready when you are." I caught him in a chat session. We arranged to meet in the school lobby later that afternoon since he had to be downtown for law review class anyway. I promised to buy him a drink after we survived finals.

I hung around the lobby for nearly an hour between classes, one eye on my Lit textbook, the other on the milling students. A guy struggling with crutches, a briefcase, and a handful of file folders reminded me I needed to follow up with McQueen and Haskins. I ducked around the corner to a quieter spot to make the call. Had to leave a message. When I turned back toward the entrance, the crutches guy blocked my way.

"Fatál?"

Good thing he pronounced it right. My increasingly paranoid brain had already calculated which direction to kick the crutches to guarantee he'd fall and allow me to escape.

"Do I know you?"

He balanced on one leg and crutch, holding out the folders with his other hand. "Phil said to give you these."

Phil's buddy. I released the breath I didn't realize I'd been holding. "Why didn't he come?" I took the files without opening them.

"He got a last-minute interview at Schuster and Schuster and was afraid to ask for a time change."

I didn't blame him. When one of the largest law firms in the city calls, you answer. "So you're Nick? He never mentioned crutches." I couldn't get past the coincidence.

"Rick. I tore my ACL day before yesterday playing basketball." He shifted his briefcase to the other hand. "Still trying to figure out how to keep from killing myself with them."

"I appreciate the effort, on all counts." I held up the files. "Thanks." I followed him to the door and pushed it open while he edged through. "Need a lift?"

"No, I borrowed my grandmother's placard." He pointed to a beat-up Honda in the first handicapped slot.

I waited till he backed out. He stopped in front of me and rolled down the window.

"Almost forgot. Phil said the party's a week from Saturday, eight o'clock until they kick us out of The Pub over at The Greene. His class reserved the patio room. He said unless you want to get hit on by drunk law students, you should bring a date." He grinned. "See you then."

After dinner, ensconced in my room with more Red Bull while Zigana went to a village council meeting, I read through the documents Phil had sent. Rick was thorough, I'd give him that. Reams of legalese covered the formal incorporation of the Café. He'd included a few Internet files detailing how easy it is to set up an offshore account. A phone call to Lithuania or some other enterprising small country, and with only cursory personal data, I could have a corporation in Belize operating on a secure Swiss bank account. One firm even provide a list of semi-legitimate names as a board of directors in case someone like me snooped.

Most of those accounts are designed as tax shelters for people with so much money they can't spend it fast enough. Several of the offshore banks listed for the Café jived with the accounts in Tatum's database. I highlighted those for further investigation. I checked the status of my brute force attack on the mysterious Khan37 email recipient. Nothing yet, so I linked to a new rainbow table and started a second attack using one of the rouge software packages from my usergroup.

Back to the corporation files. I needed the Red Bull to ward off sleep while wading through all the pages. After an hour of mind-numbing scanning, I tossed them aside and reconsidered my approach. Without knowing who or what I was looking for, I was wasting my time. I opened the name file I'd extrapolated from Tatum's database and added a new field. Starting with the ten biggest account totals, I went back to basics. I ran a Google search on the names, one at a time, and followed the related results whenever they looked promising. After another two hours, I'd still found nothing to tie them to each other, much less to the corporate papers. All that told me was the shareholders were smart enough not to owe their soul to the company store.

"I'm home," Zigana called up the stairwell at eleven-thirty.

I eased out of the desk chair, stretched my aching muscles through a few yoga poses, and met her in the kitchen.

"Late night for council." I set out tea mugs while she plated our evening crumpets. "More pastries from Jocelyn?"

"Emergency committee meeting after," she said. "The AG's office decided there was 'insufficient evidence' to tie the notebook to the drilling company. They didn't even look at the pages, only the statements from Jocelyn and her roomie." She slammed the cutlery drawer. "What a joke."

"So, what's next? Is there someone higher up to kick it to?"

"Governor's office, like that'll happen. His campaign took so much money from the energy lobby last year they probably have a desk in his office."

"All politicians do that. I don't see why you're surprised."

"That doesn't make it right." She brooded over her tea and left the sweets to me.

I was happy to oblige. Midway through my second sticky bun, an uncomfortable thought struck. I peeked at Zigana to gauge her mood before asking. Her color was better so I chanced it. "Was Patrice there?"

"Yes." She shifted away from me.

"And?" I couldn't imagine why she seemed uncomfortable.

She busied herself refilling our mugs before answering. "I wonder if you've misjudged her."

"How can you say that?" I sputtered. Tension crackled between us as we hovered at opposite ends of the kitchen, wary, uncertain. In twenty-five years, she'd never defended those who'd wronged me. It was an unpleasant experience. I took a deep breath and reconsidered. This was Zigana. She knew me better than anyone else did. Knew Patrice better than I did maybe, certainly in a different context. I pulled back my initial disappointment and tried again. "What'd she say?"

"She didn't mention you at all, if that's what you mean." Zigana leaned against the sink and stared into her tea. "She gives off nothing but sincerity, and a level of insecurity unless she's defending a cause. Nothing malicious."

"Sure wasn't insecure when she fired me." Images of Patrice drumming on the table, on the desk, on Carmen's box clashed with my response. Jealousy reflected the ultimate insecurity. It had motivated her first request to spy on Tatum's email. She did as he asked and let me go without a fight. Needing to be needed, to be loved. Lame, but probably accurate. Maybe Zigana was right. I sighed. She usually was. "Tell me what happened."

As she told me about the committee's debate, I had to admit Patrice came off sounding pretty good. Sure, her activism earned good press for herself and for the school, but that didn't mean it wasn't sincere. My studies in Kant's deontological ethics taught me that. To combat the drilling company's full-court press, Patrice had offered the school's resources for research and information dissemination. She connected Zigana's committee to more established anti-fracking groups in Arkansas. And she presented a younger, polished, media-savvy spokesperson, someone not easily dismissed as a regular Yellow Springs activist, on the rare occasions when the press cared what opponents thought about the issue.

The longer Zigana talked, the more her admiration for Patrice broke through the reticence she held on my behalf. I conceded defeat as graciously as I could.

"Does this mean we have to invite her to dinner?"

Zigana's laugh erased the last of the tension. I took my tea and the lingering remnants of her hug to my room. With this new vision of Patrice, my to-do list needed updating. An email from Adam continued the warm fuzzies. He was stuck in Florida chauffeuring his mother while she tended to *her* mother's broken hip. But he missed me.

"You could come down for the weekend. I have frequent flyer miles to use up," he wrote.

With the blowing flurries outside my window, whistling through the gaunt branches, his grandmother's address in Pensacola sounded like a great idea. I saved the email to answer when I could come up with a good reason *not* to accept.

———

The hack on Khan37's account broke late Wednesday afternoon. It was the first real progress in two days, so I pounced as soon as I could. When I escaped from a mandatory lab hour and settled into the quiet of the bookstore for my evening shift, I tapped the neighborhood wifi and a third-party proxy to keep Matthew in the clear as I logged into my usergroup. The password got me into the email account, no problem. I downloaded the address book and message history, took a screen shot of the user profile, and logged out. Wiping the access IP took another few seconds, but I left no traces.

Now I had a name: Charles Grechko, and a location: Dayton, Ohio—a hometown boy. Next I hit Google, which led me to Facebook, LinkedIn, Twitter, and MyLife. His user names were different, but he apparently had a thing about Genghis Khan. His avatars were all variations of the same theme—Khan37, GK1227, so even when he went with a basic hash like T3muj1n or G3ngh15, he wasn't hard to trace. I scrolled through his public Facebook profile and found out he was single, at least on line. I sent a friend request from one of my fictional identities, a sultry redhead with an innocent pout who magically shared his interests in alt-rock, Doctor Who, and microbreweries. It didn't take long. He accepted his new "friend" before Matthew and Sammy came back from AA.

I was in.

The search continued when I got home. Grechko was a tech sergeant at Wright-Patterson Air Force Base. Depending on his security clearance levels, frequenting the Café would certainly be frowned on—according to Tatum. Made him a prime candidate for Tatum's blackmail efforts, too. I compared his other user names with the database client list, but he didn't show up in any form. When I opened his email messages, I hit the jackpot.

After an initial exchange of cryptic messages with Tatum, referenced as "DT," about "mutually agreeable terms," every email carried an attachment that matched a file in Tatum's encrypted documents. An early message from DT laid out the steps for Diffie-

Hellman encryption. Tatum was a patient teacher, but his student—Grechko—had ignored the final instruction to delete the message after implementing the code. Careless, or mindlessly arrogant.

Now that I had the key, breaking the encryption would be a cinch. It was almost midnight and an early class loomed, but I couldn't resist cracking at least one file.

I should have waited, because once the document was unlocked, sleep was impossible.

I took in the first screen in one glance and jumped away from the desk, knocking over my chair. My bedroom wasn't really large enough to pace in, but I circled it three times before returning to the computer to verify what I'd seen.

Grechko was funneling classified military documents to Tatum.

I opened a second. And a third. One showed specs for the latest experimental attack drone planned for the Air National Guard base in Springfield. Another contained final bid data for the hotly contested in-air refueling tankers. A third outlined plans for Wright-Patt that were wending their way through Congress and the Department of Defense under the Base Realignment Commission.

Shock fueled my actions. I closed all the open documents and dumped copies onto four flash drives, trashing a year's worth of music files to make room. I logged out of all browsing sessions on the desktop and laptop, wiped my access history and changed the proxy settings for both machines. I shuffled the flash drives on my desk like an elaborate shell game, waiting for my heartbeat to return to normal. What to do next. Where to turn. Who to trust.

Who to protect.

Exploitation: Countermeasures

"Preventative technology or controls that hinder the ability to successfully complete an exploit avenue"

After five long, slow breaths to still my racing heart, I unplugged the network connections and turned off the wireless router before restarting the computers. I backed up all my school and personal files onto my external hard drive and still another flash drive and set them aside. After I made sure the desktop files were redundant, I wiped the hard drive and swapped it out for a spare from my parts box in the closet. I did the same thing to the laptop. While the configuration programs ran, I raided Zigana's shop supplies for four padded mailers. One I addressed to TK, another to an anonymous post office box I kept in downtown Dayton for hacker correspondence. They each got a hard drive and a flash with Tatum's files. I sealed the external drive and another flash in the third envelope with no address. The final flash drive with Tatum's files needed a good home, but I was out of ideas. I couldn't involve Zigana or Matthew any more than they already were.

When the systems were up and running, I configured a new proxy and reconnected the wireless router and modem. I logged in to my regular email account to verify TK's snail-mail address. A new message from Adam was time stamped only an hour earlier.

Adam. I clicked through to the saved email and jotted his mother's Pensacola address onto the fourth envelope. I added a Post-it: "Save this for me. Thanks. F" and sealed the envelope before I talked myself out of it. Zigana's postal scale and the USPS online app took care of postage. I used my anonymous P.O. Box as return address on the envelopes to Adam and TK, bundled up in my parka, and headed out into the night. I left by the back door and kept an eye out for anyone dumb enough to be on the streets of Yellow Springs at three-thirty in the morning. Even the bar crowd had made it home by now. I dropped the package to TK in the mailbox on the corner of Xenia and Short Street. Adam's I stuck in the mail drop in the post office lobby. I'd mail the third, to my P.O. Box, from school.

I tightened the scarf around my head and neck before plunging into Glen Helen to hide the unmarked envelope. As much as I loved the forest, the nature reserve is not my favorite place to be at night, especially alone. Too many shadows, and if the local cops or the park ranger spotted me, there'd be unwelcome questions to answer. I made my way by streetlight and the waning moon, using the flashlight on my phone when darkness closed in. A pair of raccoons skittered across the trail in front of me. I paused long enough to watch them disappear into the underbrush before following the rough-hewn stone steps to the bottom of the gorge. Icicles hung off the boulders over the eponymous yellow springs, glistening stalactitesin the pale light. I stuffed the unmarked envelope into the crevice next to the dried flowers we'd left for Carmen and shoved a rock into the opening to hide them. A few minutes of mental communication with whatever spirit of hers I could connect with assured me she'd take good care of it. My return trek involved a prudent detour around a marauding skunk, but I made it home without incident.

Two hours of what could laughingly be called sleep got me through morning class. I went by the bookstore to give Matthew an idea of what I'd found so someone would know to look for me if everything imploded. The worry on his face when I finished tore at me. "Don't tell Zigana yet, okay? Please." Only after I promised to tell her everything at dinner did he agree.

I holed up in the computer lab for the rest of the day as much to filter searches through the network as to finish my last assignments. I had 10 days to submit my senior project, one week to pass the last Cisco exam, and one more week for finals. My Lit paper was in shambles. I chugged another Red Bull and attacked the mess. To stem my impatience, I made a deal with myself: one hour of academics earned me fifteen minutes of as much hacking as I could fit in.

After what I'd already found, additional details on Khan37 were scarce. Bit of an egomaniac, hence the Khan reference, with a taste for high-maintenance women and poker, not much else. His Facebook history carried a few interesting links, and posts that were a bit more disgruntled and militant than a standard flyboy. All political references had stopped eight months ago. Right about the time he hooked up with Tatum.

Fascinating as that was, the classified documents spooked me more than I'd like. I stayed out of dark-web chat rooms—and restricted files on the school network—until I had a better handle on the danger. By the end of the next week, my Lit paper was ready for the required critique swap. Thursday morning, I was in the lab nailing down the Cisco practice tests when Dayton PD Officer Haskins called.

"We found him," she said. "The guy on crutches."

I stepped out into the hall, relieved to hear one piece of good news. My elation didn't last long.

"His name's Howard Zalenski," she said. "He claims the boyfriend shoved him out of the way right before your friend fell."

"And you believed him?"

"No reason not to." Haskins sounded impatient. "I know you want someone to blame, but sometimes there isn't anything that clear-cut. Without more to go on, the case is closed. Let it go."

I tried to see the logic in her insistence and failed. "What's his story?"

"Why should I tell you?"

"Because I found him."

She sighed. "Retired Air Force, on disability. No record other than illegal gaming a few years back. First offense, probation. Clean since then."

Illegal gaming. I hadn't told McQueen and Haskins about the Café. It was too close to Tatum. Without that connection, I'd never convince her it wasn't an accident. As much as it frustrated me, I had to let it go. For now.

I finished another two rounds of studying alternated with hacking without much progress on either. As I left the lab, a classmate from Yellow Springs bummed a ride home. I figured another body was good insurance at this stage. Her non-stop chatter didn't require more than the occasional nod or "Uh-huh, really?", so my mind could juggle Tatum and Grechko while my subconscious drove.

When I got home, Matthew and Sammy were huddled around the kitchen table with Zigana. She shot me an annoyed look, and I swatted Matthew.

"You promised," I scolded him. My annoyance bounced off his thick skull. The worry I'd wanted to avoid now lurked in Zigana's eyes.

Matthew pushed a chair toward me. "I didn't spill your story. Sit down. Sammy's got something to tell you."

I accepted the coffee Zigana offered but waved off the food.

Sammy fidgeted with a spoon, rolling it through his fingers, tapping it like a drumstick. I waited as long as my nerves would let me before pinning his hand to the table.

He grimaced and pulled free. "I followed Bruce this afternoon."

"You what?"

"It was his idea." He nodded at Matthew. "Picked up the tail at the apartment I followed them to last time."

"What were you thinking? He knows your truck," I said.

"I'm not stupid," Matthew said. "I got him a Rent-a-Wreck from Jack over in Riverside."

I rolled my eyes and turned back to Sammy. "And?"

"He went to the Café." At my gasp, he added, "No, I didn't go inside. I'm not stupid either."

Annoyance simmered, but I pulled back and let him talk.

"Tatum got there about ten minutes later. He's never there during the day. Another half hour and Bruce runs out, jumps in his car, and tears away. Had a hell of a time keeping up without getting caught." Sammy puffed out his chest. "Never spotted me though, I'd put money on it."

"Yeah, you're a real James Bond." I couldn't help it.

"Fatál! They're trying to help." Zigana switched from anxious to pissed in a flash. "If you let Tatum turn you against your friends, he wins in the long run."

I slouched in the chair and swallowed my growing frustration. Most of it was directed at myself anyway. Sammy was just a convenient target. "I'm sorry. Go on, Sammy. Where'd Bruce end up?"

"At an apartment off Wayne. Picked up a guy on crutches." He smirked when I jerked upright, slopping my coffee. "Oh, sure, now you're interested. Maybe James Bond here knows what he's doing after all."

"I *said* I was sorry. Where'd they go?"

"I dunno. I had to return the car before Jack closed up shop. I went back with Matthew's truck, but they were gone."

It didn't add up. Bruce's obvious fear when he told me he thought Tatum was responsible for Carmen's death, afraid he'd be framed for it, concerned enough about Crutches-man to mention the stranger to me. Now he was running the guy around town.

"What kind of game is he playing?" I didn't realize I spoke out loud, but Sammy answered.

"Tatum's pulling the strings, looks like."

No, duh. I made sure that comment stayed in my head.

"Why would Bruce cooperate, especially if he thinks Tatum killed Carmen?" Zigana refused to consider personal betrayal until it was the only option.

Nervous energy pushed me to my feet. "Bruce is greedy, likes his big-ticket toys, but I can't imagine he'd give up Carmen." I prowled the kitchen, looking for answers in the wine rack and the crockery shelf.

"When are you going to tell Zigana what you found last night?" Matthew broke the silence.

She looked to me expectantly, hope tinged with fear, and waited me out.

I moved behind her chair, stuck my tongue out at Matthew, and laid my hands on her shoulders. I needed the tactile input. I didn't need to see the growing concern. Or want her to see mine. "It looks like Tatum's blackmail includes dealing in classified military files."

She tensed under my hands.

I kept going. "He's got a mark on the inside funneling stuff to him. I haven't figured out yet where he's selling them."

Zigana pulled away and turned to face me. "You're serious?" One look at my face and she answered her own question. "You're serious." She clutched my hand. "You need to let the authorities handle this."

I hooked a foot around my chair and pulled it closer so I could sit at eye level. I didn't let go of her hand. "It's not that easy. Bruce was afraid he'd be framed for Carmen's death? Well, Tatum could frame me for all kinds of things, with the work I did on the database, the school hacks. I covered my tracks pretty well, but not that well. Not at first."

Across the table, Matthew stiffened. I'd avoided mentioning that possibility to him earlier, left that elephant feeding in the living room and hoped he wouldn't notice. Now it nosed into the platter in front of us.

My cell phone rang. I swiped it to voicemail without checking the caller ID. The wall clocked ticked off the seconds. The phone rang again. This time I glanced at the screen. Haskins. I waved an apology to the group and answered.

"I'm here, don't hang up."

"What the hell aren't you telling me?" Her voice was loud enough everyone in the kitchen heard the anger if not the words.

"I don't understand." *Dayton Police*, I mouthed to Zigana. She nodded and relayed the words to Matthew and Sammy. I lowered the volume to save my ears.

"Where have you been since we talked this morning?" Haskins asked.

Because of my experience with the Feds I knew the Miranda drill, but if I wanted her help, this wasn't the time to invoke said rights. I gave her the rundown of my afternoon, the drive home, and the past hour or so with present company. "Why do you want to know?"

McQueen grumbled in the background as Haskins repeated my answers. She came back calmer, harsher. "Walker and Zalenski are dead."

I dropped the phone and choked on the name. "Bruce—"

Matthew grabbed the phone and punched the speaker button. Haskins' voice filled the room.

"...railroad crossing at Linden and Woodman. A witness says an older guy driving a beat-up yellow pickup rammed the car from behind, pushing it onto the tracks like something out of an old movie. Traffic was backed up on the other side. They didn't stand a chance."

Three pairs of eyes locked on Sammy. A flash of confusion, quickly replaced by hurt, darkened his face. He shoved his chair back and left the room, his heavy footsteps down the stairs echoing in the sudden silence.

"Riverside Police found the truck out by the warehouses. We're dusting it for prints now," Haskins said.

Matthew swore under his breath and went after Sammy. "My truck's out front," he called before leaving the apartment.

I hung my head in my hands and didn't say a word.

"We need you at the station first thing tomorrow with some answers," Haskins said. "And Fatál? You might want to bring a lawyer."

Matthew returned before a new pot of coffee brewed. "Sammy's gone. He must have hitched a ride."

"Should we go after him?" Zigana asked.

"I'll check his usual haunts later, after he's had time to calm down."

"And forgive us for suspecting him?" My words hung in the air.

Matthew cleared his throat. "Reasonable reaction, given the circumstances."

"Was it?" Zigana handed around full mugs and sat down heavily. She stirred her coffee, staring at nothing. "And he was finally opening up to me."

"We'll find him. It'll be okay," Matthew promised.

When the coffee was gone, the final cups fortified by shots of Jameson, we spent the rest of the night considering and discarding ways to handle the larger issue.

Tatum's motivations.

"The cops showing up at what's-his-name-Zalenski's door about Carmen must have spooked him," Matthew said.

"But to kill them both, in such a horrible way?" Zigana shuddered, eyes bright from the liquor she usually avoided. "Seems harsh even for him."

"He's getting desperate," Matthew said. He took over Sammy's planning expertise, sketching outlines and charts on sheets of legal pad that covered the table. Put my lists and flow charts to shame. "We have to find out who Tatum's working for, who's buying the classified shit."

"I doubt they're the same people," I said.

"With his two sets of books, you can bet the Café owners don't know about any of the blackmail. He'd be in more trouble with them over the money." Matthew drew another line connecting two boxes on his chart. "He could be caught in the middle. If the Café finds out about the documents, they find out about the money."

"And if the document buyer finds out he's skimming at the Café, it gives them leverage to demand more information, maybe cut off his income." I used a red pen to add a couple of arrows to Matthew's notes as the hacker in me took over. "If he's using Café resources to shop classified documents like he's doing with the school computers, then he's putting them at risk for a boatload of shit they want nothing to do with." Even in her mild alcohol haze, Zigana scowled at my language. "Sorry, 'Gana."

"The owners would shut that down pronto, even before they cut him off at the knees for skimming," Matthew said. "They don't want the Feds nosing around."

"Too late." I hadn't shared everything about my visits with DHS before, didn't want to add to the general anxiety. Now, when I told them how I'd been warned off the Café, Matthew looked disgusted.

"I thought we were all in this together. What else are you hiding?" He glared at me. "Didn't we talk about communication?"

"This isn't about family communication. This is about not putting more people in danger because I can't control what's going on." My voice cracked. I shoved away from the table and curled up on the loveseat, my back to the kitchen.

After a muffled conversation between the two of them, Zigana knelt next to the loveseat and wrapped me in a hug. "You don't have to control any of this," she whispered into my hair. "You're not alone here." I sank into her embrace, soaking up her positive energy.

"Coffee's ready," Matthew called from the kitchen a few minutes later.

We regrouped and started again at the beginning. This time I left out nothing, from Patrice's jealousy to Bruce's apparent double-dealing to Tatum's misleading suggestions about his "commander-in-chief." *Wonder what army* that *commander led.*

None of us slept.

It was a hard sell, but I insisted they let me handle offense at the police station.

"This all started because of my hacking at school. It's grown tentacles. I'll have a hard enough time living with myself after what happened to Carmen and Bruce." I turned to Matthew. "And now he's trying to frame you and Sammy." My emotions were back in check, harnessed by a growing determination to bring Tatum to justice, and not for my petty concern over being fired as a scapegoat. Zigana had taught me one thing above all: do *not* mess with my family. "Don't let him find other ways to complicate things, using you guys to keep me from doing what I need to do."

My words sank in, eventually, but only to a point. Matthew insisted on following me to the police station and staying with me until my lawyer arrived. Then he'd find Sammy and hole up at the store with other people as much as possible. Zigana would mind the shop, her part-timer brought in as a buffer.

"I'll call Ed, too," she said as we cleared the dishes. "He'll send an extra patrol around for the next couple days, no questions asked." Ed was a Yellow Springs police officer and a former beau. Zigana could handle him.

As daylight broke, I made a few calls myself, the last one to the lawyer who had handled my case with the Feds. Zeb Kutcher growled at the early morning summons until I spelled out what I was up against.

"Nine-thirty, I'll meet you there. They can wait that long," he said.

While I showered away the sleepless night, I ran through all the possible outcomes I could think of, only a few of them worth pondering. Zigana pushed me to eat before I left, so I choked down half an omelet. I couldn't face more coffee, but a Red Bull on the road kept me going. I was beginning to hate my traditional caffeine sources.

Kutcher met us in the parking lot at Dayton Police headquarters. I made the introductions before Matthew left to start hunting for Sammy. Kutcher and I spent ten minutes in his car reviewing details before going inside where Haskins led us to a smelly, claustrophobia-inducing interview room.

"Wait here," she said before leaving us alone.

I tried to pick up our conversation from the car, but Kutcher nudged my foot. Of course. Behind the blank interior window on the wall, the room was monitored. We sat in silence until the officers returned with a stenographer. McQueen stood by the door, arms folded, while Haskins sat across from me, back to the faux window. Probably decided I'd open up more to a woman. She waited until the stenographer nodded in readiness, fingers poised over the tiny keyboard.

"No digital recorder?" I couldn't help asking.

Kutcher kicked me under the table.

"Technology's great when it works," Haskins said. "I prefer a human being when I can find one." She slapped a legal pad on the scarred wooden table. "Ms. Wood, you're not under arrest, and you're not a suspect *for the moment*. However." The pause following her disclaimer hung in the air for a long second. "However, since you've brought counsel, we'll go through Miranda to cover all the bases." She pulled a business-sized card out of her pad and read aloud. "You have the right to remain silent."

Kutcher interrupted. "We waive the reading, Officer. Ms. Wood understands her rights."

Haskins looked to me for confirmation.

I nodded.

"You have to speak for the record," she said.

"Yes, I waive reading, and yes, I understand my rights under Miranda." I bit off the sarcasm that crept into my voice.

"All right then." She returned the crib note to her pad and picked up a pen. "On the third of March, you contacted Officer McQueen and myself about concerns you had over the death of your friend, Carmen Lowery, is that correct?"

"Yes."

Haskins knew her stuff. She retraced our every discussion, making me repeat the information I'd given them about the man on crutches. She brought out a written statement from the witness in Waynesville describing our meeting. She covered it all. Kutcher listened and took notes. I'd given him most of it in the car, but he had to earn his fee somehow.

When she was finished, Haskins flipped through her notepad. "One second." She stepped away to consult with McQueen at the door.

Eavesdropping wasn't so easy here. I craned my neck to read the upside-down scrawls on Haskins' notepad until Kutcher nudged me again and shook his head in one quick motion. I leaned back and studied the walls, anxious for the interview to be over.

Haskins returned to her seat. "At four-thirty Sunday afternoon, you called my cell phone to relay the information you had learned in Waynesville. I told you we'd follow up on Tuesday, is that correct?"

"Yes." This was getting old.

"Did you hunt down Zalenski in the meantime?"

She had my attention now. And Kutcher's. "I didn't know who he was until you called me Thursday," I said.

"And after I gave you his name, did you go looking for him then?"

"No, I didn't."

"Yet less than three hours later, he gets creamed by a freight train while a passenger in a car driven by your buddy Bruce Walker."

"He's not my buddy...wasn't, that is." I stumbled over the thought of Bruce's death almost as much as I did over Carmen's. "He was my friend's boyfriend." I took a gamble. "Honestly, I didn't like him all that much."

Kutcher stopped writing and glared at me.

"Why is that?" Haskins asked.

"He took advantage of Carmen, sponged off her. When she told me she was pregnant, she worried about his reaction."

"When was this?"

I swallowed hard. "Two days before she died."

"Was there a witness to the conversation?"

"No."

McQueen leaned over her shoulder and whispered. She listened and nodded, never taking her eyes off me.

"When did you last talk to Walker?" she asked.

"Maybe two, three weeks ago. I'm not sure."

"You didn't tell him we'd found Zalenski?"

"No, I didn't trust him." Now came the hard part. I had to bring Tatum into the mix without mentioning him by name or talking about the school.

"Why is that?"

"I found out he was working for someone at the Cyber Café who put pressure on him for his gambling debts. I was afraid that's what got Carmen in trouble. They were after him, and she got in the way." I forced myself to breathe normally while Haskins considered the implications. No body language tips off a lie quicker than a change in breathing. Flushing can be blamed on the thermostat. Gasping not so much.

"How did you hear that?" she asked.

"He told me last time we talked."

"Walker told you."

"Not in so many words, but when I picked up my stuff from Carmen's apartment, I saw he'd sold everything of value in their place, including most of Carmen's things that her folks didn't claim. And he asked for money, said he was in trouble, somebody wanted to frame him for Carmen's death. That's when he mentioned the guy on crutches. He was scared." A little truth, mixed with a little lie, is always the best basis for a good falsehood. It was the same story I'd given Kutcher. If nothing else, it would buy me some time while they checked out the Café, maybe scare Tatum into leaving us alone.

McQueen leaned in again. Haskins brushed him away. "Why didn't you tell us this before?"

"Because I didn't want to get mixed up in his gambling problem." I let indignation spill over. "I told you I didn't like him much. Whatever trouble he was in was his own fault. All I wanted to know was who hurt Carmen, or if it really was an accident." The catch in my voice wasn't phony.

The rest of Haskins' questions were a replay of what she'd asked on the phone. Where was I between three and five-thirty yesterday afternoon, did I have access to a yellow Chevy pickup. I had to give up Matthew at that point, but with his truck intact, it didn't matter. Tatum's clumsy attempt to implicate him had fallen apart.

"Far too many coincidences here for my liking," Haskins said as they turned us loose. "And believe me, we'll check every one of them."

I never doubted it for a minute.

Exploitation: Precision Strike

"Simulate an attacker in order to represent a simulated attack against the organization"

I parted ways with Kutcher in the parking lot after promising to keep him in the loop with any further developments, and another fingers-crossed promise to stay out of trouble.

On my way to the college, I stopped at the bookstore. Sammy was at the front counter with Matthew, but he disappeared into the office when he spotted me.

"Give him time," Matthew said.

"Is he sober?"

"Wishing he wasn't, but yes. I found him at the dive bar he used to hang out in, staring at a shot and a beer."

My heart sank. I turned from focusing on Sammy's exit and frowned a question.

"He said if Zigana thought he'd kill Bruce and Zalenski, he might as well drink." Matthew ran a hand through his fuzzy hair. "When I told him she didn't think any such thing, and got her on the phone to confirm it, he handed me the glasses. I took care of them." His bloodshot eyes told me how.

————

I tracked down Patrice in her office. When I closed the door and pulled the blinds over the hall window, she reached for the phone.

"Don't bother with security. We need to talk about Tatum before someone else dies."

She gasped and dropped her hand into her lap. "You're crazy."

"He's dangerous," I said. "Three people are dead. You want to be number four?"

She paled. "Three? I mean, who...I thought...you still believe...he didn't have anything to do with Carmen's death." She struggled to put together a coherent sentence. "I wish you'd leave Derek alone."

Patrice's use of Tatum's first name spoke volumes about her mental state, as did her now-balled fists, thumbs tucked inside. I scoured my memory for the chapter on body language in Social Psychology. The hand movement signaled insecurity. Or lying. I couldn't remember. Either way, her vulnerability flared.

"He's using you, and the school, to blackmail gamblers from the Cyber Café." I pushed on, forcing her to listen. "His database, your 'special project,' has all his records. You've seen them. What did he tell you they were for, fundraising? You're not stupid, Patrice."

Her hands unclenched and she started finger drumming, eyes vacant.

I did as Zigana taught and let her mind run wild. Likely she'd come up with worse than anything I could suggest. She was quiet for so long though, I thought I'd lost her.

"Where's Tatum?" I asked.

My question pulled her back to the present, but it took a moment for her to focus. "Derek's in Vegas for a technology convention until the 15th."

Good news, if it was true. "Are you sure?"

"I took him to the airport yesterday, four-thirty flight." She met my gaze. "You mentioned three deaths."

I made note of the flight time. *He couldn't have killed Bruce.* "You didn't see the news this morning."

Her head shake was timid, fearful.

"Carmen's boyfriend Bruce was in a car-train wreck with another guy."

Her eyes widened, horror reflecting in their depths. Like Haskins said, too much coincidence. "Number three?" she whispered.

"Guy named Zalenski."

Patrice clutched at her throat. "Howie?"

Her pallor sent me rummaging for a bottle of water from the mini-fridge under the credenza. "You know him?"

She took a sip and blinked back tears. "He did odd jobs for Derek, mowed the lawn and such. He could fix anything." She shifted her attention back to me. "What was he doing with Carmen's boyfriend?"

I wasn't sure she was ready to hear it, but I'd promised Zigana I'd warn her. "Bruce told me right after Carmen died that he thought Tatum had something to do with it. He mentioned a guy on crutches who was on the street with them right before she fell."

She snapped the plastic bottle cap in half, slicing her finger in the process. She watched it ooze for several seconds before wrapping the cut with a tissue. "There are lots of people in town who use crutches." Her voice shook.

"The police connected Zalenski to Carmen's accident a few days ago." I left out my part in that discovery. I needed Patrice fighting with me, not against me. "I'm guessing Tatum threw them together again and got rid of them. Even tried to make it look like my father had a hand in it. I spent all morning in an interrogation room talking them out of arresting him, or me."

Patrice spun her chair around to face the window instead of me. It was raining, a dull March drizzle not quite heavy enough to warrant an umbrella for a dash from the parking lot to the building. Students cowered under newspapers and book bags as they splashed through puddles. Would have been fun to watch if not for the sharp tension in the office.

I checked the time and settled back to wait her out. It took a while. I'd given her an awful lot to think about.

She spoke to my reflection in the window. "Your father. The Sammy Zigana talks about?"

"His friend, Matthew. They went to school together." Her shift to a personal link gave me hope.

A shove against the windowsill, harder than necessary, and Patrice rotated back to the desk. "You're very sure of yourself, aren't you? Confident in your choices." Her laugh held no amusement as she added, "I try to be. It rarely works."

"Zigana says you're a great organizer, a big help to her committee and all."

She dismissed the compliment. Throwing back her shoulders and lifting her chin, Patrice reverted to the consummate professional she was whenever Tatum wasn't involved.

"I won't let Der...Dr. Tatum take down this school over a *gambling* problem."

Okay, we'll ignore the deaths for now, if that's what you need. I waited.

"I assume you have a plan or you wouldn't be here," she added.

I had fifteen minutes to explain before making my next appointment. One I couldn't miss. She wavered when I asked her to let me into the network unobstructed.

"It's too risky," she said, fear returning. "I can't lie to him directly. And he'd be suspicious."

"Not as much as if he finds me hacking in. You said he's out of town. Tell the desk you've hired me back till the end of the semester to wrap up loose ends or something. He doesn't have to know. I'll be in and out before he's back from Vegas." I stood to leave. "Think about it. I'll be back in an hour or so to finish up my labs."

I hated leaving it hanging, and her doubting, but I didn't have a choice. I made it to the bookstore only five minutes late. Bratton and Reynolds were waiting, flanked by Matthew and Sammy in a testosterone-fueled stand-off.

"It's okay. I asked them to meet me here. Safer than the rooftop." I tossed my coat onto the rack and shoved my backpack under the counter. "Can we use your office?"

Matthew nodded once, not breaking his stare-down with Reynolds until Bratton nudged his partner to follow me. Sammy ping-ponged a glare from one agent to the other.

Men.

When the door closed behind us, Bratton said, "You could have warned them we were coming."

I pointed to a blinking light on the phone. "I tried."

"We're not at your beck and call, you know." Reynolds' pent-up hormone surge hit me full on.

Bratton shut him down with a look before turning to me. "You said it was urgent."

"I think I found what you're looking for." I handed him a printout of what I'd hoped was the least dangerous of the classified documents.

He barely masked a surprised reaction before passing the papers to Reynolds. "Where did you get that?"

"Tatum's database. There's a whole list."

"We've got the list. How'd you break the code already? Our guys have been on it for a week."

"Not so fast." I scooted onto Matthew's desk while I organized my thoughts. "I need to know you're not going to hang this on me."

"We ought to." Reynolds shook the document in my direction. "This shit's classified."

"No, duh. And Tatum's dealing it, and a lot more, from what I can tell." I looked to Bratton. "Assurances, or I wipe everything and you never get him."

"Turn off the recorder in your pocket and we'll talk." He laughed when I grabbed my side. "Think you're pretty smart, don't you?" Bratton straddled a side chair and leaned his arms on the back, waiting for me to comply.

I did, displaying the power light as it faded away before tossing my Droid onto the desk.

"You don't know as much as you think you do," he said. "We already knew Tatum was selling this stuff. Question is where he gets it, and where it's going."

"Assurances," I said again. "And I'll answer the first one."

That shut up Reynolds. They exchanged a long look, then Bratton nodded. "We don't care how you found the stuff. Anything in those files our guys will decipher eventually, so your name doesn't need to come up."

I weighed his words, ignoring Reynolds and gauging the sincerity on Bratton's face. Satisfied with what I saw, I tossed him a flash drive. "The encryption key's in there, along with a bunch of emails and identifiers for an airman named Grechko. He's not too bright."

Bratton fingered the drive. "How'd Tatum get to him?"

"He took a gamble."

They were ready to charge out the door to haul Tatum in for questioning until I dropped the next piece.

"Tatum's in Vegas till the 14th. And you may have to fight the locals for him." I laid out details of the three deaths, all linked to Tatum now that a motive had been discovered. "Must have really spooked him when he found out I hacked his files. Allegedly, of course. Not that I'd do such a thing."

Bratton laughed grimly. "All because of a jealous girlfriend."

Reynolds just looked more annoyed.

I didn't share his laughter. "I feel responsible for Carmen, at least. Bruce and Zalenski got themselves into it by choice." I turned away to collect my Droid and my emotions. "He'll probably try to pin the documents on me like he tried to frame Matthew for the train wreck. I can't let that happen."

"Then don't." Bratton laid a hand on my shoulder and steered me to face him before I jerked away. "He's out of the office until next Friday, right? We'll be busy with paperwork and protocol on this until he gets back. I'm sure a smart gal like yourself can find a way to fix things." He silenced Reynolds again and opened the door. "We'll be in touch."

The jangle of the bell over the front door still echoed when Matthew poked his head into the office. I straightened from my slouch on the desk and forced a smile. "Got any more flash drives? I keep giving mine away."

Later that afternoon in the computer lab, as I struggled to focus on my final Cisco review, Patrice appeared at my workstation. She dropped a master key and pass card on the desk.

"You're on second shift tomorrow night. Don't be late."

Not likely. I wanted to dive in immediately, but it had to wait. It was Zigana's birthday, the big six-oh. I'd made reservations at The Winds Café in Yellow Springs, an elegant establishment saved for special events because artisan organic is usually out of my price range. After the way we'd botched things with Sammy, I had offered to include him and Matthew in the outing. Zigana demurred.

"This is for us," she said. "We could both use a quiet night talking about something other than Tatum."

So that's what we did. Over the olive plate we reviewed the latest movie scheduled for The Little Art, debating whether to suffer through the subtitles. During the entrée, we argued amicably over the new Franzen blockbuster, and a spirited critique of the latest indie band playing at Peach's occupied us through an incredible mousse. We killed a bottle of high-class wine, and Zigana blushed when I said her homemade stuff was better. The sincere compliment and dinner had to stand as her birthday present. I was broke.

I waited until Zigana turned in for the night to open Tatum's database again. If I was getting into the network at school tomorrow, I wanted to be sure I knew what I was looking for, tags he used to ID client records, stuff like that. Even if I would be there semi-legally, my actions would push the limit. I needed to get in and out of his files as quickly as possible. I noticed a stray document in the last batch Carmen sent wasn't encrypted with the same key as Grechko's classified materials. I ran a basic cipher against it and broke the code in less time than it took me to dash through a wake-up shower so I could work a few more hours.

While not as shocking as the military documents, the file was just as confusing. It contained all the pages from the oil company notebook Jocelyn had found in her driveway. Tatum wasn't an oil man, but apparently one of the Café's owners was. Looked like he helped orchestrate the misinformation campaign to get fracking into Yellow

Springs. But that didn't explain how this file ended up in a lost notebook in the driveway of the chief activist against the drilling.

Or did it?

Patrice had access to the database files, too. Either she was in on the whole thing, which didn't seem likely considering Zigana's assessment, or Patrice swiped the document and planted it so Jocelyn and her group would know what they were up against. If that were the case, it had backfired, allowing the company to ridicule the notebook as a desperate attempt to discredit them in the press. The media played along, and the activists looked foolish. *Maybe she* was *in on the whole thing*. My head spun with the new subterfuge.

The shower hadn't helped my mental fogginess. Too much wine and good food combined with a string of restless nights left my thoughts in a whirl. I moved a copy of the clean file to my back-up drive and went to bed.

Zigana was still sleeping when I left for the bookstore Saturday morning, so I couldn't tell her about the notebook. I scribbled a note for her to call me when she had a break. The shop opened at ten, and with the Spring Fling sales lining the streets, she hoped for a busy day. It might be dinnertime before I'd hear from her, but since I was going straight from Matthew's to the computer lab evening shift, it was better to leave the tag at her end.

I made it to the bookstore as Matthew signed off for the UPS delivery.

"Sorry I'm late." I started opening boxes.

"Too much party for Zigana's birthday?"

"How'd you know about that? Sammy tell you?"

His hands stilled over the books he was sorting before he shoved a stack my way. "Yeah, Sammy told me."

"Where is he, anyway? I could use some coffee. Unless he's still mad at me."

The front bell jangled a few minutes later. Sammy appeared with a tray and four cups. Adam followed.

"You're not supposed to be here." Panic fought with pleasure when I saw him. I'd hoped he was safe in Florida, away from Tatum.

"Good morning to you, too," Adam said. He handed round the coffee and perched on the edge of the table to watch us work.

"How's your grandma?" Matthew asked. "And your mom."

"Gram came home from the hospital day before yesterday. She refused the rehab center, so a physical therapist is supposed to come to the house three times a week." He sipped the coffee and grimaced. "You really drink this flavored stuff?"

"Here." I handed him my cup. "This one's plain. I figured Sammy forgot my hazelnut."

"Did not," Sammy said.

Adam made a show of peering through the sip hole in the lid. "You didn't spit in it, did you?"

"I can if you like." I tasted my coffee, savoring the flavor he ridiculed. "I could ask you the same thing."

When the front bell jangled again, I searched for a spot to park my cup so I could attend to customers. Matthew waved me off. "Finish unpacking. I got this. Give me a hand, Sammy?"

They trailed off to the front of the store, leaving us alone. I stuck out my tongue at Matthew's back. "He's still matchmaking." I concentrated on sorting the stacks to avoid meeting Adam's eyes.

"I think he's done enough, don't you?"

Another gulp of coffee gave me an excuse not to answer. I searched for a better topic of conversation while marking off the inventory sheet.

"We never got to have dinner. What're you doing tonight?" he asked.

My heart sank. "I have to work."

"I thought Matthew closed up at five."

"I've got second shift at the computer lab."

He squinted in puzzlement. "The one you were fired from?"

Now I was puzzled. I knew we hadn't discussed the lab. "How much did Matthew tell you about me?"

"Just that you got fired because of hacking by a boss who asked you to do it. He said you were taking care of things." He grinned. "Are you?"

"It's a lot more complicated than that, and you don't need to know." Bruce's wrecked car flashed through my mind. "It's safer that way."

"You're worried about me? How sweet."

"It's not sweet." I stopped, flustered. "I'm serious, it's dangerous. I hoped you were in Florida where he couldn't connect you to me."

"He who?" My growing tension made an impact on Adam as his face reflected the worry I felt.

"It's a long story, and I have work to do, here and tonight." I handed him a stack of books, and he followed me down the aisle while I shelved them.

"So tomorrow? I'm only here through Monday morning."

I shoved another *Twilight* collection onto the teen shelf a little harder than necessary. "Back to...oh, that reminds me." I took the last half-dozen books from him and circled around to the self-help section. "I sent a package to you at your grandmother's. Don't open it."

"You sent me something I can't open." He dropped into the wingback chair next to the stacks so he was facing me while I arranged the books. "Should I wait for a midnight visitor in a trench coat to appear with the secret password?"

"This is serious," I repeated. I peered around the corner to see Matthew and Sammy in deep conversation with Georgio, the claustrophobic pawn-shop client. Dropping to one knee next to Adam's chair so I could slip a book onto the bottom shelf, I lowered my voice and said, "Trust me on this. I'll explain tomorrow." With any luck, the mess with Tatum would be out of my hands by then.

Adam leveraged himself out of the chair using my shoulder, then helped me up. "Tomorrow night then. I'll pick you up at six. You like Thai?"

———

Raymond was suitably confused when I showed up to relieve him in the lab at four, but he had his orders. I was in a generous mood, so I listened with quiet respect while he lectured me on computer protocol *I'd* written. When he started the tour of the office area, I cut him off.

"I can take it from here, thanks. Why don't you go on home?"

End-of-the-semester cram session students kept me busy all evening. I managed to enter a few preliminary lines of escape code to pave the way for my later incursions, but that was all. By eleven-thirty, only a handful of workstations were occupied. I was able to spend the last half-hour tapping the network from the admin account which got me past the student firewall. When I made it through Tatum's extra barriers, I sucked in my breath. He'd planted a string of code that made it look like the blackmail files were mine. My home IP address and my laptop name showed up in the user log. He was trying to frame me for whatever documents were in the database. At the very least, it provided him a plausible deniability of ownership, making it look like I framed him. *Damn him.*

I barely noticed the last students filtering out of the lab as I scurried to make screen prints, copy files, and wipe as much code as I could. I ran out of disk space, so I dug through the storeroom off the lab for a few of the one-gig flash drives the school gives to every student. I'd just finished dumping all the stuff that was time-stamped since my last incursion when I realized I wasn't alone in Tatum's online files, and the lab was empty.

I struggled to keep a few strokes ahead of whoever was out there. *Tatum.* I snuck a quick glance across the hall to be sure he wasn't in his office. It was dark. Must be logged in from Vegas, if he actually went there. I'd believed Patrice without question. *Should have checked.* Instead, it looked like I'd walked into a trap.

His reverse-attack coding could erase all the evidence I'd gathered to clear my name. The flash drive in the USB port had been wiped through his external access. I couldn't let that happen again. I pulled up my laptop and rerouted my network access through three proxy ghosts and a server hi-jack, adding a few lines of code to protect my external port. I launched another flash drive on the laptop and resumed copying files. He was fast, but I was faster, so far. I kept an eye on the blinking light from the flash drive at my wrist. It fluttered in pace with my heart rate. The download box onscreen showed 3.9 gig of 4.5 copied and safe.

Only a few more seconds.

I inhaled sharply as he executed a reboot command trying to force me off the system.

Not yet, you bastard.

I overrode his code, relieved I'd had time to configure that special admin account earlier. 4.2 gig...4.4... The download box flashed full, the USB light shown steady. I hit my escape key sequence to disconnect and the screen went blank. I pulled the flash drive with one hand and dropped it in my pocket while yanking cables free with the other before shoving the laptop into my backpack.

On my way out the door, I dropped a second flash drive onto the front counter. I was counting on Raymond's efficiency and the lab's lack of high-end security. When Raymond found the flash drive Monday morning, he'd plug it in to see who it belonged to. The auto-run BackTrack program I'd installed on the drive would wipe Tatum's private network and leave nothing to trace the shambles to me, linking instead back to the computer lab itself and scrambling some of the system files. I'd carried it as insurance, hoping I wouldn't need it.

Sorry, Raymond.

I took advantage of the security guard at the door and had him walk me to my car in case Tatum was around. It was late. He was bored. I smiled my thanks and we parted happy. I made sure to hold my Droid visible from the driver's window like I was talking to someone until I reached the parking lot next to the Dublin Pub. The place was packed as usual for a Saturday night, and I ended up in the back row adjacent to the apartment complex next door. Bratton and Reynolds pulled in across from me five minutes later as planned. Gave me time to copy the last flash drives.

Reynolds didn't argue this time. He held the front car door open for me with an exaggerated bow before moving to the backseat.

I shivered and pulled my coat tighter. "Don't you guys believe in heat?"

Bratton failed to hide a grin. He flipped the fan on high. "Well?"

I dropped a pair of flash drives into his outstretched hand. "I'm not so sure Tatum's in Vegas." As I told them about the network battle in the lab, Reynolds made a call.

"Did you physically see him anywhere?" Bratton asked.

"No, but it had to be him online." I pulled back. "Unless it was your guy?"

"No, not us."

Reynolds leaned back into the conversation. "He's in Vegas, on a noon flight home on the 14th, back in Dayton at six-fifteen. Left the convention floor an hour ago, stayed in his room for thirty minutes, alone, and went back to the show."

Tension eased out of my shoulders, knowing he was far away. For now.

"I'm out of it, right?" I asked. "You'll handle it from here?" I didn't mention the flash drive I'd left for Raymond. DHS had enough to nail Tatum in the files I'd provided and what they were able to find through other channels. Wiping his network would protect the school. Figured I owed the institution that much for taking me in. Might come in handy, too, if I had to negotiate for my degree after the story broke.

As for Patrice? I'd wait and see what DHS dug up before taking her on again. If she'd double-crossed me by telling Tatum I'd be in the network, Zigana's sixth-sense had produced an epic fail. Not likely, but any other answer eluded me for the moment.

Bratton and Reynolds left me with assurances Tatum would be brought in as soon as the data had been verified. His emails with Grechko were the link they needed to tie buyer and seller of the classified materials together.

"We'll give Dayton PD what we can, but don't be surprised if it's not enough to pin your friend's death on Tatum," Bratton said. "They have to meet a higher standard of proof than we do with national security issues on the line."

As much as I wanted Tatum to pay for killing Carmen, and Bruce and Zalenski for that matter, I knew McQueen and Haskins would have a hard time connecting him to the deaths. This was one time I wished common-sense justice prevailed over the letter of the law. *Sorry, Zigana.*

I met Matthew and Sammy inside the pub and drowned my disappointment in a Guinness. Or two. Matthew stayed sober enough to drive me home, Sammy following behind in the pickup.

———

The aroma of Zigana's cinnamon rolls broke through the haze of sleep mid-morning Sunday. I splashed water on my face, saving a shower for later before dinner with Adam, and joined her in the kitchen.

"You didn't call me yesterday," I said over a second cup of coffee and another homemade roll.

"I got sidetracked." She scrubbed the baking pan in a sink full of suds. "The shop was busy, wine had to be bottled, Hank took me to the movies. Was it important?"

"Hank? I thought you were done with him."

She shrugged, her back to me. "It was for my birthday. I could hardly say no."

"What about Sammy?"

Zigana straightened away from the sink but didn't turn around. "What about him?"

"I thought…." My words trailed off. For all I knew, Sammy's crush was one-sided. "You seemed so worried about him."

Drying the pan absorbed her attention for several minutes. I finished my coffee and waited.

When she finally sat down at the table, her expression was flushed, wary. "Why don't you tell me what happened yesterday at the lab?" She nibbled on a roll while I described the online scene with Tatum in the simplest terms I could think of, ending with the meeting with DHS.

I finished with, "He might never be charged with murder, but selling classified military secrets will lock him up for a long time." The idea didn't sit any better with me in the pale morning sunlight than it had the night before, but I had to live with it. My fatal errors set in motion a chain of events I had never imagined, and the consequences would haunt me forever.

"It doesn't matter," Zigana said. "We'll know why he's locked up." She took my hand. "Carmen will know."

Her soothing words eased the pain a little. I returned the favor by not mentioning Sammy again. When she was ready, we'd talk about him.

"Are you sure you can trust the Feds?" Zigana asked as she cleared the table. "It seems like you're opening yourself up to another double-cross."

"Not this time." I laid my burner phone on the counter and pressed the memo key. The recording wasn't as good as on the Droid, but Bratton's voice was recognizable.

"We don't care how you found the stuff. Anything in those files our guys will decipher eventually, so your name doesn't need to come up."

I sighed in relief. "He caught on to my recording him earlier, but he didn't know I had another phone on stand-by."

Zigana laughed. "That's my girl." She went off to open the shop with her worry eased.

Wish I shared her confidence.

I spent the rest of the day reviewing for my last two exams before graduation. Didn't seem possible, after an interrupted six years of trying, but I could see the finish line. I flipped through my desk calendar. Four weeks till graduation, then I could accept the job at Teradata. The prospect didn't excite me like it once had. Half an hour of yoga followed by a long, hot shower lifted my spirits. I refused to contemplate how much of my elation was due to Adam.

We were past the appetizers and through a round of drinks at Thai-9 in Dayton's Oregon District when the gently rising euphoria fled. I'd finished relating the Tatum and Patrice saga, skimming over Carmen's death as lightly as possible, when he dropped a bombshell.

"You're moving to Florida?" The empty sushi boat between us mocked me like the shipwreck of my life.

"Mom needs to be with Gram. She doesn't have anyone else. Frank's on the road three out of four weeks," Adam said, referring to his stepfather. "He doesn't care where home base is, so she's decided Florida's the answer. She hates the winters here anyway." He forced a laugh I couldn't share. "Don't we all."

"Florida." May as well have been on Mars.

He toyed with his fork, watching me from lowered eyes. "You could come with me."

"What?" I shook my head, trying to clear the muddle my thoughts had become. "Excuse me." The ladies' room was downstairs, across the room, and behind a set of hand-painted screens. High heels I wasn't used to wearing made the trip twice as long. I locked myself into a stall and leaned against the wall, trembling with a combination of anger, fear, and disappointment. I fingered the edge of my leather skirt, cursing myself for wearing it, for falling for him so fast, and pounded the wall behind me in frustration.

"You okay over there?" A disembodied voice floated in from the next stall.

I took a deep breath and pulled myself together. "Yeah, sorry." At the sink, I splashed cold water on my face and used a paper towel to wipe away the out-of-character make-up I'd applied so carefully when dinner with Adam had sounded like a good idea. I touched up my eyeliner, left the rest of my face bare, and returned to the table. No sense letting good food go to waste.

Adam tried, I'll give him that. Through the salads, which I hardly tasted, to the dessert tray I ignored, to the brandy-laced coffee, he laid out his reasoning why my moving to Florida was a good idea.

Lots of tech jobs in the defense industry because of the air base near his grandmother's.

Got that here in Dayton, I countered.

Great weather.

Also hurricanes, I pointed out. "Tornados with lots and lots of water."

He would be there, so we could get to know each other better. I stumbled on that one, since I'd hoped that's where this was going. Then he stumbled. Big time.

"You don't know what it's like," he said. "Mom needs me, like her mom needs her. And Dad won't miss me. He hasn't been around much since I was a kid. Kind of like you and Matthew. That's not a big deal since you just met him, right?"

My fingers itched to throw the dregs from my wine glass into the face I'd found so attractive at Peach's. "I don't know what it's like—having a mom who needs me, you mean? Giving birth does not a mother make."

He pulled back, eyes darting to the interested parties at neighboring tables trying hard to act like they weren't listening. "I didn't mean it like that. I'm sure you and Sigma are very close."

Butchering her name was the last straw. "Zigana. And 'close' doesn't begin to describe it." I stood up and yanked my coat off the adjacent chair. "I'll find my own way home."

Adam didn't follow me. Blind Bob's was only a few doors away, which was fortunate considering the weather and my ridiculous heels. I slid onto a stool and kicked off the offending shoes.

"Shot of Jameson, water back," I told the bartender. I downed the whiskey before the glass had time to leave a ring on the rough wood surface in front of me. After the burn subsided, I slipped back into my shoes and carried the water to an empty table away from the bandstand. I couldn't call Matthew for a ride. Adam was his buddy. At least his father was. The ice water chased the lingering alcohol from my mouth and chilled my anger.

"I thought that was you."

I spun around, on alert. The tall guy looming over my shoulder didn't look familiar.

He hung a polished ebony cane on an empty chair next to me. "Mind if I sit down? My knee's still pretty sore."

"Do I know you?"

"We missed you last night. Phil was disappointed you didn't make it."

Phil. The law review celebration. "Nick." Without the suit and crutches.

"Rick." He grinned. "But you seem to like Nick. I can live with it."

"Rick, right, sorry." I drained the water glass and pushed it away. "It's been a rough night."

"And you're drinking water? Braver man than I, Gunga Din. Sorry, guess that should be 'person'." He flagged down a server. "What can I get you?"

However I managed to get home, I sure wouldn't be driving. And he was right. Water wasn't enough. "Jameson, rocks."

"Make it two."

"I don't think I thanked you properly for the work you put in reviewing all those corporate documents," I said when the server was gone. "And I promised an explanation."

"Why don't you save it till Phil's here, too? He was pretty worried when you didn't show up."

"Last minute shift at work. I'm really sorry I missed the party, though."

"Come for dinner on the 29th. It's my last final for the semester, and he figured I needed a celebration, too. He's making his famous lasagna."

Phil's cooking was hard to turn down. "I'd like that."

"It'll be just a few of us. Phil and Marcella—he proposed Saturday, by the way. My partner, Jeremy." He pointed to a stocky redhead in a group clustered near the bandstand. "And you. Bring a date, if you want."

I grimaced at the thought. "Not likely, but I'll be there."

Drinks arrived as the band started its next set, so we sipped in silence rather than shout over the noise. At the lull between songs, I said, "I don't want to keep you from your friends."

"Not a problem. You look like you could use one yourself right now."

Such perception from someone I'd met twice unnerved me. I'd always prided myself on keeping my emotions in check. I nursed the Jameson and considered how the past few months had changed my response patterns. Until Patrice fired me, I'd thought I had life under control, knew where I was going, what the future held—at least as far ahead as I cared to consider. Maybe I'd been too cocky. Zigana always said it tempted fate if you became over-confident, too sure of having all the answers. Look at the big picture and consider consequences you can hardly imagine, she'd told me more than once. I seem to forget that gem of advice on a regular basis. I'd almost blown it with Sammy, pushed him into a bender because of my uninformed interference. And then there was Carmen.

I took a huge gulp of the whiskey and coughed hard. "S'ok," I said to Rick, who jumped up to thump my back and promptly winced at the pain in his bad leg. "Sit down, I'm fine."

My Droid buzzed. A text from Adam. I started to delete it, but "consider the consequences" echoed. I ignored the message. For now.

During the break, the redhead identified as Jeremy joined us. We shook hands, made small talk, and I fidgeted. Before the band started up again, Jeremy said, "We should be going."

"Any chance somebody in your group is headed toward Yellow Springs?" It was a long shot, but it was that or suck it up and call Matthew.

"Let's find out," Rick said. He led us over to them for more introductions. Everyone was headed west or south, nowhere near Yellow Springs.

I'd resigned myself to calling Matthew when Adam walked in. I spotted him right away, but it took him a minute to find me in the crowd.

"Everybody, this is Adam," I said when he edged into the group. No sense trying to remember names I'd already forgotten.

He gave a half-smile and a wave before pulling me aside. "We need to talk."

"I'm not so sure about that."

"Let me apologize, okay? I walked up and down the street looking for you. I've been to the Taproom, the Dublin Pub. This was my last stop."

Even in the bar's dim light I could see regret in his eyes, and I caved. "I need a ride home."

The walk to the car was quiet, but once he was behind the wheel, Adam talked nonstop.

About his misunderstanding.

"I called Matthew after you left. I didn't know your mom died. Shit. I figured she disappeared like Dad did when I was nine. I must have sounded like an insensitive jerk."

He did, but I let him ramble.

About his mother and Grams.

"It sounds like a bad melodrama, I know, but until Frank showed up when I was seventeen, I was the man of the family. Grams lived with us until she retired to Florida after Mom remarried. I feel responsible for them. A lot like you and Zigana."

About his father, and mine.

"After my folks split when I was little, Dad was around for a few years, taught me to ride a bike and stuff. When wife number two got her claws into him, he vanished. Other than an occasional phone call, usually a week after my birthday or whatever holiday was close, I never saw him again. He showed up, single, at my high school graduation and acted like he'd never been gone." Flashes from the streetlights lining US 35 revealed glimpses of a lingering pain. "Matthew was around more than Dad when I was growing up. He's the one who taught me to drive. Mom refused to get in the car with me behind the wheel."

"You haven't run over anyone yet." My first words since we left the bar made him smile.

"Yeah, well, it's early." He checked the time. "Really early. My flight's in four hours."

Mention of his imminent departure left a chill. "Can I return the favor and take you to the airport?" Anything to give us a few extra minutes to work this out.

"Don't you have to be in school?"

"Not until ten."

"I guilted Dad into getting out of bed to take me so I didn't have to use Uber at that hour. He'd appreciate the offer." Adam reached over to squeeze my hand. "I do, too."

He didn't let go, and I didn't complain.

"We should leave by quarter to five," Adam said as he dropped me off at home.

I managed to close my eyes for an hour even though I checked the clock every twenty minutes or so. Good thing no exams were scheduled for Monday. All I needed to do was drop my senior project off at my advisor's office.

On the ride to Dayton International Airport, I did all the talking, giving Adam the whole story about Tatum and Patrice, Carmen and Bruce. For once, I held nothing back, not my hacking, not my guilt. He had that effect on me.

"I won't be back until the end of the month, maybe late Thursday, early Friday, so I'll have the weekend here," Adam said while we waited at the ticket counter. "I'm driving Mom's van back for the rest of my stuff. Maybe we can have dinner, actually enjoy it this time?"

I told him about Phil and Rick's invitation. "I can't ditch them again. Would you maybe want to go with me?" His ready acceptance added another point in his favor. The disastrous comments at Thai 9 were almost forgotten.

As he moved into the security line, I surprised us both with an impulsive hug. "Remember, don't open that package. Stow it somewhere safe for now, and bring it when you come back, please." I watched until he was through the goofy full-body scanners and into the concourse before I left.

I treated myself to breakfast at Ohio Coffee before school. A quick stop at the print shop to pick up my senior capstone project, and for dessert, I relished the look on my advisor's face when I dropped the eighty-page document on his desk a full six hours before deadline. First time for everything. By noon I was back home in bed catching up on sleep as a reward.

For the rest of the week, I stayed as far away from the computer lab as I could and avoided Patrice's increasingly urgent phone calls. Her voice mail was proof my planted flash drive with the BackTrack software had done its job. Tatum's files were gone, and she was the one who had to tell him. What she didn't know was that if DHS didn't drag their feet, Tatum should step off the plane Thursday evening straight into custody.

But Friday was the last day I could access practice tests. I still had to graduate. I entered the tech building through a service entrance to avoid Patrice's office and made it to the computer lab without seeing her. I signed in while Raymond was occupied, slid into the least desirable workstation, behind a pillar but with a view of the hall, and went to work.

An hour into my review, all the coffee I'd had wanted out. I plopped my backpack on the chair to make sure no one disrupted my work and went down to the restroom. Patrice's office door was closed, as was Tatum's. His was dark. I took care of business, washed my hands, and when I opened the door to the hall, Patrice was waiting.

"My office, please." She didn't wait for an answer, all but dragging me inside and closing the door before moving behind the desk. "You've ignored my calls."

"I've been busy getting ready for finals."

Her lips thinned. "There was a…problem in the computer network on Sunday. I don't suppose you know anything about it."

"Really? This is the first time I've been in the lab all week." I breathed through the intense stare-down she hit me with and waited it out.

Patrice narrowed her eyes, breaking the locked gaze, as she sat down, hands folded tightly on the desk. She motioned to an empty chair.

I stayed standing. "Is there anything else? I have a practice—"

"About Carmen…"

Now she had my attention.

"It appears you were mistaken. According to the official report, Carmen's death was an unfortunate suicide."

I sucked in a breath, blindsided by her change of topic and tone. "Suicide? She was run down in broad daylight."

"Witnesses have reported she was depressed, what with all the commotion your misunderstanding caused. Not that anyone would blame you for what happened. I'm sure you meant well."

"You brought me here to insult me?" I clenched my fists to keep from throwing her commemorative granite-and-steel paperweight through the window. "What about Tatum? Bruce and your buddy Howie died, too."

"At least two people saw her step off the curb deliberately. As for Bruce," she faltered over the name. "Before the accident, I understand he gave the police a note Carmen left. They're investigating the possibility he committed suicide as well."

"Bullshit. *Witnesses* saw his car pushed onto the tracks."

Patrice drew in a breath. Her smile was taut. "Be that as it may, the official report will likely read suicide."

"Who told you all that? Tatum? He's lying. He should be locked up and you know it."

She ignored my comment and spun the trio of bracelets on her left arm, avoiding my gaze. Her movements released a waft of expensive perfume into the air. Reminded me of the sandalwood incense I avoided in the local head shop. I wrinkled my nose and realized she was doing that watch thing again.

"Dr. Tatum has explained the miscommunication he had with you, and he regrets it. That's why he didn't argue when I asked to bring you back on staff."

"Did he also tell you how he's selling classified military documents to who knows what rogue army? And how he tried to frame me for his dirty work?"

Her gasp told me I'd hit the mark. Her bracelets rattled louder as conflicting emotions chased across her face.

My mind raced through possible set-ups, discarding most of them. "What's this really about?"

"Classified…that can't be! Derek said…you've been wrong about so many things. He'll explain it all, I'm sure. Why don't you sit down and we'll discuss this like adults. I'll have Becky bring us some coffee." She punched the intercom button.

"I don't want coffee," I said. My sixth-sense added to the pounding in my head. *Leave, now.*

While Patrice talked to her secretary, she looked at her watch again—one too many times. Before she could stop me, I bolted out the door, her anxious voice trailing behind.

I charged into the computer lab, ready for a fight. My backpack was unzipped, the laptop missing. Raymond was at the counter, and he bore the full force of my fury.

"Dr. Tatum took your laptop a few minutes ago," he said, backing away from me. "He said you asked him to upgrade the software. I think he's in the storeroom."

"Call security, now."

Rather than pick up the phone, Raymond scurried out of the lab. The heavy door clicked shut behind him, leaving me alone. The storage room door in the back of the lab was ajar. I approached it silently, held my breath, and peeked around the jamb.

A single overhead fluorescent tube cast weird shadows on the discarded computer equipment stacked on the metal shelving lining the walls. Barely bigger than a closet, the room was filled with clunky CRT monitors, CPU boxes scavenged for parts, and the odd broken desk chair. A rickety worktable took up what little floor space was left. Tatum was bent over the table fidgeting with my laptop. He jumped when I shoved the door open wide.

"What the hell are you doing?" I stepped into the room and slammed the door closed. *No more games.*

Tatum backed away from the computer, and from me, his face showing a gratifying flash of panic before his pretty-boy blasé charm reemerged.

"Fatál, I didn't hear you come in. I,uh, took the liberty of updating your laptop with our new network configurations. Things have changed since you left us. So glad to have you back on board."

I scooped up the tiny screwdriver he'd dropped on the table when I came in and threw it at his feet. "You cracked the case. Why?"

For once Tatum seemed nonplussed. He edged toward the door, but I planted myself in front of it. I could see him sizing me up, wondering if he could take me. I straightened my shoulders and stretched my five-foot-nine to the limit, eyes locked on his. His raspy breathing echoed in the niches between the dead monitors.

When he looked away, I reached for the power button on the laptop. "Let's see what updates you installed."

"No!"

Tatum's vehemence startled me. I squinted at him, trying to read his mind. I slid the laptop across the table, never taking my eyes off him. When it got to the edge, a memory chip clattered to the floor.

He inhaled sharply. "That is, I don't have time for this now. I'm sure you have studying to do for finals." Beads of sweat peppered his forehead, his eyes shifted nervously.

I stared at him, more repulsed than usual as the scent of his fear filled the room. I couldn't prove it, but I knew he had orchestrated Carmen's death, knew he was behind the train wreck that killed Bruce and Zalenski, knew he had tried to frame me for his dirty work. With his cloak-and-dagger cybersecurity work for the military, what else was he capable of?

A too-long pent-up anger, simmering beneath my consciousness, found a focus. *No more games.*

I thrust the laptop at Tatum. "Turn it on."

He lashed out, trying to knock the computer out of my hands. Keeping it just out of his reach, I edged between the table and an old floor safe and backed him into a corner. The more I closed in, the more he shrank away, until he was wedged next to a jumble of hard drives and keyboards.

Enough.

Cracking the case. The memory chip. *What's he up to?* Instinct took over. In one fluid motion that would have made my old *sensei* proud, I punched the power button, threw the laptop at Tatum, and flipped the worktable on its side. The milliseconds it took for the circuitry to connect were just enough for me to squeeze between the metal table and the safe, head tucked under my arms, shielded from the explosion I somehow anticipated. His screams were lost in the reverb. Shards from the monitors rained down on us.

It took a few seconds for my head to clear enough to react. I crawled to the door and yanked it open, sucking in gulps of smoke-free air as I fell out into the lab. One more gasp and I dove back into the storeroom for Tatum. I dragged him into the lab and beat out his flaming clothes before security showed up. By that time, enough smoke and heat had escaped from the storeroom to set off the fire suppression system, and the guards hauled us both into the hallway. The ringing in my ears merged with the fire alarms, all mercifully muted by a residual numbness from the blast. I leaned against the wall, sliding into a nauseated heap on the floor as the impact of Tatum's booby-trap hit home.

He tried to kill me.

The last thing I remember was Patrice running down the hall toward us, her eyes wide in terror, before she crumpled to the floor next to Tatum.

Post Exploitation

"Determine the value of the machine compromised and maintain control of the machine for later use"

I woke up in the Miami Valley Hospital emergency room. Zigana hovered on one side of the bed, Matthew on the other. My forearms were swathed in bandages, fingers sticking out the end like spiny octopus legs.

Zigana said something. I saw her mouth move, but nothing registered.

"What did you say?" My voice was little more than a raspy sigh. Fire and smoke do that to a throat.

She leaned in closer. "I said, how are you feeling?" It sounded like a whisper at the end of a tin-can-telephone string.

I took an inventory of my body parts before croaking out an answer. "Hurts," was all I could manage. I lifted one arm a few inches and questioned Zigana with my eyes.

"Burns from putting out the fire on Tatum," she said.

"He owes you for saving his life." Matthew shuffled his feet and cleared his throat. "Should have let the bastard fry."

Zigana's glare silenced him. "Why don't you go tell Sammy she's awake?"

When he parted the curtains to leave, I caught a glimpse of a blue uniform standing guard.

"Police?"

"For Tatum," she said. "He's across the way."

I slipped in and out of consciousness, taking a sip of water after Zigana cajoled the nurse into allowing it, nodding at the doctor's questions when I could, letting Zigana answer when I couldn't. A round of x-rays, more needles than I could count taking more blood than I knew I had, another doctor or two. Eventually I ended up in a private room on a ward somewhere in the maze of the hospital.

It was dark outside when I finally woke up and stayed that way. I tried to sit up, groaning aloud at the effort. Matthew's worried face appeared at the edge of my vision. He adjusted the bed to a gentle incline and offered me a plastic cup. I pushed it away.

"Need to pee," I croaked, glad I hadn't been saddled with a catheter.

"You have to wait for the nurse." He pushed the call button.

"She'd better hurry." I ran swollen fingertips over my face, wincing at the light touch. The skin felt like a bad spring sunburn. My head throbbed. My arms were leaden and achy. "How bad am I?"

"Second degree burns on both arms, singed your face and hair a little."

"My hair?" I fingered the crispy edges. "Wonderful."

"Concussion, but mild, no internal injuries." Matthew leaned over the bed rail and hung his head. "Apparently, Tatum didn't know there was a security camera in that room. Recorded the whole thing. Police say you were lucky."

I didn't want to ask, but I had to know. "How's he doing?"

"All I know is what we overheard in the ER. They're not telling us a lot. Second and third degree burns to his face and arms, top half of his body is scorched pretty good. Probably has a concussion, too."

An aide arrived to help me into the bathroom and back, maneuvering an IV pole on the way. I eased back into bed and scrunched the pillows under my shoulders. Matthew tried to help. He meant well, but his nursing skills are lame. I accepted the water this time as much to make him feel useful as to soothe the sandpaper in my throat.

"Want some food? The doctor said you were allowed to eat when you woke up."

I shook my head ever so carefully. "Maybe later. What time is it, anyway?"

"Ten-thirty."

Almost twelve hours since my confrontation with Tatum. Matthew pulled his chair closer and took my hand. I tried not to cringe at the pain his light touch shot through my forearm. My hearing was coming back. Nighttime hospital noises filtered in, a chorus of beeps, coughs, and the occasional moan. The PA system chimed, asking Dr. Koothrappali to please call the nurses' station.

"Where's Zigana?" I asked.

"I sent her home."

"Sure you did."

Matthew chuckled. "Sammy helped. We convinced her she'd be more help to you during the day with doctors and tests and stuff. She'll be back in the morning."

"Is he here?" I craned my neck to peer into the darkened corners of the room.

"He's playing chauffeur."

Someone else who wanted to do something useful.

The nurse arrived for the never-ending temperature and blood pressure readings. After the numbers were duly recorded, she asked, "How's your pain, on a scale of one to ten?"

I compared my current aches to what I'd been through earlier in the day. "I don't know, maybe a six? I'm not dying."

"No, but you don't need to suffer, either. The doctor left orders if you need something." She checked the bandages on my arms for seepage. "Looks good. We'll change them in the morning. Don't wait too long to ask for meds." She wheeled her computerized record stand into the hall, leaving the door ajar.

"Nice cow," Matthew said.

I sputtered. "How rude."

"Not her. The computer thing. Computer on Wheels they call it, C-O-W, cow." He laughed. "I'm not that crass."

"I didn't think so." I laid back and tried to focus on the IV monitor for distraction. "But after the way things have turned out, I'm not so sure of myself anymore. Made a shitload of mistakes lately."

"Not so much as you'd think." Matthew leaned in between me and the monitor. "None of this is your fault."

"Yeah, whatever." I patted his hand with as much pressure as I could tolerate. "I don't suppose you'd go home if I told you to." His expression told me the answer to that. "Figures. Well, I'm going to sleep now, if that's okay." I carefully rolled over to face the wall, arms akimbo, and buried my tears in the pillow.

Minus the periodic temperature and BP visits, I slept through the night with only one call for pain medication. Exhaustion warded off all but the worst nightmares. By the time Zigana arrived, followed by the breakfast trays, my appetite returned. She had to feed me, which irked, but we only spilled a little orange juice and a few bits of scrambled egg. My throat was still raw, but coffee helped. I made another bathroom trip, this time without waiting for the nurse. Zigana hovered but let me go it alone. Couldn't manage a toothbrush though and had to settle for a swish of institutional mouthwash. The overpowering cinnamon scent chased away lingering traces of the fire and the worst of the hospital's antiseptic odor.

Mid-morning, Sammy trailed in behind the nurse. He took one look at the equipment on her tray, dumped a vase of flowers on the windowsill and left again, muttering something about putting change in the parking meter. Just as well. I hate anyone to see me cry and changing the bandages on my arms was unpleasant. Angry red burns darkened to black at the edges, warning of more pain to come as the wound peeled. Awful as it looked, they decided I didn't need advanced methods, just careful treatment. Two to three weeks, the doctor said, with fresh gauze and a saline flush twice a day after I was discharged. Zigana watched diligently as the nurse showed her how to clean the area without damaging new skin as it emerged like a phoenix from the ashes.

About the time the doctor was due to sign off on my release, I spiked a fever, which meant another 24-hour stay that stretched into 48 until antibiotics kicked in to fight the infection. Kept the police at bay, too. Even they couldn't buck medical protocol and invade my room.

"They'll be around tomorrow after we take you home," Zigana said as she left with Sammy. "Don't let anyone in tonight," she told Matthew, who'd already settled into his seat next to my bed.

"Yes, ma'am." He sketched a salute and grinned when she rolled her eyes.

Matthew's duties were light. No one invaded. My fever broke and I napped for a while. We played hearts, now that my fingers were freed from the worst of the bandages on my arms. It was slow, and I propped my cards on my knees rather than hold them, but I managed to beat him three out of four hands. By nine-thirty we were both yawning. It took a bit of guilt-play, but I convinced him not to spend the night in the chair.

"Go home, please. I won't sleep if you're here," I said. "You snore."

"It didn't bother you last night."

"I had drugs."

He laughed and patted my knee through the thin cotton blanket. "If that's what you want, I'll go. Call me if you need anything." He left my Droid on the nightstand within reach.

The flashing message light on my phone mocked me for an hour before I gave in. I fumbled with the tiny keys and managed to scroll through the accumulated text messages. Phil, TK, a few classmates. Apparently local media covered the explosion, but there were no updates to the online story and it was too early for the eleven o'clock news.

The last text was from Adam, "Just saying hi!" It was two days late, but I owed him a response. Now to figure out what to say. After a few minutes of mental debate, I settled for non-committal. Speech-to-text eased the strain on my singed fingers. *Hello! Hope Grams is well. Lots to tell you when you're back.* That way he couldn't say I didn't warn him. I shouldn't care about what he thought, shouldn't care about him much at all since he was moving fifteen hundred miles away, but I did. I took Zigana's wisdom to heart and considered the potential consequences of my foolish emotions until it was time for the news broadcast.

I dug out the remote from where it was lodged between the mattress and bedrail, wincing at the immediate finger pain, and turned on the television. The local CBS station carried the story right after a lengthy report on the weather—always a hot topic in southwest Ohio. Facts about the explosion were vague, lots of "allegedly" and "reportedly" thrown around. Somehow they ended up with my mug shot from five years ago. Tatum appeared on screen in a photo from the school's publicity department. By comparison, *I* looked like the criminal. I turned off the set and lay in the darkness for a long time.

A vague rustling woke me hours later, disoriented from unsettling dreams. I squinted at a figure sitting by the window, outside the pool of light filtering in from the hall.

"Thought I told you to go home, Matthew." Dry throat brought back the raspiness to my voice, and I reached for the water pitcher to refill my plastic cup. A hint of fragrance drifted in over the hospital's antiseptic. Water sloshed on my hand as I recognized the scent. Sandalwood.

Patrice moved into the dim light and stood staring down on me, arms crossed. She was wearing the same clothes I'd seen her in before passing out in the hallway at school two days earlier. Her usually meticulous hair was wild—like her eyes.

I groped for the call button on the remote.

"Don't," she said. "I just want to ask you a question."

Her pleading tone was low, shaky. I laid the remote down, but kept my hand on it. I had to clear my throat and swallow hard to get past the dryness. "What do you want?"

"Derek did this on purpose?" She didn't meet my wary gaze.

"Yes." I shifted into a sitting position to bring me to her eye level, take away the sense of physical disadvantage. With an embarrassing hospital gown, miles of bandages, and several bruises to overcome, I must have made a comical sight. Neither of us were laughing.

"He said he needed a few minutes to get some files off your laptop, that you were trying to make trouble for him. Someone named Chaz was threatening him about it." She wavered and caught herself on the bedrail. "I've never seen Derek frightened before."

"Charles Grechko threatened Tatum?" My brain buzzed. Another miscalculation on my part, if it was true.

"I tried to get him to explain, but he just kept saying he had to give Chaz access to some kind of off-shore account, or someone else would die. Howie trusted him, now he's gone. He told me to be careful, he couldn't stop him." She ran her hands up and down her arms, rattling those damn bracelets.

"Who couldn't stop who?" Between the pain meds and the concussion, I had trouble following her rambling.

Patrice took on a faint look of surprise as her eyes searched my face. She leaned over the rail. "You could stop him, couldn't you? Derek knows you're smart. That's why he made me fire you."

"Stop who, Patrice? Chaz? And why should I help Tatum?" Without breaking my gaze, I fumbled for the water cup and took a long sip. "I hear he's burned pretty bad from that little explosion he tried to kill me with."

"It wasn't his fault." She pulled away. Her hands gripped her upper arms, knuckles stark white in the relative darkness. Reality, what little there was of it, slipped from her eyes to be replaced by something I couldn't identify.

Something that frightened me. I'd pushed too far.

Consequences.

I scooted as far away from her as I could, covertly leaning on the call button at the same time.

"You have to stop him." Her voice sounded distant. "Derek and I take care of each other. He's all I have since Father died. I can't lose him, too."

"Did you need something?" The aide's voice, along with the glare from the workstation light she flipped on, shattered the tension.

Patrice started and stepped back, hands clenched at her sides. "I was just leaving. Could you bring her some water?"

The aide nodded and left with the pitcher.

Patrice locked eyes with me again for an instant. "You have to stop him." Her parting words echoed for what was left of the very long night.

I didn't mention Patrice's visit when Zigana arrived in the morning to take me home. Didn't say much of anything, other than to answer the endless medical questions and to ease her worries.

"I'm fine, really. Tired is all. Ready to go home." The smile I pasted on couldn't fool anyone, but she didn't push.

It was after noon before all the papers were signed, but the police were on the ball. They would interview me at home, graciously allowing me a few hours to get settled first—at Zigana's insistence. Back in the apartment, I refused her suggestion of a nap and prowled restlessly. I didn't want to be alone in my room.

"Where's my backpack?"

She brought it out of the closet. "Sit down and you can have it."

I sat.

My flash drives and papers were in the bag, apparently untouched. I thought for sure the police would have confiscated everything. Media reports notwithstanding, maybe I would be treated as the victim.

I missed my laptop. Fortunately, my capstone paper was already turned in, and I'd backed up my Lit papers after the critique session. I still had the last Cisco exam to pass. I'd need software to create a virtual machine for practice if I couldn't work at the school lab, but I doubt my old desktop could handle it. Growing obstacles between me and graduation overwhelmed. I pushed the backpack aside and curled into a ball on the loveseat. Zigana spread a quilt over me, and I slept.

Matthew and Sammy were there when she woke me up an hour later.

"I'm sorry, *chey*, but the police will be here in an hour."

The police. *DHS wouldn't like that one bit.* "Where's my phone?"

Sammy passed me the Droid from the side table. I found Bratton's number and worked my way through the automated receptionist and a live gatekeeper before he picked up.

"You're home?" he asked. I heard papers shuffling. "Damn, missed the message. Who's coming?"

I relayed the detectives' names Zigana gave me.

"We're on our way. Keep DHS out of it as much as you can until we get there."

Zigana charged Matthew with making coffee and sent Sammy down to Current Cuisine for sandwiches while she helped me change clothes. I'd come home from the hospital in sweats, not exactly proper attire for a police interrogation if I wanted to come across as credible. I managed to brush my teeth with only minor discomfort. My hair was another matter, tangled and charred. I leaned over the tub in Zigana's room and she scrubbed my head like she did when I was a kid, only more gently. The memory, and my beat-up emotions, brought me to tears. When she twisted a towel into a turban to dry my hair, I wrapped her in a hug as best I could with bandaged arms. As always, my tears led to hers. It's a family tradition.

We cried together for a few minutes, releasing the anguish and fear bottled inside. Eventually I caught sight of our reflection in the full-length mirror and the tears erupted into laughter. The towel had come loose from my head and hung down over one shoulder like a misplaced sarong. Splotches of dampness showed dark on Zigana's shirt, and her long hair escaped in messy tendrils from the ribbon she'd used to tie it back. My purple underwear glowed in the harsh fluorescent light.

"Good thing there's not a security camera in here," I said, wiping my eyes with the edge of the towel.

We made ourselves presentable and followed the scent of Matthew's coffee to the kitchen. As we ate, we talked about everything but the explosion. Book sales, Zigana's wine, the weather. As much as I dreaded the coming interview, it was a relief when the doorbell rang.

For a change, I relished the opportunity to be the victim, and I played my role to the hilt. I huddled on the loveseat, cocooned under my quilt, bandaged arms prominently displayed, and let Zigana handle the host duties. She made introductions and served coffee. Matthew sat next to me, the stalwart guardian. Sammy parked in the corner, out of range but within earshot.

The lead detective refused coffee, his professionalism barely masking his displeasure. "So, Ms. Wood, we have orders to wait for DHS to arrive before we begin. Could you tell us why that would be?"

Matthew stepped in. "Should her lawyer be here?"

"You have a lawyer?" He turned to his partner. "This gets better all the time."

Bratton and Reynolds' arrival rescued us. Our compact living room overflowed, and the ambient temperature wasn't the only heat rising. Sammy brought two chairs from the table and let the suits haggle over them. I hugged the quilt closer and watched to see who won the battle of the badges.

"Detective Garcia, could I speak with you in private?" Bratton led them into the kitchen for a whispered conversation. Lecture was more like it, since he didn't let the detectives do much talking.

Score one for the Feds.

I almost felt sorry for the local police. When they came back to the living room, Bratton and Reynolds took the armchairs and left the wooden dining chairs for the detectives. *Make that two for the Feds.*

Bratton continued his lead role. "Ms. Wood, you will answer the questions these officers put to you about what occurred on April 15th truthfully, completely, and to the best of your ability. If at any time classified information we've discussed previously is compromised, I'll call a halt. Is that clear?" His question took in all of us. At the group nod, reluctant as it was from the detectives, he added, "Detective Garcia, it's all yours."

The look Garcia shot Bratton telegraphed his opinion of the situation. He placed a pocket-sized digital recorder on the coffee table between us and pushed the button. "Ms. Wood, beginning with your arrival at the Gem City College computer lab on the morning of April 15th, would you *please* give us a rundown of what happened up to and including the explosion and fire?" His exaggerated emphasis on "please" brought a smirk to Reynolds' face. Bratton sat impassively.

I took a sip of coffee and studied the officers over the rim of my cup. How much to say, what to leave out.

"Monday morning, I arrived in the lab about eight, eight-thirty, to work on my test prep for finals. A while later, maybe ten o'clock, I took a break to go to the bathroom. I left my backpack with my laptop in it on my chair at the workstation to save my spot."

"You left your laptop unattended in a college classroom?" Garcia broke in.

I shrugged. "Happens all the time in the computer lab. There's an attendant at the counter, no one walks off with anything."

He scribbled a note on his pad. "Go on."

"On my way back, Patrice called me into her office."

"Patrice Gerrard, the department supervisor?"

"Right. She wanted to make sure there hadn't been any problems with my first shift back in the lab Saturday night after she rehired me."

"Why were you fired in the first place?"

Bratton intercepted Garcia's question. "Let's come back to that. Stick with what happened Friday for now."

Garcia glared, but motioned for me to continue.

"Anyway, we talked for maybe five minutes. When I got back to the lab, my laptop was gone. Raymond, the tech on duty, said Tatum— Dr. Tatum—took it to the storage room. I went to find him." I paused for another sip of coffee, annoyed to see my hand shake and hoped no one else noticed. "Somebody said you have a security tape of what happened. Do I have to go through it?"

"Please." This time Garcia's request was more cordial.

I took a deep breath. Matthew grabbed my hand and smiled encouragingly. "I asked Tatum what he was doing with my laptop, and he said something about updating the configuration files. Nobody updates my computer but me."

Garcia pulled back at the force in that statement, and I eased back into victim mode.

"I found a screwdriver he'd used to crack the case on the laptop, which didn't make sense because you don't do that for software updates. I asked him to turn it on and show me what he'd done. He refused. So I pushed the power button."

I couldn't help it, my voice quavered as the explosion flashed in my memory. Zigana's face was pale, tortured. Matthew squeezed my hand, and the pain brought me back. I swallowed.

"Anyway, the laptop exploded. There was fire everywhere, lots of printer paper and files in the room. I dragged Tatum into the lab, tried to beat out the flames on his clothes. That's about all I remember." I gingerly pulled my hand free and touched Matthew's knee in thanks. "I woke up in the hospital with a concussion." I held up my arms. "First- and second-degree burns, and here we are."

"Dr. Tatum is the chancellor of the college," Garcia said. "Why would he sabotage your laptop?"

"You'd have to ask him." My answer earned me the glare previously reserved for the Feds.

"Why do you *think* he sabotaged your laptop?"

I looked to Bratton. He nodded once, so I spoke carefully. "In the course of my duties as tech in the computer lab, I was asked to create a special database for Tatum, but I never added actual data. He, or Patrice, maybe, did all that. I later learned it contained files relating to illegal activities at an Internet café in Dayton. When he learned about my…special computer skills, he had Patrice fire me."

"Special skills. You mean hacking."

No way I was commenting on that.

"So, why did Gerrard—why do you *think* Gerrard brought you back on staff?" Garcia's careful language had Reynolds smirking again.

"I asked her to."

"Why?"

Trying not to raise suspicions by being too evasive was tough. "I heard rumor Tatum might be trying to frame me for something to do with that database. I wanted to find out, put a stop to it."

"By hacking the college computers."

"By accessing the system she was legally authorized to in her status as a lab tech," Bratton said.

Garcia scowled. "And after being ordered to fire you, Gerrard rehired you because you asked."

I shifted and pulled the quilt around my shoulders. Zigana pointed to my coffee cup. I nodded and passed it to her. Gave me time to think.

"I'd had conversations with Patrice about the fracking controversy here in town. She's on a committee to derail the drilling. I thought we'd learned to trust each other, that she didn't know what Tatum was really up to. I wanted to warn her so she didn't get mixed up in something illegal. I *thought* she rehired me because she believed me and wanted to help." I burrowed deeper into the quilt and hung my head. "Now I'm not so sure."

"What makes you say that?" Garcia asked.

Zigana's mantel clock ticked loudly while everyone waited for me to answer. Waves of exhaustion swept over me, and I struggled to ward them off. For some reason, Patrice's double-cross—her second, I realized—stung more than Tatum's. I threw the quilt aside and gulped the coffee, scalding my mouth and clearing my head.

"She called me into her office to give Tatum time to plant the explosive."

The detectives exchanged looks. "Do you have any proof of that?"

I grabbed Matthew's hand again and locked eyes with Zigana. "She came to the hospital last night and told me."

Zigana's frightened gasp hurt as much as the vise grip Matthew planted on my hand.

A weak apologetic smile to them both. "She claimed she didn't know what he was really up to. She was…confused, almost deranged, or something. I don't know. Kept talking about off-shore accounts, saying Tatum was scared."

"Of whom?" Bratton asked.

I shot a sideways look at him. "I'm not sure."

"Did anyone else see her?" He had a notepad out now, too.

"An aide came in, but I don't think she heard what Patrice said." I slumped back and closed my eyes.

"Isn't that enough for now? She needs to rest." Zigana to the rescue.

Garcia turned off the recorder. "We'll need to have this signed after it's transcribed." He looked to Bratton. "I assume you have the computer files in question?" Bratton nodded. "Then we'll finish this up when the statement's ready."

Everyone stood up but me. Goodbyes and future scheduling whirled by in a blur as I huddled on the loveseat. When it was quiet, Zigana led me upstairs to bed. I didn't argue this time.

It was dark when I woke up. I found Matthew engrossed in an old Sean Connery James Bond movie, and Sammy snoring in the armchair.

Zigana came up from the basement with a batch of wine bottles as I tried to rummage through the refrigerator.

"There's a casserole in the oven," she said. She unloaded the bottles onto the counter. "Let me get it for you."

"You need to stop waiting on me." I gave her a gentle hug and stifled a wince at the pain that shot through my arm. "After you change these damn bandages."

"We probably should eat first, or we'll lose our appetites."

Matthew shook Sammy awake, and we gathered around the table. Zigana poured two glasses of wine and two of lemonade. "No alcohol for you till you're off those meds." We demolished the enchilada casserole with very little talking, scraping up the remnants with warm slices of *pan pueblo*. I filled them in on Patrice's mystery man, Chaz, while we ate. When that opened up a whole new rabbit hole for us to needlessly get lost in, I switched topics.

"You guys have been here all day?" I asked Matthew. "Who's minding the store?"

"We're on vacation," he said. "Family comes before business."

"And you?" I directed my question to Zigana.

She shrugged. "Nora can handle the shop alone this time of year, and there's nothing wrong with closing for a few days when she's not available. Like he said, family."

I pushed away from the table, careful not to aggravate my burns. "Enough. I'm on my feet, more or less. Tatum's out of commission. The Feds are after whoever...did this." My arms flailed. "Did they ever explain why they didn't pick up Tatum at the airport like Bratton said they would?"

Matthew snorted. "All I got was there was a mix-up in when his plane landed, and they missed him."

"Wonderful." I gathered the plates and nudged on the faucet with my elbow to rinse them.

"What about Patrice, and this Chaz guy?" Matthew asked.

I dropped a handful of silver into the sink with a clatter and let the water run longer than it needed to. "I don't know."

"The detectives said they'd bring her in for questioning," Zigana said.

"Not until they've confirmed Fatál's story." Matthew brought the empty casserole to the sink.

"So until we figure out what she's up to, you've got a round-the-clock companion." Special Ops Sammy joined the discussion. "School, work, here at night—if that's okay with you?" he asked Zigana.

"There's a futon mattress in the basement, if you can make do with that. The loveseat's awfully short," she said.

"Oh, sure ask her for permission," I groused. "What about me? I don't need a bodyguard."

"Yes, you do," they said in unison.

Three against one. It was pointless to disagree.

I gave in to Zigana's TLC and let her pamper me. It was good for both of us. I slept, I lounged, I watched old movies. When I tried to study for finals, Zigana took away my books.

"Not yet," she said. "When you can stay upright and awake for more than an hour at a time, you can have them back."

No matter how much I railed at being incapacitated, my body had other ideas. After I stopped taking the pain meds that knocked me out, muscles I'd ignored for too long got angry—painfully so. My hearing returned fully, eventually, but an annoying, sporadic ringing in my ears hung around. The concussion spawned a migraine the likes of which I hadn't experienced in years, and I lost two full days.

Our usually roomy apartment got very crowded that week. Sammy slept on the futon in the living room every night and spent the days watching old movies with me or reading Raymond Chandler. Matthew and Zigana kept their respective shops open on reduced hours, and we all spent evenings playing cards.

By Friday, I'd met Zigana's prerequisite of sleeping versus waking hours, and she returned my textbooks so I could study.

By Sunday I was climbing the walls.

When Zigana gathered the supplies to change my bandages after dinner, Matthew and Sammy retreated to the living room. She peeled off the gauze, apologizing with each congealed thread. I tried to avoid looking at my wounds, but it's like a pile-up on the highway. Hard to resist rubbernecking.

"I have an exam tomorrow at ten," I said through clenched teeth.

"No, you don't." Zigana ran the saline flush over the burns. "I talked to your advisor. You have an appointment in his office Friday at nine to pick up the paperwork for your professors and then finish your exams."

"But my laptop is toast. I still need to get to the computer lab for practice tests and stuff."

She patted my left arm dry and started on the right. "Sammy is your chauffeur until further notice. He'll take you to your follow-up with the doctor tomorrow, and once they release you, you can go back to school."

I grudgingly agreed, but balked when Zigana insisted Sammy drive her sedan instead of the Fiero.

"My car's in decent shape," I said. "Why should you give up yours?"

"He's six-three and has to fold himself in half to get into that thing you call a car," Matthew said. I was outnumbered again.

"Can we go shopping after the doc, Sammy?" I called through the doorway. "I think I have enough on my Visa for a cheapo laptop."

He exchanged glances with Matthew, who pulled a Dell computer box out from behind the armchair and laid it on the counter between the rooms.

"I hope it's the right kind," he said. "TK helped pick it out. He said to let him know if you need any more software. Consider it an early graduation present from all of us."

I couldn't hug anyone until Zigana finished wrapping my arms. I made up for the delay.

The medical release came through Monday morning, and after brunch with Sammy at the Sunrise Café down the block, I spent the day configuring the new laptop. TK knew his stuff, and knew what I liked in computing power. The latest Alienware model from Dell made my old machine look like an overclocked 286.

Bratton called Tuesday morning. Tatum was still hospitalized under police guard, Patrice had been cleared of any charges, and they were hunting for Grechko, federal warrant in hand. Since all the characters were accounted for—or being pursued, Sammy removed the tracking units from the cars. After dinner, he and Matthew hauled the futon mattress back to the basement and went home. Zigana and I shared a glass of wine to celebrate the return of silence to our little world before turning in.

Because more than a couple of hours upright siphoned all my energy, I slept through most afternoons. It took the next few days to finish restoring all my document files to the laptop. I managed to finish my Lit paper Thursday evening while Sammy and Zigana haggled over a cribbage game and Matthew dozed on the loveseat. Zigana accepted the encroachment of technology by my temporary workstation at the kitchen table with a gentle sigh.

As I fumbled through my nightly bathroom routine with stiff but healing limbs, my Droid buzzed with a text from Adam. *At Dad's. Need sleep. Call you later.* The prospect chased the nightmares that had dogged me since the explosion, and I slept peacefully until the alarm sounded at seven.

When we got to school Friday morning, Sammy parked in the handicap zone outside the main entrance.

"We'll pay the ticket," he said. He hoisted my backpack onto his shoulder and held the door. "Let's go."

My advisor made all the appropriate social niceties over my injuries. He wasn't sure what to make of Sammy, who I simply introduced as a friend. The vagueness kept him from fishing for details of the explosion, though.

"Well, Fatál, I have good news and bad news," my advisor said.

I cringed. After all my efforts, they weren't going to let me graduate. My senior project had been rejected. Something. "I can't take any more bad news right now."

"Okay, then the good news: You'll be graduating, with honors. Final exams are a formality at this point." He all but preened, obviously enjoying the upper hand. "And I hope you don't mind, but I shared your capstone paper with a friend of mine—with your name redacted, don't worry. He's on the editorial board at *Wired* magazine, and he was quite impressed. They'd like to use your piece as a feature article in a special issue they're doing on forensics in the fall."

Sammy grinned and patted my shoulder. "Congratulations, Missy."

For once I didn't know what to say. "Thank you," was all I could manage.

My advisor enjoyed our reactions for a moment before his eyes clouded. "Now the bad news. My contact at Teradata called. In light of the recent...incident, they've withdrawn the job offer. He hoped you'd understand."

"Of course he did." My elation evaporated in a hurry. An honors degree with no job wouldn't pay the bills.

We finished all the paperwork to allow me to test out late, although my signature was even less legible than usual because of the burns. As we mimed a handshake over my gauze-covered arm to end the meeting, he said, "I've already forwarded your resume to a number of other recruiters. With your talents, I'm sure something will turn up."

"Sure. Thanks again for the *Wired* thing."

Sammy and I made the rounds to complete my requirements. The Lit final was proctored in the library by a grad assistant. I don't remember what I wrote, but thankfully they let me use a computer rather than the prof's preferred Blue Books. Typing was hard enough. I couldn't have survived two hours of handwriting.

We had an hour to kill before my Cisco exam, so I bought Sammy a late lunch in the cafeteria while we waited. Funny how most of the students avoided our table. A few let their curiosity overcome hesitation, but they left disappointed when I deflected questions about Tatum.

Our last stop was the computer lab. Raymond's nervousness had him stuttering as he signed me in for the Cisco test, front and center workstation again. Sammy sat at the desk next to me to surf the 'net and keep an eye out for Patrice. She never appeared. After another two hours of testing, my final score was eighty-two percent, just enough to earn a passing mark. I was now a college graduate, a Cisco Certified Internet Engineer with Security credentials—and unemployed.

To cap off the day, the handicap ticket on the windshield when we got back to the car would cost me a hundred and fifty bucks, and I refused to let Sammy—or Matthew—pay it. It was a quiet ride home.

I managed to squeeze in an hour nap before dinner at Phil's. I didn't want to pull Zigana away from the shop any longer than it took to change the bandages, so I managed to wash up and dress on my own. Adam arrived at five-thirty. I gave him the nickel version of why I looked like the Mummy, and once the shock wore off, he hugged me carefully.

"I'm glad you're okay." He handed me the packaged hard drive I'd mailed to him in Florida.

It took me a second to realize what it was. "Yikes—forgot all about that. You don't want to know what it is." I locked the package in Zigana's office safe until I could hand it off to Bratton.

Lots of celebration was in order, so we stopped at the Wine Cellar to pick up a couple of bottles of champagne before leaving Yellow Springs. No more Tatum worries. Phil's law review publication and engagement to Marcella. Rick surviving his first year of law school. *Wired* magazine and my CCIE-Security. Adam's new job.

He refused to let me dwell on my lack of employment. "There's always Florida," he said, dodging my half-hearted swat at his shoulder.

Adam understood now why I could never leave Zigana. We'd reached a comfortable relationship level I'd never experienced with any of the men who'd passed through my life, few as that number may be. The thought of putting fifteen hundred miles between us in the next week was too unsettling to contemplate. So I didn't.

Phil's lasagna lived up to its legendary status. Combined with the champagne and a few more bottles of wine, the evening flowed by in a haze of camaraderie and laughter. *Maybe Matthew was right. I should get out more.* I half-listened to Phil's new fiancée Marcella gush about their wedding plans and tried not to stare at Adam. He leaned on the mantel debating common law with Phil, Rick, and Jeremy. The male-female division was annoying. He was holding his own in a complicated theoretical discussion while I was stuck with color palettes and floral arranging.

In the middle of late-night dessert, Adam excused himself to take a phone call. He was back in an instant, leaning over Phil to whisper something. Phil jumped up and produced a notepad and pen.

Adam scrawled a note and pocketed his phone. "We need to go." He held out the shawl Zigana had insisted I use instead of a jacket over the bandages. "There's been an accident."

I froze. "Zigana."

The sympathy on his face was my answer. "Matthew's on his way to Southview Hospital. We'll meet him there."

In the fifteen minutes it took to get from Phil's apartment to the medical center in Centerville, I imagined every gruesome scenario possible. Zigana was right. The mind can create more horror than reality could ever produce.

"It was a car crash, that's all I know," Adam said.

Sammy met us in the lobby, anguish emanating from him like a cloud.

"I only went home to take a shower," he said. "I didn't know she was meeting Matthew."

"Matthew? Where is he? Are they okay?" Confusion threw me into further panic. "Were they both in the car?"

"I'm right here." Matthew grabbed me from behind. "Come on, she's back here, giving the doctors hell."

As soon as we passed through the double doors separating the lobby from the treatment rooms, I heard Zigana and relaxed a bit. If she was that vocal, she was fine. Out-of-the-ordinary swearing made me grin.

"Get this damn IV out of my arm now, before I yank it out myself. All I did was bump my head."

Matthew pulled open the curtain to reveal an angry Zigana facing down a determined nurse.

"'Gana, calm down. There are sick people here." I edged around the beeping monitor to give her a hug. "What happened?"

The nurse took advantage of our presence to slip out, leaving the IV in place. Zigana flopped back on the gurney and scowled.

"Somebody ran me off the road."

"Patrice?" I turned to Matthew for confirmation.

"I wasn't there," he said.

"No, some guy in a goofy Cossack hat driving a big-ass Hummer," Zigana said. "I'm afraid your car's totaled."

"You were in the Fiero?"

"I had her car," Sammy said.

A light dawned. "He thought it was me."

"I'm glad it wasn't. You've been through enough." She closed her eyes and sighed. "I didn't see him coming until it was too late."

The nurse returned. "There's a police officer here."

"We'll go talk to Adam." Matthew touched Zigana's foot in farewell and followed Sammy out.

The intimate gesture reminded me of Sammy's comment. "You had a date with Matthew?"

Zigana's eyes stayed closed, but her breathing shifted. "What makes you think that?"

An Ohio State Patrol officer derailed the conversation. I mulled her non-response while she answered his routine questions.

"Registration and insurance information on the car?"

She pointed to me.

"It's in the glove box." It was the first time he'd looked directly at me, and I saw the double-take. Apparently he watched local news. "If you don't need me, I have to make a phone call."

He nodded uncertainly, and Zigana waved me out. I returned to the lobby and called first Detective Garcia, then Bratton. Since it was eleven-thirty on a Friday, I had to leave messages for both. "It's urgent," I told the DHS desk. "They told me to call if anything happened." They hadn't, not exactly, but then neither of them had thought Patrice's ranting held a real threat.

The OSP officer cornered me in the hall outside Zigana's cubicle. "She says this is related to the explosion at the school downtown. Is that true?"

"Probably." I gave him the numbers for Garcia and Bratton, hoping he'd have better luck. "They can explain everything." I passed the nurse as he carried the IV equipment away. Zigana had won that round.

"How come your car didn't have an airbag?" she asked when I sat down next to her. "The officer said I was lucky I didn't go through the windshield."

I shuddered at the thought. "You *were* lucky. None of the Fieros have airbags. They weren't standard equipment in the eighties."

"All this time you've been driving a deathtrap." Like me, Zigana preferred to worry about others.

"It's one of the safest small cars on the road, and you survived. Look, can we talk about something else?" I massaged my forehead, trying to ease a fast-emerging headache. "What did the doctor say? Have you had x-rays yet?"

"X-rays, blood work, they wanted to do a CT-scan. I told them it wasn't necessary, and that if they insisted, I wouldn't pay for it."

I forced myself to speak more calmly. "Tell me what happened."

Zigana heaved an exaggerated sigh. "For the umpteenth time, I was coming off the exit ramp from I-675 onto 725, headed for…the Dayton Mall. I have no idea how long he'd been following me. I was probably down to twenty miles an hour when he barreled up behind me. I saw him swerve out and then jerk the wheel back—laughing, if you can believe it!—and clipped my back bumper. I hit the guardrail." She fingered the knot under her scalp. "And my head. At least the seatbelt worked." The querulous tone was back. "When can I get out of here? I have no idea how you put up with all this medical nonsense for two days."

I brushed her hair back and frowned at the discolored bump. "Let me see if I can find the doctor. Don't beat up on anyone else while I'm gone."

They turned her loose two hours later AMA—against medical advice. No way she'd stay unless they tied her to the bed. Sammy drove us in Zigana's car, Matthew following in the pick-up.

I sent Adam home. "You've had what, four hours sleep in two days? I'll call you."

The kiss he planted on my forehead did more for my headache than any massage.

After I put Zigana to bed, her protests losing steam as the accident caught up with her, I curled up in her club chair in the living room. Matthew handed me a mug of coffee. Should have known it would include Jameson. I didn't complain.

"Garcia called. They found the stolen Hummer in the parking lot at the Dayton Mall. Not a lot of damage, given the vehicle's size difference, but there's red paint on the bumper," Matthew said. "No prints but the owner's, and he has an alibi."

I nursed the coffee and my thoughts in silence until the mug was empty. After refilling the mugs, I turned to face Matthew and Sammy. "This has got to stop."

The remaining hours until daylight were split between arguing and planning, with occasional checks on Zigana like I'd promised the hospital. She slept through our muted wrangling. Special Ops Sammy faded in and out of the discussion. The instability was disconcerting, but it was nice to know his talents appeared when needed. It took two hours to track down Patrice and another thirty minutes of wheedling to convince her to cooperate.

By noon, it was time to act. I logged into Tatum's email, found Grechko's account, and sent a terse message with Patrice as the signatory. *Seven o'clock tonight. Lookout Point, Woodland Cemetery. I have the account numbers. No BCC.*

Matthew drove back to Dayton for a nap and to find Adam. Sammy crashed on the futon mattress on the living room floor again, and I tossed and turned in bed until I heard Zigana stirring. I steeled myself for her reaction to our plan. It was worse than I expected, woke Sammy from his snoring, but in the end, she admitted it made sense, in a karmic sort of way.

Darkness shrouded the gazebo at Woodland Cemetery's Lookout Point when Patrice pulled up at six forty-five. I'd been there plenty early, visited Harmony's grave for inspiration before settling in to wait. The lone nearby streetlight cast eerie shadows over the mausoleum plaques ringing the walls. Zigana would've hated the surroundings as much as Patrice appeared to when she climbed out of the car. We had fifteen minutes, maybe less, to review things before Grechko showed up—if he took the bait. Twelve minutes later, as Patrice wavered between playing along and bolting, a second car drove in.

A man I assumed was Grechko got out and hovered next to the vehicle, checking the area for intruders, maybe for ghosts. Patrice nodded in confirmation of my silent question about his identity. I grabbed her wrist for a moment to keep her from running, took a deep breath, and waited.

We stood alone at the highest point in Dayton, far enough above the cityscape to see the Miami River glistening in the distance. The cold, clear sky held only a sliver of silver moon. Patrice stepped forward into the pool of light while I stayed in the shadows as planned. Let him come to us.

He was a short, stocky man in a dark trench coat that nearly brushed the ground. The furry hat Zigana mentioned added to his Genghis-like appearance. His footsteps echoed off the surrounding concrete as he climbed the steps slowly, watching Patrice, wary. He stopped when he reached the gazebo landing.

"Interesting choice of locations," he said. Then he spotted me. "You must be the hacker bitch." Hands stuffed into the pockets of his coat left bulges that I hoped didn't conceal a handgun.

We faced each other for a long minute, sizing up the opposition. The words I'd rehearsed all afternoon stuck in my throat. Something told me to wait.

I waited.

He strolled to the benches encircling the gazebo and sat down. "So why did you bring me here? I certainly hope you have the numbers I want or scorched arms will be the least of your concerns." His laugh was ugly. "Think you're so smart, all your hacking shit."

I waited.

"Stupid bitch. Nosing around where you didn't belong." Grechko thrust his chin up. "Tatum said he'd fire you and you'd leave us alone. What a fool. The girl and the bus? That was your fault, you know, her and that idiot boyfriend. Couldn't even finish you off like I told them to."

A damp breeze rustled through the budding trees carrying a scent of cherry blossoms and setting the memorial flames fluttering.

I waited.

"What kind of game are you playing?" Tension in his voice ratcheted up a notch. "We're going to sit here in the cold staring at each other?" He snapped to his feet and strode closer. "Give me the account numbers and *maybe* I'll let you walk away. It's my money. I won't let Tatum hold out on me anymore."

"Derek's dead."

Patrice's words shocked me as much as they did Grechko, but he recovered with a laugh that chilled me more than the frigid wind.

"Good. One less loose end I need to take care of." He leered at her. "Now that he's out of the way, you can help spend all that money. There's a private jet waiting for me at the airport. We can get to know each other better on the way to Argentina."

"I'll see you in hell first," she said.

Grechko stiffened and turned back to me. "Enough of this shit." The bulge in his coat pocket revealed a wicked-looking handgun. He waved me over next to Patrice and pointed the gun at her. "Give me the account numbers or I add another dead body or two to the list. I don't care so much, but I'm betting you do."

No more waiting.

I tossed a flash drive onto the concrete between us, into the center of the diffused beam from one of the spotlights. Grechko stepped forward and bent down to pick it up, eyes and gun fixed on us both.

"See now, was that so hard?" he asked.

Without a sound, Sammy dropped out of the rafters where he'd secreted himself earlier and tackled Grechko before he could straighten up. I watched helplessly, bandaged arms keeping me from the struggle. Best I could do was kick away the gun Grechko lost when Sammy landed on him and hit the panic button in my pocket. Red lights and sirens erupted from three different spots in the surrounding cemetery, converging on the gazebo while Sammy wrestled with the out-matched Grechko. Time did that weird shift where seconds seemed like hours before Garcia, Bratton, and a slew of uniforms arrived to take a battered and bruised Grechko into custody. Special Ops Sammy *might* have gotten in a few more punches than necessary to subdue him.

After they hauled Grechko away, Sammy pulled down the night vision security camera mounted on the post overhead. He handed it to Bratton and turned to me where I huddled on the cold concrete. Fear and adrenaline combined to produce tremors that had sent me to my knees. Sammy lifted me up, careful to avoid my injured forearms.

"You okay?"

When I nodded, I saw Special Ops Sammy slip away, his eyes morphing from sharp and hard to a vague disorientation.

"You done good, Missy," our old Sammy said.

"So did you."

After a short debrief with Bratton, he sent us all home. He had enough to do booking Grechko at the moment, and agreed to conduct what would likely be the first of many police interviews for each of us the next day. He was more interested in Grechko anyway, and the local police would follow his orders.

Matthew arrived with Adam and played the father card, insisting on driving me home in the sedan. Adam drove Patrice in her car since she was in no shape to handle it herself. Sammy followed along in the pickup and made sure Adam got home. We detoured past Harmony's grave so I could say thanks. As we left the cemetery grounds, I called Zigana.

"It's over."

Reporting

"Communicate the objectives, methods, and results of the testing conducted"

An endless round of police interviews filled Sunday as we justified our scheme first to the local police, then to DHS. I'd given them enough information to bring them to the cemetery without explaining what we were up to, and more than a few egos were bruised. My attorney and a few of his partners earned a hefty fee before all the legalities were satisfied, but we pooled our funds, juggled a few things – as much as I hated seeing family funds depleted because of me. Eventually we were vindicated.

I didn't know it at the time, but Patrice hadn't lied about Tatum. I'm still surprised how much his death unsettled me. Too many people had died – Carmen, Bruce, Zalenski, now Tatum. How could I *not* blame myself? Even though Grechko was directly responsible, I'd set it all in motion and earned myself a slew of sleepless nights.

Patrice had come straight from the hospital to the cemetery, told me later that losing Tatum gave her the strength to confront Grechko. It was the last time I saw her. I heard she left town as soon as the police declined to press charges, accepting that she'd been a clueless pawn. When the news frenzy died down, the school offered me her old job.

I declined.

Saying goodbye to Adam Monday morning was as difficult as facing down Grechko, but in a different way.

"You could still come with me, you know." He stroked the ragged fringe of singed hair that curled around my ear. "But I understand why you won't."

Problem was, I knew he did. Zigana understood, too, and was very quiet for the rest of the day. Over dinner, she asked the question neither of us wanted to face.

"Am I holding you back?"

"No," I said, too quickly, I knew, when disbelief flared in her eyes. "And yes, but it's my choice. I like Adam, sure. But I don't like Florida. Remember when the band went to Orlando my junior year? Hated every minute of it."

"Not all of Florida is like Orlando." She toyed with her food. "And Adam's not in Orlando."

I gave up pretending to eat and concentrated on the wine. "Neither are you, and your special vintage. How would I survive?"

Her smile was a ghost of its usual brilliance. "I know what it's like to lose someone you love. I keep thinking about what Patrice must be going through, and I don't want you to feel that way."

I owed her honesty. "I don't love Adam, not yet anyway. If that happens, someday, we'll have this discussion again. Until then, you're stuck with me." I wanted to ask about her and Matthew, and Sammy, and Hank, but a lingering sadness in her eyes held me back.

On Tuesday, Zigana and I took a picnic lunch to the Glen to visit Carmen. I dug the computer drives out of the cleft of rock where I'd stashed them, surprised to see they'd survived intact for so many weeks. Eventually, I'd return them to the Feds with the one Adam had brought back from Florida, but I wasn't sure how Bratton would react. Zigana tried to act disapproving when I told her about my midnight raid to hide them away, but a grin slipped out. I took advantage of her good mood to broach the subject we'd avoided.

"So, what's with you and Matthew?"

Even in the coolness of the forest, she flushed. "I don't know what you mean."

"The night you totaled my car," I nudged her. "Sammy said you had a date. With Matthew?"

"Sammy wouldn't know a date if it hit him in the head."

"Okay then, I remember Matthew telling me *Sammy* had a crush on you. Sure seemed like you guys were getting along pretty well at Peach's."

She wadded up her sandwich wrapper and threw it at me. "Next thing you know you'll have me hooked up with the mailman."

"Nah, he's too young for you. And you don't like dreds. What about Hank?"

"Knock it off." Zigana stood up and brushed the dirt from her backside. "Let's go home."

"You're not going to answer me."

"Nope."

And she didn't.

Until Sunday after the graduation ceremony at the Schuster Center. Matthew drove us to the shelter house at John Bryan State Park where I thought we were having a simple cook-out with the three of us and Sammy. Instead, the place was packed with guests. TK and his girl, Phil and Marcella, Rick and Jeremy, half-a-dozen friends from school, a few neighbors, even my advisor and a professor or two. Balloons floated from the picnic tables and streamers fluttered in the breeze. More food than twice as many of us could eat filled tables lining one side of the building, topped off with an assortment of wine and a beer keg. A cake the size of my desk was decorated like dual computer monitors, one reading "Congratulations, Graduate," and the other, "Happy 25th."

"Yeah, we're cheap," Matthew said. "Two occasions, one party. And don't tell the park rangers about the beer." He held a finger to his lips and grinned.

Sammy cranked up a karaoke machine and rocked the crowd with his own special version of Kool and the Gang's "Celebration."

"How long did you guys plan this shindig?" I asked Zigana. She was busy organizing the food line, making sure everyone got enough to eat. I followed her orders and filled a plate. "How long?"

"It took us a couple of months," she said between restocking the plates and pouring wine. "First, I had to convince Matthew it was a good idea. He's not much of a social animal." She smiled in Sammy's direction as he launched into another song. "Sammy now, he loves a good party."

"So you were all in on it, when I thought you were playing the field." I shoveled in a bite of potato salad and thought about our talk in the Glen. "What about Hank?"

"Hank made the cake. He used to own a bakery, didn't you know?"

I scanned the crowd. "Where is he?"

"He'll be here later, with his new girlfriend."

I raised my not-plate-filled hand in surrender. "You win. You guys are good."

She kissed my cheek. "So are you."

When dusk settled over the park, Sammy lowered the tempo to allow a few brave couples to take to an impromptu dance floor. Matthew lit a log in the huge stone fireplace that filled one end of the shelter house and plugged in a string of lanterns shaped like palm trees. They reminded me of Adam, and his latest email. I refilled my wine glass and searched for someone to talk to. Zigana had her head bent over the song notebook with Sammy. Matthew seemed taken with Jocelyn. When I sat down on the hearth to stir the fire, he excused himself and joined me.

"Nice party," he said.

"Thanks to you. And those two." I pointed toward Sammy and Zigana. "Does he really have a crush on her or was that a ruse, too?"

"No, I'm pretty sure he does." He sipped his beer. "She doesn't seem to mind."

I watched them laughing together. Sammy brushed her hair back, his hand lingering on her cheek. "No, she doesn't."

With school finished and no job on the horizon, I stayed busy with additional hours at the bookstore, creating a website and bringing in some online business. I frequented the pool at the Antioch College Wellness Center when my arms were healed, started hiking at Clifton Gorge, and sent out stacks of resumes every week. The rejections didn't get any easier, but I hid my disappointment.

Mid-summer, while we were stacking new releases, Matthew broached another subject I'd been avoiding.

"Heard from Adam lately?"

"Adam has moved on," I said carefully.

Matthew tilted his head to see my expression. I turned away.

"What's that supposed to mean?" he asked.

"It means he's found someone else who's not unemployed fifteen hundred miles away." My frustrations swirled, melded.

Matthew tucked a finger under my chin and brought me around to face him. "Which makes you madder, him moving on or you not having that job?"

"Any job." The words slipped out and ricocheted back to punch me in the gut. He was right. It wasn't so much missing out on a relationship with Adam as the sense of futility I'd allowed to creep into my life. My emotions were never going to be the same after the past few months. Before the holidays, I'd thought everything was under control, all planned out, and I was working the plan. The universe laughed, set me straight big time, taught me not to ignore potential consequences when faced with decisions involving other people's lives, and left me adrift.

I'll never forgive myself for Carmen's death. For lack of evidence, since Grechko refused to confess, it was officially written off as an accident as much for the family's sake as mine. Gigi paid me a visit, let me know in rude and colorful language what she thought about said official call. I let her rage without rebuttal. She deserved it.

So did I.

Bruce and Zalenski's crash remained an open investigation while the police searched for the driver of the pickup. If they ever found him, it would lead back to Grechko.

I'd bet on it.

Life went on, like Adam did. Sammy and Zigana moved forward, too, even if it had taken each of them years to find a way. But there I was, stuck in a rut I'd dug myself. Zigana always said life is what you make it. It was time to make mine.

I expanded my job search to include tech jobs not centered on Cisco. I found a class at a local career center to earn another raft of certifications to build on my forensics experience. My advisor's friend from *Wired* emailed me about serializing part of my article for their blog, and after my first excerpt, I had three job offers for consulting work as a penetration tester. I was surprised to learn hacking is fun even when it's legal. And it pays well.

In mid-September, right after my full story appeared in the magazine's print edition, Bratton showed up at the bookstore. I'd kept my Wednesday evening and Saturday shifts when I started consulting. Keeps me in the loop and gives Matthew a break.

"Looks like you made the big time," Bratton said dropping a copy of *Wired* on the counter.

"You want an autograph?"

"Why don't you let me buy you a cup of coffee to celebrate?"

"I can't leave right now." My senses tingled. "What's this about?"

He moved across the store to glance down each aisle. "Where's your dad and his buddy?"

"At a baseball game. What's this about?"

"You don't like baseball?"

"I love baseball, what's it to you?" I was getting angry until I saw him hide a grin. *How'd he know I was lying?* I shook my head at him. "Bastard. C'mon, there's coffee in back." We emptied the dregs of the pot and settled into wingback chairs between science fiction and suspense.

"I hear you're doing some consulting," Bratton said. He tasted the coffee and grimaced. "Damn, that's awful." He took another gulp. "Why don't you come work for DHS?"

I sputtered into my cup. "You've got to be joking. Me work for the Feds?"

"Why not? You're smart, talented, barely legal most of the time. You'd fit right in." He drained the cup and shuddered. "Sure can't make coffee though."

"I didn't, Matthew did. He can hardly boil water." I tossed the rest of my coffee along with his empty cup and brought us each a bottle of water. "Why would I want to work for you? What's the catch?"

"No catch. Look at it as penance."

I caught my breath. He couldn't know how Carmen's death weighed on me. "Penance for what?"

"All the times you've snooped into computers where you didn't belong." He pinned me with a sharp gaze. "What'd you think I meant?" He bounced the water bottle off his knee and waited for an answer I couldn't give. "There are more guys like Grechko out there, you know. You could help bring them down."

"I'm not a fan of the military."

"Neither am I. Nobody was more pissed off when DHS absorbed the Treasury office in '03." He grinned again. "We'll keep that our little secret."

I sipped the water and tried to buy some time to think. I had yet to return the hard drives with all of Tatum's data, including the classified documents. Never found the right time. "Where's Reynolds?"

"At the ballgame with your dad. This isn't about Reynolds."

Wise guy. "He doesn't like me."

"So? Who says I do?" At my pointed look he sighed. "Women, always wanting to be liked. Reynolds transferred to the Cleveland office last month. Satisfied?"

"Maybe." I bolted to my feet before I could change my mind. "Wait here." A quick trip to the office, and I came back to hand him a thick lumpy package wrapped in layers of silver duct tape I'd secured in Matthew's safe.

"What's that?"

"My insurance."

He looked from the package to me and back again, and a heavy silence stretched way too long. Then he grunted a laugh and handed it back. "Got an incinerator?"

For once, he left me speechless.

"This goes no further," Bratton said, "not even Dad and Grandma." He waited for my agreement. "Grechko played Tatum to get rid of his gambling debt. When he figured out how much Tatum was raking in with his little shake-down scheme, he decided to help himself to those accounts, too. He funneled the documents through Tatum back to a dummy account Grechko controlled, then used that as leverage to blackmail Tatum in return."

I absorbed Bratton's version, thinking back to the (deliberate?) ignorance in Grechko's email exchanges with Tatum. "I thought Tatum was smarter than that, with his AFIT background and all."

"Don't believe everything he told you about his...connections." Bratton tossed his empty water bottle and stood, towering over me. "As for DHS, think about it. You've got my number."

I followed him to the front door, stuffing the lump under the register with my backpack.

He stopped by the counter. "Patrice moved to Arizona. She's agreed to testify against Grechko, if it ever goes to trial."

"I doubt she had anything to do with him, not directly. You said it yourself, she wanted to be liked. Unfortunately, she picked the wrong man, with Tatum. He's dead, and she's suffered enough."

"Awfully generous of you."

"Nothing generous about it. All I ever wanted was justice. And that doesn't mean revenge, an eye-for-an-eye and all that crap." I scrawled my name across the cover of his magazine. "What about the classified documents? Even if he was sending them back to himself, Grechko broke all kinds of laws."

He rolled the magazine into a tube and flashed another grin. "OSI's dealing with him now, and you don't have clearance. Come work for me and I'll let you read the file."

I didn't tell anyone about Bratton's job offer, but I didn't forget it, either. The glamour of consulting wore off fast. I got tired of uncovering multi-million-dollar corporations stealing trade secrets from each other. The pay was good, but the ultimate benefit was less certain.

Sammy proposed to Zigana over Thanksgiving dinner in front of Matthew and me. Not the most romantic setting, but she said yes anyway. They held a New Year's Eve wedding at Peach's, officiated by a local druid priest, and said "I do" as the clock struck midnight. Matthew and I stood as witnesses. After the first of the year, they found a cute little bungalow on the edge of Glen Helen close enough that Zigana could walk up the bike trail to the shop. Sammy got a gig running karaoke three nights a week rotating amongst the local bars.

Even with the hassle of renovating their century-old residence, Matthew and I agreed we'd never seen either of them so happy.

On moving day in mid-March, as I lugged boxes down to the car to drive them a whole six blocks, Zigana said, "The apartment's yours, you know, for as long as you want. I'm not worried about rent."

"Some businessperson you are." I squeezed the box into the trunk and bounced on the lid to close it. "I can afford to pay rent, don't worry."

She gave me a hug. "We'll talk about it when Sammy and I get back." He'd surprised her with a belated honeymoon cruise for the vernal equinox so they could watch the sun rise directly over the equator.

I manned the shop while they were away, hoping the extra inventory Zigana built up in anticipation of her absence wouldn't run out. No way I could replace it, and her assistant Nora was off welcoming yet another grandchild. I was between consulting gigs, anxious to find my next paying assignment. While I'd assured Zigana rent wasn't a problem, my bank account said otherwise. Matthew and I had chipped in to buy a dining set as a wedding gift. The nice chunk of change *Wired* paid for my paper went for the down payment on a used Honda hybrid which required a monthly payment and more insurance than my beloved Fiero. The last of the hospital bills had finally been paid off. Much as I hated shopping, I had to wear decent clothes to corporate headquarters when clients called, and the price of fashion left me with depressingly little to get by.

After my fourth night alone in the apartment, I forced myself to seek out company. Peach's had live music scheduled, so I wandered up the street. I almost left when I saw it was Bobby's group, but a masochistic streak egged me on. I hadn't heard from Adam since last spring, hadn't thought of him much since a fleeting pang at Zigana's wedding. Here I was, face to face with an older version of him, and it hurt more than I'd expected.

Jennifer spotted me at the bar and bounced over. "Hey, stranger. Haven't seen you in forever." Her perfume-filled hug caught me off guard.

I was surprised she remembered. We'd only met once, and she'd been pretty tipsy.

"Are you all by yourself? That's too bad. I never go to a bar alone. Too many creeps hit on me soon as I walk through the door. The curse of being cute, huh? You know what I mean, you're so adorable, all that silky black hair. And that figure. Bet you don't have to watch your weight like I do. Where's your friends? I brought a bunch, you can join us." She waved to a gaggle seated near the band. "It's a bachelorette party."

"Who's getting married?" I managed to fit in the question when she inhaled.

Her breath escaped in a high-pitched giggle as she dangled her left hand in front of me. "I am, can you believe it? After three years, Bobby proposed. Don't you love my ring? It was Bobby's mom's or something. Maybe his grandmother's. Anyway, it's gorgeous, and he's gorgeous. But you know that. Come meet the girls." She dragged me across the room. "The wedding's day after tomorrow at Polen Farm. You should come. Adam will be there."

I didn't hear much after that, not the introductions, not Bobby's greeting, not even the band when they started playing.

Adam will be there.

When Jennifer and her party filled the dance floor, I slipped away. The walk home passed in a daze. The bare living room, void of Zigana's club chair, fichus, and mantel clock, added to my unease. I locked up and settled into the window seat, watching the night sky. With the new moon in hiding, it was empty, too, like my life.

Adam will be there.

Next morning I called Matthew. "I ran into Jennifer at Peach's last night. She and Bobby are getting married. Are you invited?"

He cleared his throat like he does when he's nervous. "Yeah, thought I told you."

Uh-huh. "I hear Adam's coming."

"Makes sense, it's his dad."

"Is he seeing anyone still, do you know?"

"I haven't talked to his mother in a few weeks." Matthew's voice was cautious. "I suppose I can call and find out."

"No, don't do that." I took a deep breath and jumped. "Do you have a date for the wedding?"

Not that I'd admit it to anyone, but I went shopping before the wedding. I found a silk burgundy sheath that wasn't too awful, and I justified the cost as a business expense.

Matthew raised his eyebrows when he saw it, but all he said was, "You look nice."

In his role as best man, Adam was sequestered with Bobby until they walked to the front of the chapel with the minister. I tried to find a single female to pair him with and was ridiculously pleased when I failed. Then Matthew came back from a trip to the men's room and whispered, "He's engaged."

Of course he is.

The wedding march began. There were four bridesmaids, a flower girl, the maid of honor. Jennifer even wore a long white gown. It might be Bobby's third time around, but she wasn't letting her first trip down the aisle lose any of the luster.

I zoned out during the homily. A prism of light filtering through the stained-glass window splintered my dark thoughts. The tragic figures blocked out in bold colors reminded me of something. A waft of musky incense drifted through and with it, the memory of Harmony. And Zigana's Tarot reading.

"Ten of Wands. Your energy is going the wrong direction."

"Six of Cups. You're stuck on something from your past."

"High Priestess. You're hiding something, maybe from others, maybe from yourself."

"Seven of Cups…misusing your talents, squandering your life."

The scent became overpowering, choking. I whispered an excuse to Matthew and slipped out the side door before I disrupted Jennifer's big day.

The chapel was set in a wooded area far enough from the roadway to escape traffic sounds. A narrow boardwalk wound its way into the trees and disappeared. Maybe a hundred yards in, I found a Zen garden with a crooked stone bench next to a plot of sand and rocks. Probably not the best surface for my new dress, but I was past caring.

Squandering your life.

Zigana's Tarot reading rang through my head, reinforced by the scent that came from nowhere but Harmony's box. When I'd dressed for the wedding, I'd looped Harmony's scarf around my neck on a whim. It made sense now, since I was finally listening.

Half-assed decisions. Fatal errors. Consequences. And then I'd allowed the dream of a relationship with Adam to take me out of the present. It offered a fantasy escape from my growing problems when what I needed was to solve them. Like Jon Kabat-Zin, and I'm sure wise minds before him, said, "Wherever you go, there you are." I had to stop running and face the fact that everyone around me was experiencing life while I stayed mired in the past, dreaming of a shadowy future, afraid to commit to today. Zigana had a point, as usual, teaching me not to dwell on ancient history. Her lesson was sinking in.

I used the miniature rake next to the bench to stroke patterns in the sand, meditating on the mandalas formed by the tines. Each line formed a new path, only to be obliterated by the intersection of another, and another. Consequences. My life crossing paths with others.

In the distance the chapel bells pealed to signal the end of the ceremony. Excited chatter drifted in through the trees as the crowd moved to their cars, off to the reception at the American Legion Hall down the road. My phone buzzed.

Matthew's worry cut through the static. "You okay? Where are you?"

I thought for moment. "I'm here, now. Finally."

About the Author

C. L. (Cyndi) Pauwels is hoping that, as she plows through her sixth decade, she'll eventually figure out what she wants to be when she grows up. Her crime fiction "Toledo Trilogy" (*Forty & Out* (2014), *Burned Bridges* (2017), and *Unwelcome Ties* (2022)) draws on her nearly 20 years' experience working in the criminal justice field. She's also written freelance news stories, the award-winning non-fiction *Historic Warren County: An Illustrated History* (2010), several anthologized essays, and numerous short stories. A recently retired college adjunct, Cyndi served as Assistant Director for the Antioch Writers' Workshop for six years until its sad demise in 2018. She lives in Yellow Springs, Ohio, with her husband of 45 years and 14 chickens. Follow her work at http://clpauwels.com.

Curious about other Crossroad Press books? Stop by our website:
http://crossroadpress.com
We offer quality writing
in digital, audio, and print formats.

Subscribe to our newsletter on the website homepage and receive a
free eBook.

www.ingramcontent.com/pod-product-compliance
Lightning Source LLC
Chambersburg PA
CBHW031132210626
46816CB00014B/624